The Other Way

Victoria L. Humphreys

Stairwell Books //

Published by Stairwell Books
161 Lowther Street
York, YO31 7LZ

www.stairwellbooks.co.uk
@stairwellbooks

Cover design: Oliver Hurst

Paperback ISBN: 978-1-917334-04-4
eBook ISBN: 978-1-917334-13-6

Also by Victoria L. Humphreys

Not the Work of an Ordinary Boy

The Other Way

For my hero, Patricia Humphreys. I miss you.

EPIGRAPHS:

As the children of survivors are said to dream the nightmares of their parents, I inherited nameless fears

'Kinderszenen'
Anne-Marie Levine

WE ARE STILL GETTING OUR RED CROSS PARCELS BUT NOT FOR MUCH LONGER. BY NOW, WE ARE QUITE THIN AND VERY MISERABLE. I OFTEN WONDER HOW LONG I WILL BE ABLE TO PUT UP WITH THIS.

Ron Stone

Part One

Alfie and Lil

1941 – 1945

1941

1: The Diehard

It is 1941 and Alfie Edwards walks like a man who stores all his energy in the soles of his feet. His body springs along the path, his auburn hair bounces on his scalp. He thinks about Lil and his feet move faster. He darts round the pedestrians like a young leaf blasted by the wind and he thinks about the question. He thinks about all the different ways to ask the question. How should he put it? He pictures her getting off the bus and himself getting down on one knee. He imagines saying, *Lil, let's get hitched.* Then he imagines her frowning at him and telling him to ask her properly. He tries out the words, *Lil, will you do me the great honour of becoming my wife?* He thinks if he puts the question to her like this, he'll sound like a ponce and she won't take him seriously. He decides he'll keep it simple and say, *Lil, will you marry me?* He thinks about her pretty face and what it will look like when she sees him kneeling in the rain (it's a chilly, dull and wet day in Chiswick). He imagines her frowning and scolding him for making the knee of his trousers damp and dirty. He thinks she might say no to a man who doesn't do his best to keep his clothes clean. He decides he'll remain standing, try to take her hand in his, and say, *Lil, will you marry me?*

It is his nineteenth birthday. He is returning from Acton where he has just enlisted. He already feels better about being a soldier than he ever did about being a painter and decorator. Somehow, he feels more of a man than he used to, but perhaps it's only because the recruiting officer kept on saying *Good Man, Good Man.* Well now that he's a soldier and a *Good Man*, he wants a wife. Lil might be two years older than him, but so what? He's old enough to go to war. And the last time he met up with her, her best friend, Margaret, said they looked good together. She'd kissed him then, a quick but fierce kiss in front of everybody and that was the moment when she finally gave him something to think about.

When they'd bumped into each other at the Hammersmith Palais last summer, Lil had practically ordered him to dance the waltz with her even though she looked like a film star in her heels, dress and red lipstick. Next to her, he was sure he looked no more than a bigger version of his eight-year-old self, especially with that bloody paint in his hair which Louis should have told him was there. And, even though he'd trodden on her feet several times because he'd been nervous and hadn't really known what he was doing, and had been distracted by his older brother Louis and Louis' mates laughing at him from the sidelines, and though it must have felt to her as if a great weight had fallen on her dainty feet because he was built like his granddad — the one who knocked out a cart horse with his bare fist — she'd ordered him to go on dancing with her. And later that evening, when that Tom fella appeared out of nowhere and took a hold of her elbow and tried to lead her away from him, she shrugged Tom off and told him she didn't want to dance with him even though he was, quite clearly, an officer in the RAF. Then she invited him to the pictures to see *All This, and Heaven Too* and even though they weren't going to be alone because they were going with someone called Margaret and Geoff-the-toff, the invitation had still felt significant. And during the film, she needn't have touched his arm every time she whispered in his ear and she needn't have whispered in his ear because nobody else in the theatre had been so considerate. And at the dances that had followed the one at the Hammersmith Palais, she could have saved her toes from the heavy burden that had been his two left feet by asking someone else to go with her, but she didn't.

He thinks about his army wages. He's going to be paid fourteen bob a week. He wonders if this will be enough for them both. He thinks that if it isn't, they'll live with his parents, Fred and Nell, until he earns enough money for them to be able to rent their own place. In his mind, there is no question of asking Lil to be his wife another day.

He checks his watch. Her bus is due at Clifton Gardens in less time than it will take him to walk there. He steps into the road and begins to run. He has enough go in him to sprint but he doesn't want to turn up to the bus stop sweaty. He thinks she might be put off saying yes if he's dripping with sweat. He's always been dazzled by her tidiness. Never a thing out of place with Lil. He wonders what she'll say when he tells her he's joined the army. He hopes to make her proud of him. He feels happy enough to sing a song in his head, but then he sees her walking with her hands in her pockets and her chin tucked into her coat collar, on the other side of the road. He waves, but she doesn't see him. He checks his watch and concludes that she must have caught the earlier bus. He crosses the road reciting the question in his head like a man with a stutter.

2: Difference is a Disease

Lil is a typist in a small office of twelve. It is an office where the two bomb-shattered windows have been replaced with laths and black tar paper. She spends her working days bathed in artificial light and wrapped in smart layers to keep warm; she rarely removes her headscarf and types in fingerless gloves. On the face of it, there is nothing to distract the girls from their work in this office: there are only the insipid beige painted walls, the jacketed back of the person in front, or the watchful face of the office supervisor, Miss Whyte. The office is a cacophony of metal sounds and floral scents. Conversation is both forbidden by Miss Whyte and muted by the perpetual clunk and clack of the machines so the girls work in silence; chitchat, and cigarettes for that matter, are reserved for break-time. The girls sit in twos with their gasmasks at their feet. Lil sits in the second row, next to the wall, furthest from the office door. Of all the Imperial typewriters in the office, Lil's is the newest; she ministers to it as if it were a sickly child. On the desk, beside her beloved typewriter, sits a cleaning kit for her machine and a wire tray for her paperwork. Next to her sits Margaret, the girl she is in love with.

Lil and Margaret have been kissing and touching one another in secret for months. More recently, they have been making love in toilet cubicles, unlit alleyways and secluded bomb sites, and also in Margaret's dreary digs when the landlady has been out. Lil has only known Margaret's hand in hers, her fingers in her hair, between her legs and on her breasts; she has only known her tongue on her flesh. Before meeting her, she hadn't known that girls could love each other in this way. She believes that Margaret has woken her up, kissed her to life, yanked open her eyes and shown her that she doesn't have to end up like her mother: worn-out, wrung-dry, unloved. She has decided that for the rest of her life, she wants to know only Margaret.

But then Margaret arrives at work wearing an engagement ring.

She comes into the office a few minutes after Lil. Lil is already seated, gazing at the door, waiting for her. Unusually, Miss Whyte is late. Lil smiles at Margaret as she collects her work from Miss Whyte's desk and walks towards her. Though Miss Whyte is absent from the office, Margaret doesn't speak to her, not even to say hello, and though she returns Lil's smile, she doesn't touch her arm as she habitually does and these oddities make Lil anxious. Then she begins to think that there is something strange about Margaret's smile. Where is the fizz, the playfulness and the promise of later? She would like to ask, but Margaret's frostiness stifles the query.

Then Margaret removes her mittens to feed a sheet of paper into her typewriter. She keeps her eyes from Lil but makes no attempt to conceal her left ring finger and when Lil sees a small diamond solitaire there, she feels as if she is observing a stranger. Ada, also on the second row but separated from Margaret by the aisle, also notices the new engagement ring and says, 'Is that what I think it is?'

Margaret turns to Ada and, as if admitting a crime, says, 'Yes, Ada, I'm engaged.'

'Come on, out with it: Who is he? What is he? Where does he live?'

Lil stares at Margaret's engagement ring as if it is dangerous.

Margaret sighs. 'His name's Geoffrey, he's a flight lieutenant and he has a place in Maida Vale.'

'Have we heard of this Geoffrey before?' Ada demands. 'I really don't think we have.'

'I've known Geoffrey for years.'

'Do you know him, Lil?'

'Yes, she does,' snaps Margaret.

But he wasn't supposed to become your fiancé, thinks Lil.

'Rank, wings, money…you've done well, unless he's old?' says Ada.

'Really, Ada,' says Margaret, checking the ribbon in her machine. Geoffrey's suggestion that she should consider doing some other type of war work, something that will really make a difference to the country, crosses her mind.

'Well, it's no good if they're already past it. Is he a friend of your father's?' she asks with a wicked smile.

'Cripes, Ada, if you must know, he went to school with my brother. He's twenty-seven. Is that young enough for you?'

'Actually, I tend to put looks above youth. Is he very handsome, would you say, Lil?'

Like restive dragonflies, Margaret's fingers hover over the keys of her typewriter as she waits for Lil's answer. Lil considers the question. Geoffrey smells of lady's soap and has a mole above his upper lip that looks like a three-legged spider. His hands are too big for his skinny arms and his Adam's apple too big for his throat - she avoids looking at it, especially when he speaks, because it makes her want to gasp for air as if it has transplanted itself into her own throat. Furthermore, she suspects he files his nails and doubts that he's handsome. But what difference does it make whether he's handsome anyway? Their courtship isn't real. What is she playing at? She thinks back to the time when Margaret had first mentioned Geoffrey.

'I have to start courting,' Margaret declared. 'Mother's begun to wonder why I have no young man on the scene.'

Margaret was lying across Lil, her head on Lil's shoulder, her large breasts pressed against Lil's smaller ones. At Margaret's announcement, Lil's stomach lurched like an Austin 10 in the wrong gear. 'Do you think she knows about us?' she asked, as she imagined Margaret's mother storming through the door and finding them *in flagrante*.

Margaret propped herself up on her elbows and laughed before resettling her head on Lil's chest. 'Good God no, Lil, nothing of the sort,' she said, drawing a figure of eight with her index finger around Lil's navel. 'Mother doesn't have the imagination for *us*. It's men she's worried about, not women. All her friends' daughters are courting or married off so I should be too. Difference is a disease as far as my mother is concerned. She'd pass out if she could see us now. Cripes, I said "Fuck" once and the lights went out. It took smelling salts to bring her round.'

'How old were you?'

'Fourteen, if I recall.'

'Fourteen? I didn't know that word existed when I was that age.'

'Oh, Lil, you should hear yourself.'

'It's true.'

'It's not as if I used to go around saying it. There was a drunk on the train when I was coming home from boarding school once. As I passed him, he grabbed hold of my arm and asked me if I wanted a fuck and I said, "No thank you, I'm not allowed to accept gifts from strangers".' Margaret had howled with laughter at the recollection. 'I had absolutely no idea, Lil. I thought a fuck must be a boiled sweet. Can you imagine going into the sweet shop and saying, "I'd like a quarter of fucks please" and the shopkeeper saying, "Right you are, dear, everybody wants fucks today".'

Lil didn't like hearing her use that ugly word and she didn't think the story about the drunk was funny at all. Her mother had warned her about men like him when she was a little girl. 'Some men want to touch your minny,' she'd warned. 'You mustn't let them, Lil. Scream as loud as you can if they come anywhere near you.' Lil hadn't been wary of some men after that warning, she'd been wary of *all* men because her mother had neglected to tell her what these 'some' men might look like.

'Did he touch you?'

'No, I never saw him again and thank goodness for that. He'd completely messed himself; his shoes were caked in it. He was wearing white leather shoes, Lil. They were white leather, although by the time I saw them, more brown than white. But white; isn't that strange? He must have been given them. I suppose they were once summer shoes for somebody. Actually, it was summer that day on the train, but those shoes, hardly the attire of a tramp. Oh, and the stench, diarrhoea on a hot summer's day, you've never smelt anything like it; I went without supper that evening, I felt contaminated. He must have eaten something terribly disagreeable. Upon reflection, I'd have to say he was totally incapable of a fuck. You just have to wonder about some people.'

Lil found it difficult not to frown. 'What happened when your mother came round?'

'We pretended that I hadn't said it. Tom had to enlighten me. You can just imagine my brother's face when I said, "Tom, can you please tell me what a fuck is?"'

Lil managed a small laugh in spite of Margaret saying that word again, and Margaret delighted in the feel of Lil's taut stomach muscles contracting beneath her cheek.

'Mother sent a car to collect me from school after that which was a shame because we used to have such fun on the train.' She swapped drawing figure-of-eights for circles before adding, 'You have the most perfect belly button, Lil. It reminds me of a Lanyard knot.'

'Have you got someone in mind?' Lil asked, not wishing to let Margaret distract her from the details or discover that she'd never heard of a Lanyard knot.

'Possibly... Tom has a friend called Geoffrey. Mother adores him and I think it might well be an arrangement that would suit us both.'

'What do you mean, "suit us both?"'

'Well, let's just say, I don't think I'm his type.'

Lil didn't follow: Margaret was brilliant and clever and beautiful; surely, she was everybody's type?

Margaret sighed, her warm breath sweeping across Lil's stomach and giving her goose bumps. 'Think about it,' she said.

Lil wound a lock of Margaret's hair tightly around her index finger. 'I am,' she replied.

'That hurts, Lil.'

'Sorry,' she said, dropping Margaret's hair.

'Do you know, Lil, sometimes you can be so obtuse. What I'm saying is that I think Tom's more Geoffrey's type.'

'Tom?'

'Yes.'

'You mean...'

'Yes, Lil, that's exactly what I mean.'

'Is Tom one as well?'

'Tom?' Margaret laughed. 'Tom one? Really, Lil, Tom has a different girl for every day of the week, but men are allowed to, aren't they? Positively encouraged to do so, I'd say. The other evening, I overheard my parents discussing his exploits. Mother said quite seriously, "There's a word for men like Tom", and Father laughed and said, "Yes, lucky!" Even Mother had to laugh. Poor Geoffrey, how can he compete? I actually feel quite sorry for him. He's a decent sort really.'

Lil said 'yes' but she wasn't thinking about 'Poor Geoffrey' one iota; she was trying to imagine two men in bed together. What on earth did they do?

'So, everybody's happy, Lil.'

All that hair! Hairy chests pressed together and hairy legs entwined. What about their bits and pieces? Where did it all go?

'Have you gone to sleep, Lil?' Margaret demanded.

'Sorry?'

'I said everybody's happy.'

'Except me; I'll have less time with you now.'

'But that's the beauty of my plan, Lil. We won't have less time together because wherever Geoffrey and I go, you can go, too. I'll ask Geoffrey to bring a friend along and we'll all look like perfectly normal courting couples and when Geoffrey isn't around, we'll have the time to ourselves.'

'I wish you wouldn't say, "Geoffrey and I and you". *You* sound like a couple, but *I* sound like the chaperone.'

'But *you* know the truth,' Margaret said, walking the tips of two fingers down to Lil's minny. 'Don't you?'

Now, Lil is absolutely sure that an engagement was never part of the plan.

Ada's prying is relentless. 'I went out with a pilot once but the amount of coping I had to do every evening was too much for any girl. It's not that I don't like passionate men but really… Does Geoffrey know when to stop, would you say, Margaret?'

'I think I can hear Miss Whyte,' says Margaret, glaring at the door.

Ada listens, says, 'No,' and then returns to the subject of Geoffrey. She wants to know where they went dancing. She wants to meet his friends.

Lil remembers that Margaret and Geoffrey once danced in a dark corner of the Hammersmith Palais. Their prolonged seclusion and the way Geoffrey's hands snaked up and down Margaret's back made Lil cross enough to want to play Margaret at her own game that night, but with whom? Though Margaret had arranged for her brother, Tom, to act as Lil's escort, he'd ditched her for another girl as soon as the first waltz was over. Thwarted by Tom's indifference, Lil had been on the brink of flouncing out of the dance, possibly in tears but nevertheless hopeful that Margaret would notice, realise she'd gone too far, and then come chasing after her, when she'd spotted Alfie and Louis Edwards. Never had she been so pleased to see them. She waited till Louis wandered off and then 'bumped' into Alfie. He hadn't recognised her at first, having not seen her since the days when she wore plaits and long socks and he sported a snotty nose and scuffed knees, but when she told him her name and reminded him that they'd once been neighbours, he beamed with recognition and she with relief. Only then had she set about imitating Margaret by showing a sudden interest in a man she cared nothing for. She even danced the Palais Glide with him.

'We don't have a preferred venue, Ada,' lies Margaret.

'Any dark corner will do,' Lil tells Ada sourly.

Margaret stares at Lil.

Ada raises her eyebrows, sucks in her cheeks and says, 'Sounds like fun.' Then she trots out of the room saying, 'Back in a jiffy.'

Margaret waits, then whispers, 'We'll talk later, Lil.'

Lil stares at Margaret's red-varnished fingernails and thinks about how happy she was when she painted them for her two evenings before. 'I'll explain then,' Margaret adds, desperately.

Lil doesn't want Margaret to explain later. She looks at her face and mumbles, 'I know what an engagement ring means. No need to explain.'

'It's not what you think.'

'You said there was nothing real going on between you two. You said he was... well you know what you said.'

'I was wrong about that.'

Lil glares at her contemptuously. Did she deliberately suggest that Geoffrey was a homosexual to stop her from making a fuss about their courtship?

'I don't love him, Lil.'

'But you're going to marry him?'

Margaret looks at her engagement ring. 'Yes.'

'Why? Why would you do that?'

'Because I have no choice.'

Lil thinks the worst and her face shows it. She stares at Margaret's stomach and imagines it swollen with a baby that looks just like Geoffrey with a hideous baby spider on its lip to match.

Margaret flushes and says, 'I'm not expecting, Lil, we haven't done that.'

Lil feels stupid and then relieved. 'Then why?'

'We all have to get married sooner or later and Geoffrey's manageable.'

Lil shakes her head, 'Not me,' she says. 'I won't get married.'

'You will in the end. There's no other way.'

'There's *our* way.'

'Lil,' says Margaret, grasping her calf under the desk. 'Don't be silly, you must know that's not true.'

Lil pushes her calves towards the back of her chair, out of Margaret's reach, and tucks her feet behind the chair's metal legs. She has not avoided Margaret's touch before and she feels childish doing it now because it is the last thing she really wants to do. Margaret sits up and sighs and Miss Whyte marches into the office full of purpose and efficiency. Seeing Lil and Margaret motionless, Miss Whyte frowns in their direction and makes a point of looking at the office clock as if they, and not her, are late for work. Then she glares at Ada's empty chair. Lil carefully places her fingers on the keys of her typewriter and then punches them savagely as if each one displays Geoffrey's big bland face wearing a stupid RAF cap.

***

Now, Margaret notices that Lil is making numerous uncharacteristic typing errors on a straightforward letter. Mistakes are difficult to conceal in the second row and so Miss Whyte is also noticing the frequency with which Lil stops typing to use her eraser, or to transfer a piece of paper to the waste paper basket. Miss Whyte would rather have three competent typists than twelve sloppy ones and she wonders whether a verbal warning is warranted.

Lil finds Margaret's presence difficult to bear. Even though she can avoid looking at her, she cannot avoid getting a whiff of her perfume every time she returns the carriage on her typewriter. She thinks about the times she's kissed Margaret's perfumed wrists and tasted the scent. She had hoped to keep working until lunchtime but now, now that she keeps torturing herself with memories of Margaret loving her and thoughts of Margaret loving a man, she doesn't think this is possible.

She stops typing and rises from her chair. She stands beside Miss Whyte and says meekly, 'I'm going to be sick, Miss Whyte.' She claps her hand over her mouth for emphasis and sees from the corner of her eye that Margaret has stopped typing. Margaret's small hands clasp her slender neck and Lil thinks she looks as if she is choking herself. Then Margaret strokes her ear lobe with her ring finger. Lil shifts her head so that she can no longer see any part of her and does a reasonable job of a fake retch.

'Go, Lillian, quickly,' commands Miss Whyte.

She nods and flees the office at a pace she is unaccustomed to.

Miss Whyte sees that Margaret's fingers are not draped over the keys of her typewriter and says, 'As you were, Margaret.'

Margaret raises her hand as if she hasn't already got Miss Whyte's attention and asks, 'Should I go with her, Miss Whyte?'

'No, Margaret, you should not,' snaps Miss Whyte. 'Dictations do not type themselves.'

Margaret promised Geoffrey that she would never take her engagement ring off. Now she wishes that she hadn't made that promise or hadn't worried about breaking that promise. But Lil should have known that they couldn't be together indefinitely. She doesn't want to be on the receiving end of disapproving stares and ugly words for the rest of her life and she doesn't think Lil's up to it either.

While Margaret has these thoughts, Lil sticks her chapped fingers down her throat to make herself sick in the ladies loo. She does it so she can tell herself that Margaret has made her ill. She thinks she should start trying to hate her but already she understands that she'll never be able to do that. She stares miserably at her own vomit in the toilet bowl and decides that, once she's wiped her face, she's going to leave the office without a word to Miss Whyte and, more importantly, without a word to Margaret. Nothing matters now. Her life is over.

3: Love Never Faileth

Alfie blurts out the question on the busy street before Lil can lift her chin out of her coat and return his greeting. 'Lil, I've joined the army will you marry me?' he says.

A stout woman in a crisp Norland nanny's uniform with ankles the size of Lil's thighs stops pushing a pram to glance and then frown at him; he wishes he didn't speak so loudly. Lil speaks so quietly that he always has to strain his ears to hear her; he wishes he was more like her. Not wanting to draw any attention to their differences, he turns his back on the woman with the pram and then repeats more quietly, 'Will you marry me, Lil?'

Lil has spent the afternoon sitting on a bench in Green Park staring at her feet. Now, she stops walking and stares at them again. She feels as if Margaret is watching her, testing her to see if she will act wisely or act stupidly. She pictures Margaret's hand on her leg and her face inches from her lap telling her that marriage to a man is the only way. But she doesn't think of Alfie as a man, she thinks he's still a boy. Then she remembers Margaret's excuse for marrying Geoffrey, '*Geoffrey's manageable.*'

She remembers the time when she was a brand new twelve-year-old and Alfie was an inferior ten-year-old. Alfie's older brother Louis, also twelve but in Lil's opinion undeserving of the age, dared Alfie to walk along the top of a dilapidated wall. Alfie described the dare as pathetic because scaling a wall, whatever its height, was easy. She noticed that he didn't have anything to say about its condition. Louis upped the stakes. 'Do it blindfold then.'

'Blindfold?'

'You heard me. Lil'll lend us one of her long socks won't you, Lil?'

She didn't even consider it. 'No, I will not.'

Louis laughed. 'Have to make do with one of mine then, Alfie.'

'One of your stinking socks? Not likely,' Alfie responded, quite seriously.

'What's the point of this dare?' Lil asked, folding her arms.

Alfie shrugged. 'I don't know.'

'Bloody hells bells,' shrieked Louis. 'Why does there have to be a point? I dared him so he has to do it.'

'Bloody hells bells,' repeated Lil. 'What does that actually mean, Louis?'

'Bleeding Nora, Lil. Why do you have to ask so many bloody questions?

'Why do you always have to swear?' she said, bending down to her left foot and unlacing her shoe.

Ignoring Lil, Louis turned to Alfie and said, 'Are you doing it or not, cos if you're not, I'm sodding off and you can stay here and play with a stupid *girl* instead.'

'For heaven's sake, Louis, of course he's going to do it. A dare's a dare,' Lil responded, turning her forehead into a land of slit trenches. 'Keep your hair on.' Thrusting her long white sock at Alfie and staring at Louis' miserable socks with as much disdain as she could muster, she added, 'You better use my sock, Alfie, because you'll end up with a verruca on your face if you use Louis'.'

'Sod off, Lil, I haven't got a verruca.'

She said nothing.

'Your feet do stink, Lou, I'm right about that but I didn't know you could get a verruca on your face. Is that true, Lil?'

'Yes,' she said, even though she'd doubted it because her mother had told her that you caught a verruca by walking barefoot across wet and dirty public floors.

'There's nothing wrong with my feet,' protested Louis. 'I can prove it.'

'No thanks,' she said. 'I expect Alfie's right. I expect your feet do stink and I doubt you'd know a verruca if you saw it anyway.'

Alfie laughed.

Louis wondered why a boy wasn't allowed to hit a girl. It was a stupid bloody law; some girls deserved it. Then he said to Alfie, 'You can shut your cake-hole.'

'Do you think I can do it, Lil?' asked Alfie.

She shrugged.

'Don't worry,' he said, 'I'm really good at things like this.'

She wasn't worried: why should she care if he fell?

He asked her to tie the sock. She tutted but stepped forward snatching back her sock from his outstretched hand. She spun him round so that the back of his head was in front of her face. Then she whipped her sock across his eyes and with an unnecessary yank of the toe and the cuff fastened the two ends into a knot.

'Sure you can't see?' Louis said, checking for gaps beneath his eyes.

'I can't see a bleeding thing,' confirmed Alfie, 'except white dots.'

'Get on with it then.'

'I can't see where I'm going.'

Louis shoved past Lil as roughly as he thought was legal before clamping his hands on Alfie's shoulders and frog-marching him to the wall. Alfie smacked the wall with the palms of his hands. Lil watched some mortar slide out from between some bricks and fall to the ground. She sidled over to it, ground it into sand with her shoe and spread it over the path so that it looked no more ominous than a handful of scattered semolina.

'Give us a leg up. I can't reach the top otherwise.'

Louis linked the fingers of his hands and hefted Alfie to the top of the wall. 'Well that bit was easy,' said Alfie, grinning.

Lil noticed his grey front tooth.

Louis looked at Lil and she looked up at the sky.

'What are you waiting for?' asked Louis. 'Slow coach, I'd have done it by now.'

'I'm doing it.'

'Why don't *you* do it, Louis? I'll dare you if you like.'

'Why don't *you* do it, Lil,' he replied, pointing at her.

'It's rude to point,' she said.

'It's rude to point,' he mimicked. 'I'll point if I want to.'

'Are you lot watching me do this or what?' asked Alfie.

'Yeah, but I haven't got all day,' said Louis.

Lil thought Alfie looked as steady as a drunk and when his foot happened upon a loose brick and he toppled from the wall and the skin from his face, hands and knees looked as if it had been rubbed across a cheese grater, and the blood poured out of him and he bawled at the sight of it, and a piece of his grey front tooth lay on the path coated in dust from the masonry that she'd ground to sand with her shoe, and her sock travelled from his eyes up to his forehead so that he looked like a soldier from the First World War wearing a field dressing that had been applied on the hop by someone who had no idea what they were doing, and Louis looked on, seemingly at his wounded younger brother but actually at a scene in his head in which he got a hiding from their old man for daring his brother to do something stupid, and he sloped away from the scene like a fox, it was her, 'a stupid girl', that calmed Alfie down and sorted him out.

Now, with Margaret's words ringing in her head, she thinks that Alfie's always been manageable and will do what she says.

'I'm serious, Lil,' he says. 'Will you do me the honour of…'

'Yes,' she says. 'If you're quite sure it's me you want.'

She knows he can't make her happy and she can't make him happy but that she's given him a chance to change his mind.

'Am I sure?' he says, incredulously. 'Listen, Lil, do you remember that time when we was kids and I fell off the wall?'

It's when we *were* kids, not when we *was* kids. 'No,' she says.

'You do,' he insists. 'It's how come my tooth got chipped.' He curls his upper lip to expose the damaged tooth and she shakes her head like a wind-up toy on the wane.

'Well, anyway, you were so bloody…' He puts his fingers to his lips and says, 'Excuse my French, Lil,' before continuing with, 'You were really nice to me.'

'I don't remember it,' she says, tucking her chin back into the collar of her coat.

'That was the day I decided that I wanted to marry you, but then you moved house and I thought, well, I thought that that was that, but then you showed up at the Palais and asked me to dance and I couldn't believe my luck.'

She is glad her lips are hidden behind her coat collar because it means she doesn't have to pretend to look flattered or pleased. She thinks it's a ridiculous admission and she wishes she'd never agreed to go along to the Palais with Margaret; she wishes she'd never agreed to go along with any of it.

'So, you will?' he says. 'You will marry me?'

'Will you see active service?' she asks, unexpectedly changing the subject.

She looks a long way up into his bright blue eyes. It occurs to her then that the colour of their eyes is the only thing they have in common.

Now he thinks he understands her reticence. He thinks she's worried he's going to croak it and leave her a widow. His face matches his thoughts and she can't bear it; her eyes skirt away from his earnest face and find sanctuary on his stomach. She wonders why he doesn't see through her. How can he not know what she's asking? Why can't he see that she's a terrible person?

'You needn't worry about me, Lil; I'm tougher than you think,' he says, seeing that she has taken her hands out of her pockets to tightly clutch the hem of her brown box coat. Gingerly, he takes one of her gloved hands and holds it between his own. He looks at her sad face and says as tenderly as a boy can, 'What if I promise to come back without so much as a scratch on me?'

She replays him falling off the wall, looks passively at her hand, now in his gigantic paws, and decides that it's not likely. Then she says, 'Alright, Alfie, I'll marry you.'

1941

4: Consummation

Alfie and Lil are married in Chiswick Registry Office on a day of heavy showers and bursts of sunshine. Lil wears a floor length white satin dress overlaid with a donated piece of lace curtain and carries a small bunch of pink ranunculus flowers. Alfie wears his uniform. Alfie's father, Fred, organizes the railway club social hall for the afternoon reception because, being a railway worker, he gets it cheap. In the hall, the guests eat the sponge and jam cake to which each family had contributed a teacup of sugar. Alfie's mother, Nell, gets a sing-along on the go. Lil tries her best to smile. Alfie does his best not to drink too many bottles of stout. When the reception is over, Lil and Alfie help Fred and Nell put the chairs away.

They spend their wedding night in Alfie's childhood home in the bedroom he usually shares with Louis. Lil is relieved that Louis is away on exercise and Alfie's parents are spending the night elsewhere with Alfie's aunt, because she doesn't want to submit to Alfie's conjugal rights with his brother and his parents within ear shot. She's spent a lot of time thinking about his conjugal rights and she's come to think of them as *his* conjugals because *she* isn't interested in having any part of his body inside hers.

As she waits for her new husband to finish his ablutions in the kitchen below, she thinks his and Louis' bedroom is wholly predictable: sky-blue walls, grey curtains, bare floorboards, no pictures. The bedclothes on their single wrought-iron cream-painted beds match the walls as do the blankets that top them. There is a chest of drawers beside a brown tiled fireplace on the far wall. The fireplace sits between the feet of the two beds but the grate is empty. When she first entered the bedroom, she was shivering and Alfie, thinking she was cold, apologised for not being able to light a fire for her. 'Sorry, Lil, the chimney's blocked. I'm too bloody big to sweep it now,' he'd joked, but his joke hadn't raised a smile from her. This was because the thought of him being too big for a small space was too close to the bone to be funny. He thought he must have offended her with his bad language and so had decided that he must try to watch his language in front of her in future and avoid pairing every other word with 'bloody', 'bleeding,' or 'sodding'. Then, unused to uncomfortable silences, he had hastily offered her the use of the kitchen but she had declined because she'd already been down there to wash her face and clean her teeth while he was in the garden doing God only knows. So, he'd grabbed his pyjama bottoms from beneath his pillow and bolted down the stairs with them, not being able to shake the feeling that he'd done something far worse to his new wife than swear in her presence.

Now, she thinks she might as well be lying in the doctor's surgery because Alfie's bedroom feels clinical. She pulls the white starched top sheet and the scratchy blue blanket up to her chin and assumes her original position: feet together, legs together, hands against her thighs and face staring up at the ceiling. She wears nothing but a thin cotton nightie and lies in his bed like a body in the mortuary. On her mother's advice, she has slipped an old towel beneath her crotch. She feels as if she's waiting for him to injure her. She thinks about her Nan, a miserable old woman who talks non-stop about dying but hasn't got round to doing it herself, and the old bat's constant refrain: *dying's much worse than death*. She wishes he would hurry up in the bathroom so they can get it over and done with.

Then she hears his pee thunder into a metal bucket. She thinks he can't have been all day to go for so long and she wishes that he could have been bothered to use the toilet at the bottom of the garden. She feels her own bladder tingle but she won't go till after her ordeal because she's been told that she'll avoid getting pregnant if she goes straight after. She doesn't want children, if she can help it. Alfie peeing has reminded her of Killarney, the piebald rag-and-bone man's horse. Killarney pees steaming yellow rivers onto the street. A gang of local children have made a game of getting as close as they can to him without getting their shoes splashed with his urine; they squeal with delight when they misjudge the distance. Lil can't help thinking about his enormous mottled penis and how it seems to appear out of nowhere, hanging like a gymnasium climbing rope and pounced on by fat black flies. She's not seen a man's penis before but, thanks to Killarney, she's sure it's a very ugly and unnecessarily large thing.

Next, he cleans his teeth. She thinks it sounds as if he has put too much toothpaste on his toothbrush because the noise he makes sounds frothy. She gags at the thought of him with a frothy mouth and a kitchen sink covered in toothpaste and spit. Periodically, he stops brushing his teeth to whistle a tune she doesn't recognise. She doesn't understand why anybody would whistle in the middle of cleaning their teeth; she thinks he is needlessly dragging the wedding night out and gags again.

She quietly climbs out of his bed and tiptoes to the window for something to do. If she gags once more, she thinks she'll bring up her morning cornflakes. She's felt too nauseous to eat anything since breakfast. She lifts the bottom of the black-out blind from the window pane, and ducks down to the gap she has made to see if anything is happening in the street. With the help of a full moon, she spies a man, woman and four children marching down the street carrying the family's belongings. The adults carry blankets and torches and a cardboard box, and the children, wearing white arm-bands, carry cushions and a board game. They are on their way to the communal air-raid shelter at the bottom of the street. She wishes she was going with them. Every window in every terraced house in the street is black. She thinks she would be comforted by some signs of life but everybody in London knows the night-time drill and she knows she will see nobody but Alfie tonight.

She hears him charging up the stairs and hurtles back into his bed like a startled gazelle. She sits against the headboard so rigidly that it looks as if she's in a state of *rigor mortis*. She wonders whether she should have pretended to have fallen asleep; he's been in the kitchen so long it would have been feasible, but she remembers that *dying's much worse than death*. She tells herself for the hundredth time that it's better to get his conjugals over and done with, as if he's only going to want them once. Then he appears at the bedroom door bare-chested but wearing his blue pyjama bottoms. She directs her gaze above his waist. He is as muscular as she imagined, but thankfully less hairy. She thinks if she were a normal woman, she would find him and his physique very attractive. Then she wishes again, for both their sakes, that he'd not asked her to marry him that day because on any other day, she'd have said no.

Alfie can't believe that Lil is sitting in his bed in her nightie. He can't believe that she is his. He stops in the doorway and stares at her as if she's a new exhibit in a zoo. He thinks he is a bloody lucky bugger. He has never seen her hair loose and finds that it is much longer than he imagined. His eyes follow the dark waves of it all the way down to her breasts and then, as if he has seen something prohibited, his eyes dart back up to her face. He can't let his gaze rest any longer where it wants to because he feels the beginning of a problem in his pyjama bottoms. He doesn't want that sort of problem while standing in the doorway because it's not part of his wedding night strategy.

He has spent a lot of time considering his wedding night strategy. Back in January when he wrote to Louis to tell him of his engagement, Louis - Royal Marine, experienced with women, good at drawing, and fan of cartoons – had responded with a letter entitled: *Louis' Illustrated Guide To Sexual Positions For Virgins*. The coarse drawings had made Alfie laugh out loud but he could only imagine Lil, and himself for that matter, in one of the suggested positions. He'd hid the letter under the chest of drawers in their bedroom and told himself that, on the wedding night, it was perfectly acceptable to stick to kissing, cuddling and the missionary position – the position Louis had underlined and termed in capital letters, 'THE BORING FUCKERS' POSITION'. Now, he doesn't give a hoot about positions and wedding night strategies, he just wants to dash into bed, whip off his pyjama bottoms, put his arms around his wife and have a go. He is exceedingly glad that he didn't push the two single beds together to make a double because he wants to keep her close to him all night. He approaches the bed trying not to look like a starving lion and decides that he's never been so happy.

***

Lil lies on her back and Alfie lies on his left side gazing at her face. To break the silence he says, 'Hello, Mrs Edwards.'

She wishes he hadn't called her 'Mrs Edwards' because it seems utterly ridiculous. And as for the way he says it, well it's really too much, it makes her feel quite ill. He's drawn the short straw getting her, why can't he tell?

'Mrs Edwards is your mother,' she says.

He feels foolish but he laughs it off and says, 'Christ Almighty, Lil, you're definitely not Mum.'

She says nothing.

'You're beautiful,' he says, wondering if that's the right thing to say and whether he can touch her yet.

She sighs and surreptitiously checks with her left hand, the hand furthest from him, that the towel she is supposed to bleed upon is still in place beneath her bottom. He inches his body towards her as carefully and as discreetly as he can as if a sudden or loud movement might send her fleeing from the room.

'I can't believe you're my wife.'

She says nothing.

'I'll do everything I can to make you happy, I really will.'

She doesn't want to hear these impossible things so she silences him by saying, 'Kiss me.'

He doesn't need telling twice. He props himself up on his elbow and leans over her face. To begin with, they kiss like children with their lips pressed together and their faces shifting ever so slightly from side to side until he gets brave and prises her lips apart with his tongue. She decides to give his tongue a chance because she thinks one tongue must feel much the same as another. She opens her mouth and lets their tongues clash. As they go on kissing, she closes her eyes and imagines that she is kissing Margaret. She licks *her* lips, explores *her* mouth, tickles the tip of *her* tongue and teases the sides and back of it.

Alfie enjoys kissing Lil so much that he fears he will make a mess of his pyjama bottoms if they don't stop. And he knows that if he goes for the BORING FUCKERS' POSITION at this point, it will all be over in a second. He doesn't know what is best. He doesn't want to embarrass himself by advertising his inexperience. He needs her to stop making him feel so good even if it is just for a second. He decides to slow things down by telling her what a great kisser she is, but he forgets that he needs his tongue to speak. He says, 'You're a great kisser, Lil,' as if he's just suffered a stroke.

Lil opens her eyes and Margaret disappears. She pulls her face away and becomes aware of his erection against her thigh. She wants to put some distance between his erection and her thigh but she has run out of bed. If she moves away from him now, she'll find herself splayed upon the floorboards with that godforsaken thing on display.

'Where'd you learn to kiss like that?' he says. As soon as he asks the question it occurs to him that she shouldn't be such a good kisser if, like him, she's a virgin. And, as soon as this occurs to him, he forgets about his premature ejaculation fears and worries that he isn't her first. She has never spoken of another boy, but what if there was one?

Lil has a sudden compulsion to tell him about Margaret and to shout, 'I'M NOT WHAT YOU THINK I AM.' But she remembers that she is married now, that Margaret is married to Geoffrey, that she won't ever be with Margaret again, and so she says something she thinks will allay his fears. She says, 'Girls practice on each other.'

He hides his relief by laughing and saying, 'Boys don't.'

She says nothing but just as she is wondering what his next move will be or whether she should make the next move by taking off her nightie, the air raid siren sounds. He groans and says, 'That's all we need. Come on, Lil, we better not risk it.' She thinks she'd very much like a bomb to drop directly on her head while he leans over the side of the bed, puts his hand beneath it and pulls out a torch. He gets out of bed, grabs a pillow off Louis' mattress, and holds it over his groin to conceal his problem.

'Where are we going? I can't go to the public shelter in my nightie,' she says, horrified at the thought that Alfie's conjugals might now be dragged out till the morning when there is a good chance his parents will return home and catch them at it.

'We're not going to the public shelter. We're going to the lounge. We've got the Morrison now, remember?'

'Oh, yes,' she says frowning. 'I forgot.'

'How'd do you manage that?' he asks, smiling.

She ignores the question, gets out of bed and takes the pillows and the blanket from his bed. He untucks the blanket from Louis' bed and whilst his back is turned, she snatches the old towel from his mattress and slips it between the folds of the blanket. Then they descend the stairs by torchlight preceded by great mounds of bedding. She catches sight of herself in a mirror. *Oh, God, this is what I would look like pregnant.*

'I take it you haven't been inside a Morrison before?' he asks.

'No,' she says faintly. 'I haven't.'

He mistakenly thinks that the newly invented Morrison shelter and its ability to competently shield the pair of them from a collapsed roof, is the cause of her anxiety. He tries to reassure her by saying, 'It's really sturdy, Lil, and plenty big enough for us to kip the night in.'

She says nothing.

'It's better than the public shelter eh, Lil?'

'Yes,' she mumbles and shakes her head.

They enter the front room and he makes the bright torch light dart about the walls as if they are burglars who need to identify the whereabouts of the valuables as quickly as possible. The Morrison shelter takes up the entire lounge. The Edwards' furniture, two patterned armchairs and a brown Moquette three-piece suite, huddle uneasily around the twelve foot by six foot steel-topped shelter with wire mesh sides.

'Here, chuck us that bedding,' he says, his voice sounding urgent as the siren seems to get louder and louder. 'I'll make sure we're nice and comfortable down here, no need to worry about that.'

She hands him the bedding but keeps hold of her towel.

'What's that?' he shouts in relation to her towel.

'It's nothing,' she says, awkwardly.

He doesn't hear her because she doesn't speak above the siren. 'Come again,' he shouts.

'It's nothing,' she repeats, shouting and blushing and grateful for the darkness.

He lets it drop because he's got an idea he knows what her towel is for and he wishes now that he hadn't asked her about it. He lifts up the side of the shelter that acts as the entrance and throws the bedding in. She watches him hastily cover the floor of the shelter with one of the blue blankets, lay out the pillows then cover the first blanket and the pillows with the second of the blue blankets.

'Do you want any of those cushions?' he shouts, pointing to some maroon knitted cushions on the three-piece suite.

She shakes her head.

'Here we are then,' he shouts again, offering her his hand. 'I'll help you in.'

She takes his hand because it's easier for her to do that than it is for her to shout that she doesn't need his help, but as she crawls into the shelter, with him holding onto her arm as if she's some old dear, she finds herself irritated by his chivalry.

'Alright, Lil?'

She nods a lie, sits on her calves with her back slouched and waits for him to enter the shelter.

'You can sit up in this thing without hitting your bonce you know. It's bigger than you think.'

She thinks he sounds like a young boy again: a bit boastful, trying to impress her. She knows she can sit up straight without touching the top of the shelter but she doesn't want to, and she doesn't want to be reminded that some things are bigger than she might think.

'I think I'll lie down,' she says, pointing at the carpet with one hand, in case he hasn't heard her, and clutching her old towel with the other.

'What was that? Lie down did you say?'

She nods.

'Good idea,' he says, as if it's an idea he hasn't had himself. 'Once we're in, I'll turn off the torch, alright?'

She nods her approval and is relieved that his conjugals aren't going to be illuminated because she doesn't want to see any aspect of it.

He turns his back and makes a pretense of sorting out his pillow so that she can put her towel where she needs to put it without him seeing. He has mixed feelings about her old towel: he doesn't want to hurt her, it is the last thing he wants to do, but he regards its presence as proof of her virginity and he can't help but feel relieved that he's her first.

She quickly flings the towel on the lower blanket, sits on it, gets under the top blanket and pulls it up to her chin.

He takes off his bottoms because he knows he can't hide this part of himself forever. As he wriggles free of them, his erection bobs up and down and Lil, unable to look away from this spectacle, wonders how she's going to manage it.

'Ready?' he shouts and turns off the torch, plunging them into darkness.

***

Alfie enters Lil just as the first bombs of the night are dropped on London. He moves slowly inside her in an effort to be gentle but she still feels as if she is being tortured. She tries to put herself somewhere else, in Margaret's bed, with Margaret on top of her giving her pleasure instead of pain. She tries to picture Margaret's amber eyes looking up at her from between her legs and she tries to remember the feel of Margaret's auburn curls against her inner thigh and the warmth of Margaret's mouth on her flesh, but the sound of the air raid siren and the bombs, and the burden of Alfie's weight upon her thin body, and the sounds he makes, cauterizes these images, and once more she finds herself deserted by Margaret. There is only Alfie and the Morrison's steel roof when her eyes are open, and there is only Alfie when her eyes are closed. He pushes himself deeper inside her, and shouts that he loves her and promises her that he'll get better with practice and she responds by edging away from him to escape the pain and the sound of his voice until the top of her head reaches the wire mesh wall of the Morrison and she can move no further.

***

Afterwards, when Alfie has had his conjugals and insists that Lil rest her head on his arm and listen to his vision of their future together, she remembers that she is supposed to use the toilet. The all-clear hasn't sounded yet and, until it does, she knows that he won't let her leave the Morrison to use the bucket in the kitchen, let alone the toilet in the garden. He states how many children he would like and specifies how many of these should be boys and how many should be girls and what order they should be born in, while she lies there spilling onto her towel, thinking that she is lost, and wondering whether Margaret lies in Geoffrey's arms thinking the same.

5: The Picturegoer

Alfie shouts up the stairs, 'I'm just nipping out.'

'What, without your new wife?' remarks Nell from the hallway.

Sitting on Alfie's bed, Lil pummels her forehead with her fists. Why can't Nell just say, 'Lil'? Without Lil? And just because they're married now, doesn't mean they have to spend every spare minute together. And if *she* doesn't mind him nipping out, why should *Nell* mind? He can go out and never come back for all *she* cares. She wonders if she's ever going to be able to do as Nell has asked and call her 'Mum.' Why can't she go on calling *her* Mrs Edwards? Nell *was* Mrs Edwards first. Nell *is* the *real* Mrs Edwards. Lil doesn't want to be called Mrs Edwards: it is as bad as being called Alfie's *new wife*.

'I won't be long, Mum,' says Alfie.

'But it's your honeymoon,' says Nell.

Fred mutters something from the lounge. Lil doesn't catch the words, but Alfie laughs in such a way that it makes her want to slap the laughter right out of him. Her cheeks burn: it's as if Alfie's slapped them with those big paws of his. She imagines Fred with a glass against the other side of Alfie's bedroom wall and his fat ear glued to the bottom of it. Why did Alfie have to make so much noise? He sounds like a dog.

'Don't be crude, Fred,' snaps Nell.

Fred rustles his newspaper.

'I just want to get something for…' says Alfie.

'Oh,' says Nell followed by, 'Ah, course you do, dear.'

Lil doesn't want whatever it is that Alfie's nipping out to get... her. She is reminded of her Nan's Christmas refrain: *You don't give to receive.* Well, that wasn't true. Alfie would give her some small token that she didn't want and she'd be expected to give him her body in exchange. Why couldn't he just forget the present and leave her in peace?

'We've got flowers in the garden,' shouts Fred, 'if it's flowers you're after. Save your money, son, I would.'

Nell advances to the lounge door, pokes her head round it and snaps, 'Be quiet, Fred, Lil will hear you.'

Fred shouts, 'There's still a few daffs out the back, Alfie,' but Alfie's already running down the road with a pocketful of change and the wind behind him and Lil is throwing on her coat, grabbing her copy of *Picturegoer,* thundering down the stairs and running out the house shouting and lying, 'Won't be long, Mum.'

***

Lil has seen *Gone with the Wind* before, but it doesn't matter because she's rather fond of Olivia De Havilland, especially Olivia De Havilland in Technicolor. But it was impossible not to recall that she first saw *Gone with the Wind* with Margaret.

The pictures had been a weekly outing for them, especially during the winter months because it was warm in the theatre, and they could sit in the back stalls and when the lights went down, they could touch each other almost wherever they liked. And it never mattered what the film was, or how many times they'd already seen it. Except, after *Gone with the Wind,* Margaret complained that it had gone on too long and that the one bar of chocolate they shared hadn't been enough to sustain her. When they left the theatre, Margaret pretended that the daylight hurt her eyes. She shielded them with her forearm and zig-zagged down the road groaning theatrically and saying, 'fiddle-dee-dee whatever has happened to my poor lil' eyes' in a terrible impersonation of Scarlett O'Hara. Lil stood on the theatre steps, adjusting her scarf, buttoning up her coat, watching her. She laughed at the disapproving stares Margaret received from passers-by and the way they altered their course to avoid contact with her on the path. The fact that Margaret didn't seem to realize that Lil wasn't walking beside her made it even funnier: on her own, Margaret looked unhinged. When Lil caught up with her, Margaret jumped on her back and demanded a piggyback ride until her eyes adjusted to the light even though, by that time, it was dusk. She squeezed Lil's flank with her thighs and pretended to whip her as Scarlett O'Hara had done to the frothy-mouthed horse that had eventually collapsed of exhaustion and died on the desperate journey back to Tara. Like the horse, Lil collapsed too, but it was on a grass verge and it was because her shoe lace had come undone and she was worried about tripping over and disfiguring them both. Once they stopped laughing at the heap they made of themselves, and the sheer folly of it – *at their age* – they walked arm-in-arm and discussed the following: the amount of mud on Margaret's skirt; Lil's piggyback skills; Margaret's growling stomach; and the surprise discovery of two bars of Fry's Turkish Delight hidden in a book. Tom had hollowed out the monograph and sent it to Margaret during her final year at boarding school. She hadn't found them at the time because what young girl wanted to read *Rome Under the Caesars* if it wasn't compulsory? And she'd only found them the day before because Mother had been on the hunt for things to donate to the YMCA – *of all people* – and she thought she better untie the string that Tom had used to secure the book to make it appear as if she'd read it so as not to incur a raised eyebrow from Mother. When the two bars of Turkish Delight popped out, Margaret decided that the trick was not to scrutinize their condition, nor draw the attention of Mother to their existence, but to just get on and eat them, one bar straight after the other. They'd tasted delicious in spite of the slight crunch, and they'd been one of the best surprises of her life, and yes, she did still let Mother have *Rome Under the Caesars* because what possible use had she for it? And she was sorry that she hadn't saved the sweet treasures to share with Lil during *Gone With The Wind*, but she just couldn't help herself because she'd been ravenous at the time of their discovery. Lil wondered if Margaret might have worms. Margaret demonstrated a comprehensive knowledge of the tapeworm diet.

'Let's talk about something else,' Lil said with a shudder when Margaret described the worm travelling to the brain.

'Okey-dokey, who do you think is prettier: Vivien Leigh or Olivia De Havilland?'

'Olivia De Havilland,' Lil replied without hesitation.

Margaret paused and then said, 'I have to say Vivian Leigh, but only because she reminds me of you.'

Now, alone in the theatre, the organ rising from the orchestra pit catches Lil's eye and concludes her reverie. The organist plays a lively version of 'Underneath the Arches'. A woman, from somewhere behind Lil, warbles, *Every night you'll find us / Tired out and worn…* Others join in: their cheery rendition belies the sentiment of the lyrics. Lil fiddles with her wedding ring and follows the progress of those shuffling up the carpeted slope to get to their seats. An elderly woman with holes in her stockings causes a traffic jam when she stops to retrieve a dog-end from the aisle. Lil watches as the woman puts the dog-end in her mouth and lights it before making for the cheap seats. Heads bob up and down and chairs fold with a squeak as those already seated half-stand to let others pass down the rows to the nearest empty space. Lil massages her neck and shifts this way and that, hunkering down in it until the back of her head makes contact with the back of her chair. She watches the crimson and gold of the cinema grow foggy with cigarette smoke and revels in the glorious familiarity of it all.

***

The audience laughs as Scarlett gargles with a mouthful of *Cheautard's Eau de Cologne* to conceal the smell of Brandy on her breath from Rhett Butler. Lil lets the last square of a bar of Cadbury's Ration chocolate melt on her tongue, stretches her legs beneath the chair in front, and returns her hands to the warmth of her arm pits. A message appears on the screen just as Rhett is telling Mammie that he knows she doesn't like him. It reads, 'AN AIR RAID IS IN PROGRESS. SHOULD YOU WISH TO LEAVE THE THEATRE, PLEASE DO SO AS QUIETLY AS POSSIBLE.' Lil kicks off her shoes and tucks her feet beneath her. Why on earth would she want to leave? This is where it starts getting good.

1942

6: Fatherhood

Lil writes to Alfie to tell him that they have a son. She instructs him to choose a name. He chooses Henry, to be shortened to Harry in honour of Harry Curtis, the manager of Brentford Football Club. He thinks this is appropriate because in 1935, Curtis took the club to the top division and made him the happiest boy alive. He doesn't tell Lil the origin of their son's name because he thinks she would care, but the truth of the matter is she wouldn't.

Harry is nearly three months old by the time Alfie meets him. It only happens at all because he is unexpectedly given a few hours leave one Saturday in March. It is the first leave granted him since reporting for basic training ten days after his marriage in April the year before. Nobody at home knows that he is coming and so when he bursts into his parent's house and cheerfully calls out Lil's name with a vision in mind of her sitting on the sofa nursing Harry, he finds himself bitterly disappointed. His own mother and son are at home, but his wife is not.

'Lil's mother is bedridden,' declares Nell. 'All since their place was bombed. Course, it's her own fault really. She decides, see, just this once, not to go to Turnham Green. Daft I know, but she says she was fed up to the back teeth with traipsing down there every night and getting a bad night's sleep for nothing. I don't blame her; it's cold and draughty in those public shelters and you have to put up with people coughing all over you, but it's asking for trouble if you don't go, isn't it? Sod's law the night you don't go is the night you get bombed and that's what happened to them. Next thing she knows, there's an almighty bang, she jumps out of bed, goes down the landing to the top of the stairs, and instead of the staircase what does she find but a pile of bricks. So she gets on her backside and starts bumping her way down the bricks, in the dark mind and alone because Lil's father's on duty, and she gets confused about where the bricks end and the floor begins so she stands up, not being able to put up with the bumping anymore, because, let's be honest, she hasn't got as much padding as some of us…' she pauses to slap her own generous bottom, 'and she takes a step forward and of course she falls arse-over-tit. So, she ends up with a twisted ankle, two sprained wrists and bruises you've never seen the like of before, and she's packed off, with Lil's father of course, to Shepherd's Bush. God only knows why they've decided to rehouse them in Shepherd's Bush. They've got no relatives there and poor Lil's been catching the bus every afternoon since to cook them an evening meal. She's such a good girl, Alfie, she really is, but she looks done in. Course it doesn't help that she eats like a bird.'

Alfie nods and wonders why Jerry couldn't have waited till tomorrow to drop the bloody bomb on her parent's place, and why it has to be her that does all the running round after them? She's got her own family to sort out now.

'Apparently, the blast lifted a motorcycle from the street straight into Lil's old bedroom. If she hadn't married you, she might have been a goner. What a frightening thought, Alfie.'

He stares at the clock above the fireplace and asks, 'What time will she be home?'

'Oh, she's always back for the babe's tea-time feed.'

'I'll miss her then. I can only stay an hour.'

'Oh, no, Alfie, is that all? She'll be ever so disappointed. I'd better wake the babe. At least you can have a look at him. He's the absolute image of you, he really is, but don't worry if he cries because he does fret. He's got Lil's temperament see.'

As Alfie sits in the arm chair with the Morrison pressing against his shins and his arms extended ready to receive his sleeping son from his teary-eyed and over-excited mother, he can't help but feel that it should be Lil warning him to support Harry's neck with one hand and his bottom with the other and to note the length of his legs and the amount of fair hair on his head. While he has stood for hours on end in pill boxes and walked long distances on route marches and patrolled the boundaries of one airfield after another, he has escaped the tedium of these duties by imagining certain future moments with his wife. Her handing him his son for the first time was one of those moments and a passionate reunion with her was another. He had hoped to find his parents out of the house and Lil and Harry home alone so he could make both these moments, moments he has imagined in infinite detail, happen. Instead, he is handed his son by his mother and offered a cup of tea and some jam and dripping sandwiches.

Whilst Nell is busy in the kitchen, he looks upon his son's face and feels like crying. He decides that Harry looks like him. He wants to thank Lil for this as if it is her doing, as if she molded his face from a lump of clay. He feels cheated holding their child beside a place where the child might have been conceived, without her at his side. He strokes Harry's face and rests his lips on the palm of his tiny hand because touching the places on him that he thinks she might have touched before she left the house, is the next best thing to touching her. He presses Harry to his chest and wishes like a man with a fever that he and Lil had been born in a different time when there was no war to separate them.

***

He is ten minutes late getting back to the guard hut that day and is put under arrest by his sergeant. He is confined to barracks for fourteen days and is made to do four hours pack drill in full kit at the double. As he doubles around the parade square like a Nazi on tanker's chocolate, and while he still has the energy to have thoughts of any kind, he wishes he hadn't bust a bleeding gut getting back to camp and concludes that he may as well have been hanged for a sheep as a shitting lamb.

7: Marking Time

It is three in the morning and Lil, Harry, Nell and Fred are sheltering in the Morrison. Nell hogs the torchlight to knit; Fred snoozes; Harry chews on Lil's nipple; and Lil wonders why she didn't think to join the Women's Land Army when Margaret ended things. Wouldn't it have been better to milk cows than to become one? Supplying Harry with milk is all she seems to do these days. She envies those girls in the poster. She'd have been quite happy to gather crops, dig ditches and wear khaki dungarees. All the girls look happy. Even in black and white, she can tell they have more colour in their cheeks than she does. Fred wakes himself up with a snort. 'Let's hope the babe sleeps through this one,' he says, yawning so loudly that Nell drops a stitch.

'We haven't had a letter in weeks,' she says, like an accusation.

'What made you think of that?' asks Fred.

'What do you mean? It's all I think about.'

'You talking about Alfie?'

'Yes, Alfie, who else would I be talking about? Louis never writes. Well, not to us anyway.'

'Alright, gel, calm yourself, I was only asking.'

'Well, when have you ever seen a letter from Louis?'

Fred tuts and Lil decides that he must have a very strong tongue to tut so loudly. This thought starts her thinking about Alfie's tongue and other parts of him that she would rather not think about.

'I hope he's managing to keep warm. Perhaps I should knit him some socks. It's much colder than last year.'

'No, it's not. It's much the same as it always is.'

'I'm not so sure about that.'

'You never do your front up,' says Fred, 'that's your trouble. What do you think buttons are for, gel?'

'That doesn't explain the chilblains, Fred. I've never had chilblains this early in the year.'

'You're asking for trouble if you roast your hands over the fire. I've told you a dozen times but you don't listen to me.'

'Why should I?'

The last time Nell had listened to Fred, she'd been convinced that if she didn't hurry up and marry him, she'd die an old maid. There had been no courtship or declarations of love. He'd bought her a bottle of Mackeson's in The Gardeners Arms and said, 'Nelly gel… I've been thinking… you're getting on a bit now… and… well… I think it's time you got married… to me, if you like?' And she replied, 'Well… yes… I suppose so, Fred, when you put it like that.'

Now, Fred grunts and says, 'Sod this for a game of soldiers. If the bloody Krauts were going to drop a bomb on us, they'd have done it by now. I think they'd be doing me a bloody favour if they did.'

'Where are you going?'

'Back to bed.'

'Off you go then, but don't blame me if you get your wish.'

He crawls across the floor on all fours to exit the Morrison. He wears a green moth-eaten Aran-knit pullover over his pyjama top and wears pyjama bottoms that should have been turned into dusters years ago. Lil glimpses grey wiry hairs on his calves and his white bony ankles and is reminded of a stray mangy dog that she saw go under the wheels of a Tomlinson electric bread van a month before Margaret joined the typing pool.

'Silly old sod, it's you that's asking for trouble. I'd better come with you.'

'No, you don't, Nelly. You stop there and keep Lil company. Talk about the weather.'

'What do you mean talk about the weather? Oh, you do go on, Fred. Oh, you are daft, Fred.'

He emits a 'humph' sound just as his slippered feet disappear from the Morrison. He lets the side of the shelter bang shut and Nell sighs, Harry wakes up, and Lil wonders why every member of the Edwards family has to be so loud and thoughtless.

8: Reunion

It is the hottest day in July and Alfie stands on an airfield wondering if Lil's plonked seven-month-old Harry in a bucket of cold water to keep him cool. He pictures Harry's hands slapping the water and the shock on his face when the splashes he creates travel to the parts of him that are not submerged in, and acclimatized to, the cold tap water. He pictures Lil on tiptoes reaching up to the washing line in a flimsy summer dress, her hair neatly rolled up at the sides, a house apron pulled tight around her waist and her long slim fingers deftly pegging out wrung nappies. From the corner of his eye, he considers three Polish pilots from No. 303 squadron. They muck about as they saunter towards their aircraft, nudging each other and laughing as if there was no chance of them dying tomorrow. When he is dismissed, he doesn't linger. All he wants to do is go home to his family.

***

Alfie pushes open the door to his parents' house and finds Harry sitting in a nappy chewing the corner of the hallway runner. Harry finds the raised pattern more soothing on his raw gums than a bickiepeg and doesn't mind the dirt. Alfie is struck by his size; he looks colossal compared with the last time he saw him. He is almost compelled to congratulate him on his growth as if Harry himself had selected the rate of it. Not knowing what else to say Alfie says, 'Whatcha got there, son?' But he doesn't feel right saying 'son'; he feels as if he is pretending to be something he's not. He crouches down to get a closer look at his child. He thinks Harry has less hair now; it seems to have receded at the front, and when he peers around the side of his head, he finds a bald patch at the back. 'You've got about as much hair as your Granddad, but the colour of your hair is the same as your mother's.' He peers into Harry's eyes and is pleased to discover that they remain the same shade of blue as his own. 'Overall, I'd say you still look like me though. You're a handsome little bugger.'

Harry stops chewing and his chin wobbles because a very big person is ruffling his balding head. A long string of drool dangles from the runner and then attaches itself to his chest. The stranger frowns and Harry's chin wobbles more vigorously.

'You're not going to grizzle, are you?' says Alfie.

Harry thinks about it because he fears this person is going to pull the runner out of his mouth.

'Don't do that, fella.'

Harry stares at the person with his wobbly chin and waits, suspended between curiosity and fear, for him to make his next move. The person's next move will determine what his will be. If the person attempts to touch him again, he intends to scream his head off until his mother comes to rescue him.

Lil is feeding a bed sheet through a mangle in the garden. 'Is that you, Mum?' she calls.

Alfie puts his finger to his lips. Harry stuffs his gummy mouth with his pudgy fist.

'Mum? Is that you?'

'Yes, Lil, it's Mum.'

Alfie smiles at Harry and Harry half-smiles back but the joke is lost on him.

'Who is that?' snaps Lil, piling the two ends of the sheet on top of the mangle to prevent them from plummeting to the dirty ground.

Harry hears the anxiety in his mother's voice; he raises his eyelids and gazes frantically at the kitchen door. He opens his mouth, curls his upper lip and makes the sound that usually earns him her attention. Then, frowning, Alfie reaches out to chuck him under his chin and says, 'Your mum sounds cross. I've only been here five minutes and already I'm in trouble.' Harry decides that he's had enough of this person and jerks his head away from the person's huge hand. However, he forgets that his head is heavy and his neck, relatively speaking, is weak. This means that he can toss his head back but his neck doesn't always counterbalance the move. He topples backwards and bangs his head on the skirting board with a dull thud. At first, he doesn't make a sound because the shock of banging his head takes his breath away but neither does the big person and he finds this odd. Even though the cool runner feels lovely and cool against his clammy back, the pain in his head prompts him to seek some attention so he begins to howl.

Alfie hears Lil say, 'blast,' as she almost slips on the kitchen tiles. He had planned to shout, 'Surprise, I'm home,' the minute he walked in the door. But now, fearing he's about to give Lil a heart attack or get blamed for making Harry cry, he says, 'Don't panic, Lil, it's only me. Harry's fine. He just lost his balance is all.'

She arrives in the hallway with raw hands and strands of sweaty hair plastered to her pale face and whispers, 'Alfie?'

Harry is relieved to see his mother again and stops crying and Alfie is relieved that Lil can silence him with just a glance because he found the volume of his bawling quite alarming. He steps over him, throws open his arms and says, 'Yes, surprise!'

She looks at him as if he's Adolf Hitler and then says, 'What are you doing here?'

Harry looks from his mother to Alfie and back again and thinks: *What about me?*

Alfie thinks that she has grown more beautiful with time even if she is a bit thin in the face. 'I'm dying for a cuddle,' he says. 'That's what.'

She slowly steps into his open arms and bursts into tears; it takes everybody by surprise. Alfie is delighted and his heart soars because he's never really been sure that she loved him, but he is now. He squeezes her tightly and says, 'I know, sweetheart, I've missed you too.'

***

After three days at home, Alfie returns to his regiment. Seven weeks after that, Lil learns that peeing after his conjugals is a pointless exercise because she is pregnant again and miserable, and Harry stops saying 'Dada' because 'Dada' seems to have gone 'Bye-Byes'.

1943

9: A Letter Home

Lil learns that Alfie has been transferred to… a thick blue line. What did the censors think she was going to do with that information? He writes that the city greeted him with a banner that proclaimed, '*Vinereall Disease Is On The Rise.*' What a thing to tell her and he's misspelt venereal. He's met someone called Joe who lives with his old Nan in Islington. Is this really news?

She is reconciled to reading about Alfie, but reading about a boy she's never met and will never meet is asking too much. Besides, this letter ought to have been full of their daughter, Margaret, not some nineteen-year-old nobody from Islington who's good with a football. And he knows she loathes football. 'Joe,' she spits, after reading his name for the seventh time. 'If this baby had been another boy, you'd have wanted me to call him Joe. Well, I wouldn't have done it.' Then that ugly word flies deliciously into her head so she adds, 'I wouldn't have fucking done it.' Then she blames Alfie for polluting her speech. 'Thanks to you, I don't even sound myself.' She looks up at the ceiling and says loudly, 'I called this baby what I wanted to,' as if to make sure Alfie hears.

'Course you did, dear,' says Nell, appearing in the kitchen with a bag full of rhubarb. 'Whoever said that you didn't? Was it Fred? You mustn't mind him; he's as daft as a brush. I named both my boys. I thought we must have company the way you were going on to yourself. Fred talks to himself just the same; he must be rubbing off on you,

41

dear. What have you got there? Another letter? Already? Oh…was it Alfie that said you couldn't call the baby Margaret?'

'No… I didn't mean… I hope you didn't… I was just thinking aloud, Mum. I haven't finished reading Alfie's letter yet.'

'I'll have a look at that when I get back. Rakes' Greengrocers was hit last night. You know the Rakes' don't you? They live above the shop.'

She doesn't, but neither does she want to be persuaded otherwise so she just says, 'Yes,' and then, 'Is Rakes their real name? Rakes' Greengrocers?'

'Do you know, I've never thought about it like that… It's always been Rakes' Greengrocers as far as I know… Certainly I've always called them Mr and Mrs Rakes but perhaps they took their name from the shop. Perhaps the shop was named after a rake and not them at all. It's been Rakes' as far back as I can remember.'

'They were hit last night?'

'I can't ever recall hearing them called something else. Fred would likely know.'

'It doesn't matter.'

'Ask Fred.'

'What's happened to the Rakes?'

'Ah… well… I don't want to upset you, dear.'

Lil waits.

'Mr Rake was killed. Direct hit so they say. Absolutely terrible.'

She thinks about how Nell's attempt to look upset is, in the main, betrayed by the flush in her cheeks, her dilated pupils and the rapid rise and fall of her bust.

'I don't know where Mrs Rake, or whatever she's called, was at the time, but they say she's there now, picking over the rubble in her dressing gown, mad with grief, looking for him.' She hides her mouth behind her plump hand before whispering, 'They haven't found poor Mr Rake's body yet.' Then, out of habit, she fills the kettle, places it on the stove and lights the gas ring. 'So, I feel I ought to get round there and see if there's anything I can do to help, you know with the search and that, or with Mrs Rake, but don't worry I'll be back to do Fred his lunch. And, I'll stew the rhubarb too. Look at it,' she says, returning to the sack and thrusting her flabby arm in to raise a stick for Lil's inspection. 'Lovely and red, dear.'

42

Lil raises her eyebrows in mock wonder and then considers whether Nell is capable of seeing through her, as easily as she sees through Nell. Then she wonders if she's expected to offer to stew the rhubarb while Nell is searching for Mr Rake's body, and after that, if she has the energy to strip, peel and slice it.

'You like rhubarb, don't you, dear? Reckon it'll do us all a power of good. Fred's bowels haven't moved in days, that's why he's been such a grumpy old so and so lately. Don't tell him I said that, he's ever so funny about his inner workings. Oh, poor old Mrs Rake... It's such a tragedy.'

'Yes,' she says, not quite sure which of Nell's statements she's agreeing with. Then she pictures Nell searching for Mr Rake and finding nothing but the seasonal contents of his decimated shop. Some potatoes would be nice.

'Does Alfie say whether he's getting enough to eat in this letter? Did you ask him, last time you wrote? I do worry about that. I worry about Louis too but... well... you know Louis, he doesn't write so I've no way of knowing how he's keeping and Fred says it's time I stopped cosseting him. What a word for Fred to know! But I'm not cosseting him, I'm worrying about him. How am I supposed to stop worrying?' she pleads.

Lil looks down at Alfie's letter. She knows from having read the second paragraph that he's hungry. If it hadn't been for Joe stealing eggs from chicken coops during the long route marches, Alfie would have starved to death. Why must he always exaggerate? She'd paused after the second paragraph to try to remember the last time she'd had a fresh egg to eat, and remembered that it was the time she and Margaret ate scrambled eggs wearing nothing but their Cami knickers in Margaret's digs. Margaret had purposely made her breasts wobble as she stood over the portable stove smoking and scrambling eggs with an antique fork and had said with a saucy smile, 'You can't beat eggs and breasts in the morning.' Lil had responded by asking her where she'd got the eggs. With raised eyebrows Margaret had replied, 'Loose lips sink ships.' Now, she wonders if the memory is real. 'Alfie's fine. He's getting eggs, which is more than we do.'

'Oh, well, that's good. That's put my mind at rest. I feel much better now but you look terrible, dear, completely done in. You should sleep when the children do and drink some of that milk, dear, that's what it's for: nursing mothers. I won't be long. Oh, I wonder if the Food Flying Squad will be at Rakes?'

Nell knows that the hot food and warm drinks the Food Flying Squad distribute to the bombed out, volunteers and mourners – be them chief or ones passing by – beats anything she might muster for her own lunch. She leaves the bag of rhubarb on the kitchen floor and gallops out of the house. Lil returns to the letter wondering which paragraph will acknowledge the birth of their daughter. It's not the fifth. The fifth is about street-fighting in... a thick blue line, and sleeping rough in... a thick blue line, and Joe's talent for the harmonica. *I nearly forgot to mention that Joe plays the harmonica.* Well, she didn't forget to mention that she gave birth to their daughter fifteen days ago. What has he got to say about that? And Harry for that matter; he's got whooping cough.

Then she sees something crawling across the page. First, it is black in colour and then it is white. It obscures some of the letters in Alfie's words and soon after, erases whole words. Now he's given her a migraine. She takes a chip-pan from the kitchen cupboard in case this one makes her sick, and also a pudding basin. She removes the whistling kettle from the stove, fills the basin with the boiling water, and drops in a flannel. Then she crosses the kitchen to the hall and stands at the foot of the stairs listening for the children. No coughing, no crying; she could sob with relief. She sits on the stairs, takes two aspirin from her apron pocket, pops them in her mouth, crunches them like sweets, and waits until she can see again with her head propped against a baluster.

When she gets to the sixth paragraph, she finds that it is censored but for the words, *I can't dodge; useless Sergeant;* and *disembarkation centre.* She thinks of the things she can't dodge in life such as Alfie's conjugals, pregnancy and childbirth and wonders which of them is worse off. She notes a horrible taste in her mouth that makes her think of the colour brown.

The seventh paragraph contains love talk and kisses: why couldn't the censors have put a thick blue line through that? What it doesn't contain is any acknowledgement of their daughter's existence. Now, she'll have to notify him of the birth all over again and it's another job she's too tired to do. She snorts at the postscript: *You really would love Joe,* and feels the beginnings of the headache she's been waiting for.

She puts the letter down, takes the hot flannel from the basin, undoes the first three buttons of her dress, and applies the flannel to her left breast because it feels like it's stuffed with hot coals. The infection she has there makes her head swim. 'No doubt you'd have thought of Josephine for a girl,' she mutters. She decides that Fred will have to send Alfie a telegram. The telegram will tell him that their daughter has been officially registered as 'Margaret' even though this is untrue; she won't go to the registry office until she no longer walks as if Margaret were still dangling from her minny. Plus, her sanitary towels can't keep up with the amount of blood her shrinking uterus deposits on them. She's lucky if one lasts an hour, and it all still feels so raw down there and dry, despite the blood, as if the two halves of her minny are shrivelling and shrinking and retreating inside her. It wouldn't be so bad if it disappeared altogether: no more conjugals and no more babies. Why couldn't the doctor have just sewn the whole thing up? She removes the damp flannel from her breast and drops it on top of the letter.

She named the baby after *her* friend, not his.

Then Margaret starts squawking fierce little *wah, wah, wah's* because she is hungry and Lil slumps on to the kitchen sideboard because she hasn't got enough milk for Margaret, and it is agony to feed her drops of nothing.

10: Rationed

The queue at the children's clothing exchange is long and cheerful. Harry sits on the varnished wooden floor and places one wooden cube on top of another. Lil stares at him and wonders when she will stop seeing Margaret everywhere. Today, it was on the double-decker bus.

Harry had been sitting on her lap, dozing. The sound of his wheezing chest had attracted an enquiry and some suggestions from the woman sitting next to them. Lil thought the woman's breath smelled worse than a drain; her teeth looked as if they were covered in lard. She also thought the woman should pluck her chin hairs; it was impossible not to count them. Nell had said the fresh air would do Harry's chest good. The woman didn't agree. 'And he'll keep that cough until summer,' she warned, revelling in the sentence. It was only October. Would he really cough his way through another year? Perhaps he would cough forever since the preceding summer months hadn't made a blind bit of difference to him. She was glad Nell had offered to keep seven-month-old Maggie at home with her because Maggie vomited at the drop of a hat and people always seemed to want to get to the bottom of that.

'What's his name?'

'Harry.'

'Henry?'

'We call him Harry.'

'What's wrong with Henry?'

'My husband prefers Harry.'

'What do men know? I should have thought Henry was preferable to Harry. How old is he?'

Lil wanted to cover her nose with her hand but her hands were employed with keeping Harry from falling off her lap. 'Almost two.'

'Two? He's a bit on the small side for two, isn't he?'

Lil ignored the question.

'You should be in the country. Staying here is madness. It isn't safe. You should have gone a long time ago,' she said, lighting a cigarette.

Lil thought of Margaret and then rising from her seat said, 'This is our stop,' when it wasn't. They should stay on for another two. Harry stirred as she shifted him onto her shoulder to bend and retrieve the bag containing the clothes he'd outgrown and their gas masks.

'You getting off, duck?' the conductor inquired.

'Yes,' said Lil.

The conductor tugged the cord to ring the bell for the driver. 'I'd sit back down again if I were you; Fritz dropped a big 'un on Goldhawk Road. We have to go round.'

'I'm up now, thank you.'

'I'll take those then,' he said, throwing his cigarette out the window and striding down the aisle to relieve Lil of the bag of clothes and the gas masks. When he reached her, he tried to make Harry smile by pulling a daft face but Harry wanted to sleep, not be entertained by a stranger, so he began to cry. Then the crying made him cough and the coughing made him cry all the more because his chest hurt when he coughed.

'Oh, dear,' said the conductor. 'What a performance.'

'I told you,' muttered the bearded woman. 'You shouldn't have brought him out.'

Lil wondered why some people said whatever came to mind and others said nothing. Would she ever be the person who said: *You should have left well alone?* Or, *you should have cleaned your teeth?* She turned her back on the dirty woman and followed the conductor to the back of the bus gripping Harry's skinny thighs and lunging at the grab handles. As they reached the stairwell at the rear of the bus, she spotted some black suede peep-toe shoes on the penultimate step. *Didn't Margaret have the very same shoes?* Though she wasn't able to see any more of the woman, her heart began to pound and her face turned hot. *Wasn't every bit of Margaret's body as slender as those ankles?* She felt shaky, as if she hadn't eaten in days. *Why did she have to bump into Margaret en route to the clothing exchange?* She felt poor and drab in her utility coat and shoes. Her heart raced and she felt uncomfortably hot. She turned her back on the stairwell to find the bearded woman watching her. She turned back to face the stairwell wondering how best to avoid Margaret. She repositioned Harry so that his head obscured her face. He didn't like it. 'No, no, no,' he cried, before wiping his snotty nose on her cheek. The conductor raised his eyebrows. The peep-toe shoes shifted on the stairwell. Lil wiped her cheek with her sleeve. The bus stopped. The conductor jumped off swinging the bag of clothes high into the air. Lil's breathing quickened. A handle on the bag broke. Harry filled his nappy and then the bus with the smell of it. Noses wrinkled and a man complained as if Harry had broken the law. The peep-toe shoes descended. A shabby knitted vest floated into the gutter like a shot-down parachute. Lil waited for utter humiliation.

But it wasn't Margaret. It was nothing like her. It was a woman in her fifties with a mink fur stole that looked like it might bite.

Now, in the queue at the children's clothing exchange, Lil thinks Margaret's peep toe shoes were brown suede, not black. She chastises herself for being foolish and blames it on the children. If she wasn't so tired, she'd still have her wits. She reminds herself that she doesn't want any more children. She thinks about sabotaging her womb with a sharp object. The sleep and peace that a long stay in hospital would facilitate is appealing. It's not a new idea. Most nights, before she drops off to sleep, she fantasizes about receiving a hospital visit from Margaret. During the visit, Margaret promises to leave Geoffrey. She proposes they live somewhere remote. She begs Lil to agree to it. Eventually, Lil does. They never get round to discussing the children.

1944

11: The Front Line

The Latium landscape is shrouded in mist. Even though it is winter, the volume of rainfall is unusual for the region. Alfie and Joe had spent the night delivering ammunition to the top of a mountain and bringing an unconscious corporal back down. In the dark and the rain, the mountain had been difficult to negotiate. In addition to the rocks, some of which were the size of a house, there were dead men, dead mules, and German and Allied soldiers with machine guns to avoid.

'No wonder they fired at us, all the noise you made,' said Alfie.

'You're taller than me,' argued Joe.

'What's that got to do with it?'

'I have to stand on the balls of my feet to keep the stretcher level with you. Look.'

'So it's my fault you're such a noisy bastard?'

'Nah, I'd say it's his,' said Joe, nodding at the unconscious corporal.

In the grey dawn light they'd spotted a red-cross flag hanging limply from the branch of an Italian maple tree and then the first aid post itself: a small sandy coloured house with a red roof. The first aid post was chaotic and the floor had felt spongy underfoot. Alfie had expected to be glad to get out of the rain but once inside, he'd decided not to linger. Joe had noticed a nurse with red hair, thin wrists and freckled hands blanket-bathing a quivering wreck.

Now, half-way into the long walk back to battalion headquarters, Joe chain-smokes and wonders if the nurses wash the crown jewels.

He's not sure how he feels about the blanket bath. He's not sure his crown jewels would stand the scrutiny.

Alfie stalks ahead and thinks of Lil. He sets out to imagine her morning from the moment she wakes, to the moment she sits down to eat breakfast, but doesn't move beyond the moment where she dresses. He is living proof that the British government aren't lacing his tea with potassium bromide. His wet trousers accentuate his problem and seem to press on the bloody thing like a hand. He has to stop thinking about Lil. He waits for Joe to catch up with him and then says, 'Don't take a shit in the middle of the night.'

'You what?' says Joe.

'The other night I was having a shit when I felt a pistol on the back of my neck.'

'Come again?'

'I was squatting by a tree having a shit and some bloody Rupert puts a pistol to the back of my neck and asks me what I'm doing.'

'Is this a wind-up?'

'Swear on my life. So I says, "I'm doing a toilet, Sir."'

Joe stops walking, folds himself in half and has silent hysterics into the palm of his hands. He puts cigarette ash in his hair. Alfie is reminded of an elderly man he saw weeks before, in Naples, being doused with DDT by a nun wielding what looked like a bicycle pump. He'd been told it was to halt the spread of typhus. Encouraged by Joe's response to his story, he decides to impersonate the officer. 'So he says, "I thought you were Jerry, what, what," and I says, "No, Sir, Private Alfie Edwards, Sir," and he says, "Very good, Private, carry on shitting."'

'You're making it up,' laughs Joe.

'I'm not, I swear I'm not,' insists Alfie, 'and I'll tell you something else for nothing: it was the quickest shit of my life.'

12: Hide-and-Seek

Alfie and Joe's trench is full of water. Behind them, two long-dead German soldiers sit propped against a telegraph pole, their heads touching as if they are plotting something big, their machine guns pointed at the sky. In the nearby farmhouse, a *useless* sergeant shouts orders from a heavy wooden door while an officer, perched on a box containing dehydrated soup, pushes back his cuticles. To the right of their trench, three soldiers roost in a coop made from corrugated iron. Next to them, the remains of American Rangers rest in the canopies of ancient oaks and Italian stone pines. Around them, the air smells of cordite, decomposition, and muddy water.

Joe is silent in the primal-looking bathtub. His skin looks like stilton. Alfie sits with his feet suspended above the rising water. He's worried about trench foot. 'Keep your bloody feet out of the water, Joe; you'll lose em if you don't.' Joe nods but all he wants to do is curl up like a woodlouse. Alfie tries to light a cigarette but the rain makes it impossible. He wishes he could find a place to hide. He thinks about when he used to play hide-and-seek with Louis.

They hid objects rather than themselves. More often than not, Louis would decide what was to be hidden and would also be the one to hide it. Bizarrely, the thing hidden would almost always be a small dead creature that he'd found, such as a squirrel, blackbird, or mouse. Once it was a tortoiseshell cat that was missing its tail. Then, Alfie would have to seek the dead thing by responding to directions that Louis expressed in terms of temperature: 'warmer... warmer... colder... warmer... colder... colder... freezing... really...... freezing... so...

freezing you're going to die, you silly sod... bit warmer... really warm... really hot... on fire... you're boiling... now you're colder again... freezing... really freezing... you're covered in frost, you idiot!' Louis never had the patience for more than one game and as soon as Alfie reached a distance where he was deemed to be 'an idiot covered in frost', Louis would declare the game over, himself the winner and Alfie the loser. The penalty for being the loser was to pick the dead thing up and kiss its face, if it still had one, which never bothered Louis but did bother Alfie. Now, Alfie thinks that Louis should not have terminated the game until the distance between himself and the hidden object was 'hypothermic'. He frowns: if they don't get out of the rain they'll die of hypothermia.

He thinks about ignoring the *useless* sergeant's orders and retreating further back into the forest. He wishes the Germans would drop a shell on the farmhouse.

'This is no good,' he says. 'We ain't staying here.'

Joe stares at a worm writhing in the mud wall in front of him. He is too cold to think or speak. Alfie climbs out of the trench and hauls him from the water as if he's already dead. Then the Germans resume their shelling, the ground explodes and Alfie lies on the forest floor like a butterflied chicken. When he comes round, he's not sure if he's been seriously injured and can't see Joe. He wonders if he has shrapnel in his back, if his legs are standing in the trees, if he's slowly bleeding to death. He decides to make every part of himself move. He brings his knees to his chin and tells himself that in order to do this he must still have two legs. He wiggles his toes and decides he must still have feet. He puts his hands in the mud and extends his arms until there is nothing pressing against his chest and thinks about his breathing. He doesn't taste blood in his mouth nor does he feel it trickling from his nose or ears and then he realizes that he can see. He concludes that he must be one of those people who survive these things. He tells himself that it happens. He rises to his feet. 'Joe,' he shouts, but a loud whistle overhead makes it seem as if he is whispering. He says, 'I'm...' before hitting the ground again.

13: Prisoner of War

Lil sits on the twin bed, the one nearest the window of Alfie's bedroom, clasping her hairbrush because she had thought to wallop the back of Harry's legs with it, and wonders if her life will always be like this.

'Are you a horse, Harry?' she says, getting to the matter at hand.

'No, Mummy.'

'Are you a dog?'

He shakes his head.

'Why did you bite your sister then?'

He shrugs. 'Accident.'

'You accidently bit your sister?'

He nods.

'It was not an accident, Harry, don't tell lies. Why did you bite her?'

'She hurts my ears.'

'How?'

'Crying.'

'Well, she will cry if you bite her cheek. I expect she'll cry for the rest of the day now and that's your fault. Babies cry, Harry, that's what they do. You did your fair share when you were a baby but nobody bit you, did they?'

He shrugs.

'I can tell you that they did not.'

He stares at the hairbrush she is holding wondering if his punishment will be to have his hair brushed in the middle of the afternoon.

'Well?'

'Don't like babies.'

'Is that so? I don't like you very much at the moment. Shall I bite your cheek?'

He shakes his head and smirks.

'Since you think it's so funny, I think that's exactly what I'll do. Bring me your cheek.'

He hides them with his hands. Her teeth are much bigger than his. She might eat his whole face. 'Not really, Mummy?'

'Yes, Harry, really.'

'No, Mummy.'

'Come here.'

He doesn't.

'At once.'

He thinks he better start crying. It's the only option left to him. Fear makes him dance on the spot as if the floorboards are covered in drawing pins. 'No, Mummy, don't bite.'

'But now that you're crying, I should definitely bite you, shouldn't I?'

'No,' he sobs.

'But you're hurting my ears, Harry.'

She watches the tears roll down his face and his little chest judder with the effort of producing them. She doesn't want to bite him. Don't they suffer enough having her as their mother? She tosses the brush on the bed and says, 'If you ever do that to Maggie again, I'll tell Granddad Fred to bite your cheek really hard. You won't like that, will you?'

He thinks about Granddad Fred's teeth; though he doesn't have many, the ones that he does have stick out in all sorts of directions and look like broken twigs. He shows his mother the whites of his eyes and says, 'No.'

'No,' says Lil.

Harry wipes his nose on his sleeve.

'Off you go then,' she says, nodding at the bedroom door.

With renewed distress, he flees from the room shouting for the whereabouts of his grandmother while Lil wishes she could run away too.

At the same time, Alfie wonders why everything the Germans say sounds as if it is being shouted or said crossly, even when it is obvious they are simply offering one another a cigarette or a lump of chocolate. Their seriousness makes him think about Lil. Yes, she was a serious sort but she did laugh too. There was an occasion before they got married when she found it difficult to stop.

It was when he did an impression of Geoffrey's mole. Making a fist, he shoved it on to his upper lip and arranged and moved his fingers in such a way that it looked like a malevolent sea anemone was stuck to his face. 'Come here, I should like to kiss you,' he made it say. He also made it ask if she would like a ride in its aeroplane and, for the sake of propriety, and fear of inviting a slap, he stopped it from saying: *Would you like to sit in my cockpit?*

The memory of her laughing till her eyes watered makes him smile, even though he believes he's about to be executed. He conceals his smile by looking down at Joe's bare feet. His plates have perked up a bit. Miraculously, just before they were taken prisoner, it had stopped raining and the sun had come out. He had removed Joe's boots and socks and placed his feet in the sun to dry. He'd driven two sticks into the mud, impaled the boots and hung the socks over a branch. Then he'd had a smoke. He was on his eleventh cigarette when the Germans arrived. In all that time, Joe hadn't said a word, just puffed when Alfie told him to. Now, he thinks the arrangement of Joe's boots on the sticks make it look as if he's drowned upside down in the mud and his legs have rotted to the bone. He wonders if the Germans will bury their two comrades by the telegraph pole. He doesn't think they will bother to bury him. He thinks of Lil and wonders what she will be doing when he dies, and if she will somehow know that he's gone. He imagines her sitting in the armchair with the children on her lap, their little blond heads nestled in her chest, their tiny bodies safe and warm in the crook of her arms.

14: Starfish Cooked in Olive Oil

'What was your last decent meal?' one prisoner asks the others. When it's Joe's turn to answer he says, 'Starfish cooked in olive oil.'

Alfie shits into a fifty-five-gallon oil drum and says nothing. How they can talk of food with the stink, noise and mess he's making, he doesn't know, but he wishes they wouldn't.

'Come to think of it,' says Joe, 'I reckon that was the best meal I've *ever* had. No offence to my dear old Nan like, she's a great cook, but cor... that starfish cooked in olive oil... that was something else that was.'

It's their fifth day on the freight train. They are being transported from the holding camp in Rome to a prisoner of war camp somewhere in Germany. Of the forty prisoners that are crammed in to Alfie and Joe's truck, Alfie is the only one with dysentery. Joe thinks he knows how it started but he's not sure why the rest of them haven't got it: they'd all drank from the same muddy puddles in the holding camp and they'd all had a go at the rotten cabbage stumps they'd found dumped by the perimeter fence. They'd tasted like wood. During their incarceration in Rome, there had been discussions on how long a man could go without proper food or clean water. Nobody knew the answer, but by the time they were herded into the trucks of the freight train, they'd been without both for eight days. That was why when a piece of bread and a lump of corned beef was doled out to each man before the train moved off, it was eaten on the spot and without a thought for how long it was supposed to sustain them.

On the fifth day, it's clear that this meal was intended to last them the entire journey. Now, Alfie can hardly make it off the makeshift toilet. He can hardly make it on there either; it's Joe that steadies him when he drops his trousers and holds him upright when he's hovering over the drum. He's not sure which hurts more, his stomach from the cramps, his backside from the emissions or his head from dehydration.

'Sausage, egg and chips,' says the man whose turn it is to respond to the last-decent-meal question.

'When did you last have that?' says the man nominated to keep a tally of the days spent in the truck with a stone he took from the holding camp and secreted in his underpants.

'I dunno, do I?'

'Christ, Chalky, the question was: What was your last decent meal, not, what's your favourite meal. If we're talking about our favourite meal, we're all gonna say sausage, egg and chips, aren't we?' says the originator of the question.

'Ah fuck off,' says Chalky.

'Not me,' says the man who beat the *useless* sergeant unconscious as soon as he set eyes on him at the holding camp. 'Can't eat eggs.'

'And I'd say shepherd's pie,' says another.

'Cottage pie,' says another.

'Same thing,' says Shepherds.

'Don't be daft,' says Cottage.

'Surely the last decent meal was the bread and corned beef,' says the man who managed to keep his boot laces when everybody else had to surrender theirs.

'You call that decent?' says the man who licks the frost from the truck's walls in an attempt to quench his thirst.

'Compared with the cabbages, yes, I do,' says Laces.

'Need to go,' says Alfie.

A few men groan. Joe helps Alfie to his feet and tells the groaners to shut it.

'The cabbages weren't a meal,' says Frost.

'What's the difference?' Shepherds asks Cottage.

'Think about it, you daft bastard,' says Cottage.

'Who the fuck cares?' says Shepherds.

'Shepherds watch their flocks…' says Cottage.

'What?' says Shepherds.

'*While shepherds watched their flocks by night all seated on the ground, the angel of the Lord came down and glory shone around,*' sings Stone.

'Jesus Christ. Shepherd's pie is lamb. Cottage pie is beef,' says Cottage.

'*Fear not, said he, for mighty dread had seized their troubled minds, glad tidings of great joy I bring to you and all mankind,*' continues Stone.

'Give it a rest will you,' says the man most irritated by the body lice. 'We've had Christmas.'

'Charming,' says Stone.

'The train's stopping,' says the man who hasn't peed in days.

'Need to sit down, Joe,' says Alfie feeling faint.

'What about the bog?' says Joe.

Alfie's legs go from under him. 'Alright, mate,' says Joe. 'Sit down it is.'

'Thank Christ for that,' grumbles Lice.

***

Since the sides of the truck are taken up with the bodies that bagged the sides of the truck first, Alfie and Joe sit back-to-back. It's an arrangement that benefits Alfie more than it does Joe: if Joe didn't spend the entire time resisting Alfie's weight, his toes would end up wiping his runny nose. So he resists Alfie's weight and thinks about football and if he'll ever get to kick a ball around again. By the time the truck door slides open, Alfie is snoring with his head on Joe's bony shoulder.

The air that floods the truck is icy but fresh; the fittest of the men shuffle over to the gap and breathe deeply. Snow covers the ground; Frost in particular wants to get his hands on it. A Nazi stands guard, his face impassive, his gun pointed at his prisoners. He watches some activity further down the line, trying not to let the prisoners see how cold he feels because he's the master race.

'It's another fuel stop,' says the self-nominated lookout. He ducks his head in and out of the door and reports back.

'What about food? Are they giving any out?' says the man with cold sores for lips and a coveted position in a corner of the truck that he isn't prepared to risk losing by getting up and seeing for himself.

'Can't tell,' says Lookout.

'We could drink the snow,' says Frost.

The guard glances at Frost before turning back to watch his colleagues. Frost wonders if the Nazi knows the English for snow and if he's been ordered to let them at it or to keep them from it. 'Are they letting anybody out?' he asks frantically.

'No,' says Lookout.

'Shit,' says Frost.

'Wait,' says Lookout. 'Yes,' says Lookout, 'I think... they... might... be...'

'Are they, or aren't they?' demands Frost.

'Yes... to empty the crapper... one truck at a time.'

'I'll do it,' says Frost, 'when it gets to us.'

'As long as you get us all some snow,' says the man who lost a freckled earlobe at the front.

'I'll go with Frost,' says the owner of the largest hands in the truck.

***

Frost and Hands inch the drum down a slide of two wooden planks that they were permitted to place side by side. Both men cover as much of their faces as they can with the collar of their great coats to stifle the smell. The effluent sloshes inside the drum like a Love wave and streams down the outer sides.

'Fucking hell,' says Hands. 'Watch it, will you?'

'It's on me too,' protests Frost.

'It's not gone on your hands though, has it?' says Hands, staring at his shit-covered hands.

The watching men are unanimous in their disgust. One man nods at Hands and then says to the space above him, 'I ain't having any snow off him.'

There's a murmur of agreement. Joe watches the drum's progress through a gap in the men. He turns away when the drum is tilted on to its side. And just as there was whenever Alfie approached the drum to empty his bowels, there is a collective groan now as the contents of the drum are emptied on to the snow. The sound of shit hitting the snow makes one man gag. The guard views the prisoners with contempt as if they alone are capable of producing shit of such inferior quality. And it is plain to all that Alfie has been shitting blood because the snow is now red as well as brown. And it reminds Joe of the man who got strafed in the gut during the march from Nola to the front; his body also produced red and brown but for some reason, the red was darker so the brown was too. And later, once the aerial attack was over and the man had been buried, Joe found himself thinking about the fireplace in his Nan's parlour, of its mahogany mantle and red tiled surround and he realized then, as he and Alfie and the rest of their battalion walked in single file across a partially cleared minefield, that he would never be warmed by his Nan's fire again. Alfie's waste, splattered across the snow like a giant bloody cow pat, seems to reiterate this. And nobody wants a handful of snow to suck anymore and it tickles the guard no end.

'Starfish cooked in olive oil,' mutters Alfie in his sleep.

15: Ping Pong

Louis transforms the Morrison into a Ping Pong table and wonders if Nell would spare a pair of tights for a net. Lil sits on a stool in the kitchen repairing the hem on her dress. It's blue with white flowers and the flattering belted waist makes it a favourite. Harry tries to draw a cartoon for Louis on the back of an old buff envelope with a piece of chalk that Louis gave him but his speech bubbles look more like deflated balloons. Maggie has one of her terse naps in the laundry basket and twitches and whimpers like a dreaming Jack Russell. Equipped with a packet of carrot seeds and a rusty garden fork, Fred digs for victory in the back garden with a soiled hankie draped on his bald head to protect it from the sun. In a stuffy church hall, Nell crams a tin of cheese into her seventy-sixth food parcel and imagines it reaching Alfie's PoW camp in Germany. None of them are looking forward to the bloater paste sandwiches for tea.

'Give us a game, Lil,' calls Louis, from the lounge.

'I don't know how to play,' she replies to the kitchen door.

'It's not hard. You've played tennis, haven't you?'

'Once.'

'Come on then.'

'I should finish this hem.'

'I'll play, Uncle Louis,' says Harry, abandoning his chalk.

'Wash your hands before you go anywhere with those hands, Harry,' orders Lil.

He licks his hands. 'All clean now, Mummy.'

Lil frowns. Louis appears at the kitchen door.

'I want to play,' repeats Harry.

'You're too small for Ping-Pong, fella,' he says, rubbing the top of Harry's head with the rubber side of the Ping-Pong bat to make his hair stand on end. 'You can't see over the table.'

'Swing me,' says Harry, grabbing his hand.

'Later,' says Louis. 'Why don't you give Granddad a hand with his vegetable patch? I bet you're good at digging.'

'I am,' agrees Harry, even though he's never done any before. 'Will you watch me?'

'Yes,' says Louis. 'Show me what you can do.'

Harry troops out into the garden shouting, 'Granddad Fred, I'm coming to help you dig.'

'Oh, Christ,' grumbles Fred, as he pokes at the dry soil with the gardening fork.

'Try not to get too grubby, Harry,' calls Lil.

'Yes, Mummy,' shouts Harry. 'Remember to watch me, Uncle Louis.'

Louis moves to the back door. 'I'm watching, fella,' he shouts, taking a tin of tobacco from his pocket.

Lil looks up from her sewing. She's been surprised at how good Louis is with the children. She'd thought he'd find them irritating and spend most of his leave away from the house but, so far, he hasn't gone anywhere. It's a problem, really. Even though he's been nothing but civil to her, she still feels uncomfortable in his presence. She regards him as a more potent version of Alfie, a version that won't be fooled and she feels as if he keeps a constant watch on her as if he is biding his time. She tries to avoid being alone with him. It had meant turning down an invitation to go to the pictures with him. It had meant missing the last showing of *Fanny by Gaslight*.

Now, at the back door, Louis rolls a cigarette and makes sure to keep a watch on Harry in the garden. 'Why did you marry my brother?' he suddenly asks.

She wonders if he came home just to ask her this and if he already knows the answer. 'You want to tell me that it's none of my bloody business, don't you?' he adds.

'Yes,' she says.

'I know it wasn't because you had to.' He lights the cigarette and bends down to sit on the back step.

She considers leaving the kitchen but fears that, wherever she goes, he'll follow. She thinks about Alfie's conjugals. Did he provide Louis with all the details? Did other people think she was already pregnant with Harry when they married? She goes from hemming her dress with a pick stitch to a backstitch.

'I was never that sort of girl,' she says, trying to make it sound like a slap on the cheek.

'You were never the sort to marry someone like Alfie,' he counters.

She feels as if the bottom's dropped out of her. She wonders if he will name what she is with Harry and Fred just a few yards away. Then she tries to remember a time when Louis might have seen her with Margaret. She can only recall the dance at the Palais when she'd flirted with Alfie to make Margaret jealous, but what if he'd observed them some other time? She scrolls through memories of excursions and events trying to pinpoint a time when their paths may have crossed or when she and Margaret might have been indiscreet. But she can't think of a time and she and Margaret were good at playing just-best-friends. She thinks about their other places. It was easy to imagine Louis knowing places such as those. She pictures a bomb site and she and Margaret on one side of a scorched wall, and Louis and some faceless girl on the other. She loses the thread from her needle. She'd never been comfortable making love outside. She wishes she hadn't let Margaret convince her that nobody would ever see them. It was naïve of her to think they had the monopoly on a space like that.

'I don't know what you mean,' she says unconvincingly.

'I just mean, Lil, if he comes home… when he comes home… promise me you'll be good to him, no matter what.'

The glimpsed escape from the anticipated accusation propels her into action. She pins the needle to her apron, scrunches her dress into a ball, rises from the kitchen stool and tells herself to get away from him.

'He's not like us, Lil, so promise me.'

'Why?' she asks, playing for time as she tip-toes towards the hall. 'Where will you be?'

Harry stops tossing the carrot seeds into Fred's trenches to check that Louis is still there. Louis reassures him with a wave and then says, 'Dead.'

1944

16: On Strike

Everything in the work camp is the colour of sludge. The only exception is the Feldwebel's white Alsatian dog, Brigit. Brigit snarls half-heartedly at Alfie as if to acknowledge that the amount of meat on his bones isn't worth the effort of the kill. He shivers in the feeble November sun and decides to ignore the bitch. The wall at his back feels clammy. He stands beside a faded patch of blood that looks like brown ink on grey blotting paper. He wonders why it should be his cracked hands that sting the most. The smell of the latrines creeps up on him like a ghoul. He watches a brittle leaf swirl around his feet and is reminded of a childhood visit to Kew Gardens with Louis.

Louis had announced that he wasn't going to school that day because the previous afternoon the headmaster, Mr Cunningham, had caned him for deliberately throwing a cricket ball at another boy's head. He'd caned the hand Louis had thrown the ball with. Alfie had agreed to skip school with him because he hadn't wanted to have to lie to Mr Cunningham about Louis' whereabouts. But scaling the fence of Kew Gardens hadn't been easy for either of them because Alfie was chubby and Louis had a livid hand. When Louis had to pull a splinter from his welted palm, he spat it on the ground and said, 'I'm going to kill him.'

'Who?' asked Alfie.

'Cuntingham.'

Alfie was shocked at Louis' alteration. 'No, you're not.'

'D'you dare me?'

'No, you can't kill Mr CUNN... ING... ham.'

'I could if I wanted. If you dared me to do it, I'd do it, you know.'

'I'm not daring you to kill somebody.'

'Sissy.'

'You'd be one of those murderers, Louis.'

'Better than being a sissy, Alfie.'

They started walking, making a beeline for a pile of raked leaves that stood taller than Louis. He burrowed into the centre of the pile like a mole and Alfie jumped on top of him. Steadily, like the leaves they kicked and threw, Louis' mood lifted as they returned the vast majority of the leaves to the verdant regions of here, there and everywhere. At that moment, an elderly patron of the Gardens, who shuffled along with the aid of a stick, left the Temple of Bellona where he'd stopped to rest his legs, smoke his pipe, and consider the main achievements of his life and began his slow campaign to the Berberis Dell. He wanted to survey the shrub's variegated autumn fruit and sample the berries because he'd been told that they were a rich source of vitamin C. But when his route took him close to the mess that Louis and Alfie had made of 'his' lawn, he forgot about the Berberis Dell and shuffled towards them. 'What do you think you're playing at?' he shouted.

'Run,' said Alfie, with a jumper full of leaves.

'No,' said Louis, throwing a fistful of leaves in his face. 'We haven't done anything wrong.'

Alfie thought of all the wrong they'd done that morning and felt the onset of a stomach ache. 'Let's go,' he said, tugging Louis' sleeve.

'Wait a minute,' Louis replied, holding his arm. 'What's it to you?' he shouted to the old man.

'It's everything to me, boy,' he admitted, waving his stick.

Louis thought of Mr Cuntingham. Cuntingham had called him 'boy' as well. Louis imagined the old man was Mr Cuntingham and coming at him with a walking stick. He shouted, 'Mind your own fucking business.'

Alfie coated the leaves with his morning porridge.

'Jesus, Alfie, what's the matter with you?'

Alfie retched again.

'What did you just say to me, boy?'

'You heard.'

'What's your name?'

'Don't tell him,' Alfie advised, trying to get rid of a morsel on his tongue by licking his sleeve.

'I don't have to answer to you.'

'You wait till I get hold of you.'

Louis sniggered, 'I haven't got all day.'

'I'll teach you some respect, boy.'

'Thanks for the offer, but it sounds bloody boring. I think I'll pass.'

'I'm going,' Alfie declared, wrenching himself from Louis' grip.

'Alright, sissy, I'm coming as well.'

Now, Alfie can't remember if they climbed the fence or walked out the gate, but the old man never did get hold of Louis. He remembers feeling glad for the old man's sake. He looks up at the Feldwebel and repeats, 'Doctor.' He won't return to work until a doctor is summoned to examine Joe. He wants a doctor to confirm that Joe was shot at point-blank range while lying face down in the dirt. That he was murdered when nobody was looking and dragged to the perimeter fence and not, as the guards had claimed, whilst trying to climb it. He knows that Joe was too ill to attempt an escape. He'd been feverish and delirious for days and had had septic ulcers the size of 2/6 coins on the soles of his feet. Joe couldn't have liberated a maggot from the turnip soup let alone himself from the camp. He knows who killed him. He just wants to wipe the smile off that guard's face.

The Feldwebel orders the firing squad into position. There is a scuffle and Alfie is joined by a gaggle of emaciated men. Standing together, they look like a consortium of indignant scarecrows.

'He's a brute, but he won't shoot his work force,' says one.

'Don't you believe it,' says another.

'Doctor,' repeats Alfie.

1945

17: Picking up the Pieces

At this moment Alfie cannot see his feet. He stands on a filthy black road in Dresden staring down at the ground while the devastated city looks on grimly from gaping holes and flattened walls. Since daybreak, he's grasped and tugged rubble from the remains of the buildings. The buildings look like chipped teeth in gaunt faces. Enveloped in plumes of white smoke, he's breathed in the smell of cooked human flesh and has touched monstrosities with his bare hands. He started the day searching for survivors but long before this moment, the moment where he stands with his eyes fixed upon the ground, he got wise and began to look for the dead.

The day is cold, but he doesn't feel it. Blistering heat leaps from every scorched brick and every charred piece of timber. It bleeds out of every crack in every building that he clears, and hurls itself at him, and all those involved in the clean-up operation: the PoWs, the German guards and those who survived the allied firebombing of the city. He feels like a hot water bottle and thinks he might have wet himself but with every thread of his clothing already sopping, he isn't able to tell for sure and, in the end, has decided it doesn't matter. His toes throb against the leather of his boots and his eyeballs feel like poached eggs. He has spent many moments since daybreak trying to imagine his body buried in snow.

When he has found a body he's given it a number, then carried it past small groups of vocal onlookers and delivered it to a designated pyre in the middle of the street. It has been the job of the guard, the vicious one with a facial birth mark the colour of rotting grapes and the size of Alfie's hand, to protect him from these onlookers and give Alfie's bodies their official number. The guard has been recording his numbers in a notebook blackened by carbon. Alfie has been keeping his numbers in his overheated head. The numbering system of each man has not been the same. Alfie has been counting in quarters, halves, three-quarters and wholes. When he has found a leg or an arm, or a head or even half a head, he has counted it as one quarter of a human being. When he has found a torso with a head, or two legs with two feet he has counted it as one half of a human being. But he has found deciding what makes three-quarters of a human being tricky. Should he count a body with a head, two arms, a torso and one leg as three-quarters, or should he count it as one whole body with a missing leg? Whatever he has found by way of a body, his guard has counted and recorded it as one. Alfie has added his quarters, three-quarters and halves to make wholes. In his head, he has been putting the bodies back together again. Alfie's number and the guard's official number have been as different as the men themselves.

The guard has been satisfied with the English PoW because the Englishman has lived up to what he has been told, and has been taught to believe, about the English. The Englishman has demonstrated discipline, resolve and reserve. He has demonstrated not only his Englishness, but also that the Fuehrer's theories about race are right. The guard has a particular fondness for English idioms. He has compared the American with the Englishman and has concluded that the American is what the English would call a different kettle of fish. Never mind that the American has been half-starved, hosed down with human excrement and subjected to regular beatings since he was captured. What cannot be overlooked is that the American is a weak-bodied, girl-faced homosexual who weeps and mutters to himself as he pulls the bodies from the wreckage. He has the figures in his notebook to prove that the American homosexual has not brought as many bodies to the pile as the Englishman has. This means that he is work-shy, and being work-shy *and* having oily black hair means that the American homosexual must also be a Jew. He has been told, and is very willing to believe, that Jews are spineless, corrupt profiteers. He has spent many moments since daybreak imagining a world polluted by homosexual parasites and dominated by lazy filthy Jews. He has grown more murderous by the minute. While the Englishman stares at his feet, the guard watches the American homosexual Jew and wishes that the stinking mongrel would just get on with stealing from the dead so he can exterminate him on the spot. He smiles at the thought of a future where just one kettle of fish exists.

Alfie and the American have been clearing a street close to a zoo. Alfie has no experience of zoos. Most of the animals he's seen that morning he's never seen before, but he's been able to identify a dead elephant with her calf, several dead monkeys of unknown breed and a vulture whining in the sky, circling the piles of fire-bombed bodies in the street. He has also seen a vet, with a red bushy moustache and a broken headlamp strapped to his extensive forehead, put some sort of horse out of its misery and a dead monkey into a box. He has wondered what the vet will do about the vulture; how he will catch a bird of that size. He has spent some of the morning thinking that zoos are not where animals belong.

Now, he cannot see his feet because ash clings to his boots and ankles. He looks as if he is wearing dirty grey socks but it is a long time since he wore socks. He thinks about man-made fibres. He doesn't know much about this sort of thing but he's read that the Americans use them to make parachutes and ladies' stockings. He decides that his new socks are made from man-made fibres because they are made from the incinerated remains of men and women and young children and tiny babies. He wonders how many human beings cake his feet and ankles. *How much ash does a burnt body make? A cupful? A bucketful?* He doesn't know. He knows a lot about dead bodies now, but he doesn't know that and he doesn't want to know. He wants to stop asking himself these types of questions because he fears the answers will send him mad. He thinks of Lil and Harry and of Maggie - the child he's never clapped eyes on. He imagines them as ashes that cling to his sodden clothes and are made damp and salty by his sweat. He wants to stop thinking about the people he loves but he is frightened of the alternative thought. The alternative thought is somebody else's baby in a soiled nappy and the tattered remains of a lemon-coloured nightie. The memory of her has grown stronger than his mind. He tries to think of nothing. *I will think of no fucking thing.* But when he puts Lil, Harry and Maggie out of his mind, the alternative thought sails on in.

He found her in a small cellar among dozens of other bodies. He thought she was a child's doll at first because she was pale pink and her skin gleamed like a child's doll. The floor of the cellar was slippery with a thick layer of human fat and as he reached out to her, he lost his balance and fell over. Then the American appeared. He looked at Alfie's hands and knees inches deep in the mess, and vomited up his stomach lining. Alfie stood up and considered his hands.

'Jesus,' said the American. 'They've melted in here.'

Alfie closed his tattered fingers over his bloody palms and nodded.

'I can taste em,' said the American, retching and spitting.

'Yes,' said Alfie, thinking that melted flesh was as sticky as glue. Seconds later, when the cuts on his hand reacted with the human grease that covered them, he decided that the dead had become part of him. 'You're spitting on them,' he said.

'I can't get the taste outta ma mouth,' said the American.

Alfie spied a length of brown fur coat and wiped his ruined hands on it. 'Don't let the goon see you,' he said. 'He's a vicious bastard.'

The American nodded and wiped his mouth and nose on his dusty black sleeve. Though the two men were out of sight of their guard, they heard him then, shouting in German, his angry words pelting the cellar like bullets. The American crouched down. 'I'm tired,' he said. 'I can't lift another.'

'Take the baby.'

'No,' said the American, with a face like a screwed-up hankie. 'I got kids.'

Alfie shrugged. The American thrust his hands into the mound and grasped a body. As he pulled the body free from all the others, it made a sucking sound as if it were stuck in mud. Alfie shuddered and a river of sweat swept past the collar of his shirt down to the waistband of his trousers. Once the American had disappeared, he returned to the baby in the lemon-coloured nightie.

The hem of her nightie covered her face. He saw the withered stump of her umbilical cord and her own waste plastered to her skinny legs. He lifted her nightie from her face and covered her blistered knees with it. He found an embroidered yellow duckling on the skirt and three warped buttons on the bodice. He brushed the buttons with his fingers and dislodged one. He held the button in the palm of his hand and wondered what to do with it. He imagined discarding it and watching its slow submersion into the viscous human soup that covered the floor. He dropped the button into his pocket and set about picking her up. He held her as he'd held Harry that day when Lil wasn't home. He put one great bloody and calloused hand beneath her bottom and one beneath her sticky neck and did his best to cradle her stiffened form to his chest. He presumed her parents were somewhere in the mound. He was sorry to take her from them. He carried her to the pyre and was struck on the head by a brick. He didn't look to see who had thrown it and he didn't stop to check the damage.

Now, looking at his ash-covered feet, he hears the American say, 'I'm hot.' He lifts his head and watches the American unbutton his shirt. The guard strides across the road shouting and lifting his rifle; his birthmark looks dull against his florid face. Alfie wishes he could do something to stop him from stripping in the street but his boots feel as if they have been subsumed by the molten surface beneath him and he can't move. He wishes he could open his mouth to say something helpful but his mouth is dry and his lips may as well have been sewn shut. He closes his eyes and finds his morning on replay. He frowns and tries to imagine himself someplace else but the sounds and the smells and the heat make it impossible to imagine that. He pictures the guard spitting as he shouts. It gives him an idea: he will think of water. He thinks of the Thames at Kew Bridge but the image is fleeting. He thinks of himself and Louis combing the river bank looking for pennies but Louis won't appear and he begins to wonder whether his absence is significant. What if he's dead? He pictures him as a dead and ugly mess in the style of his own cartoons. This image is worse than the ones he's trying to avoid and he knows there is only one way to be rid of it: he pictures the PoWs he saw earlier that morning, fishing braised bodies out of the city's static water tanks. Tears gather beneath his eyelids. The guard fires a shot. A cheer goes up and clapping done by large and healthy hands follows. When he opens his eyes, a single tear from each mingles with the sweat that drips from his forehead and winds its way down his grimy face. The American is lying in a heap on the ground with a shattered skull; his ragged shirt lies beside him, the frayed edges lift with the breeze.

The guard marches over. 'He was hot,' he says. 'Now he is not.'

Alfie says nothing.

'Tell me, are you also feeling hot?'

Of the ones that he knows, he wonders which country the guard's birthmark most resembles. He decides he'll say France if he lives through this war and has to describe it.

'I suppose you wish it would now rain dogs and cats? To cool you down.'

He feels a dangerous urge to smile so he glances at the American.

'Cat got your tongue?'

He shakes his head and the guard lifts his rifle.

'Well, are you hot like the American? Do you also wish to remove your clothes?'

'I'm cold,' he mumbles.

The guard prods his forehead with the tip of his gun. 'I didn't hear you.'

'I'm colder than a witch's tit,' he shouts.

18: The Homecoming

Alfie knocks on the front door of his parents' house, and waits on the step. It is summer and their small front garden smells overwhelmingly of mint. The street is full of English voices, tunes being whistled, children playing hopscotch and the sound of drowsy bees. A bleeding heart is in bloom beneath the bay window among a tangle of stinging nettles. The doorstep is dusty and the nets at the open windows look grey. He wears American clothes in shades of brown that are made of rayon and make him sweat. He hears his father say faintly, 'Was that the door? See will you, Lil.'

He steps forward to look through the stained-glass panel. The wallpaper on the hall walls is the same orange patterned paper that Fred put up in 1932. The shape of a child appears. The child speaks, 'I think there's a man at the door, Mummy.' Harry. Then he hears the sing-song voice of a much younger child call out, 'There's a man at the door, Mummy.' Maggie. Alfie walks back down the path to wait at the gate.

'I just said that, Maggie,' shouts Harry.

'I just said that,' shouts Maggie, laughing.

'Not again,' sighs Harry. 'Mummy…'

'Don't start, the pair of you,' warns Lil.

'Maggie's copying me again.'

'Not,' says Maggie, joining him in the hall.

'Yes, you are,' says Harry. 'You said there was a man at the door after I said it.'

Lil comes down the stairs feeling hot and bothered. 'Shall I find you both a job to do? Is that what you want?'

'Yes, please,' says Maggie.

'No, thank you,' says Harry.

'Go and play,' she says, but they don't.

She opens the door and sees Alfie standing at the gate. It is almost three years since they last saw each other. Harry, now aged four years and five months, and Maggie, now aged two years and one month, hide behind her wide skirt and wait for their mother to speak to the man. Lil doesn't know what to say so she just says, 'Hello, Alfie.' Her response seems inadequate, even to her, but it is all she's capable of.

Harry knows a man called Alfie. It's the name of his dad. Granddad Fred talks about Alfie his dad all the time. But this Alfie doesn't look anything like his dad. In the hand-coloured photograph, his dad has yellow hair and pink cheeks and all of his teeth. He worries he might have to kiss this man. He covers his mouth with his mother's skirt. Maggie has no idea who the tall old man at the gate is; she doesn't recognize the name or the face. She copies Harry and wonders where the pudgy stuff that should be under the man's skin has gone. She'd quite like to pinch what's left, or to prod it at the very least. It probably feels like raw pastry.

Alfie sees three uncertain faces and wonders whether it might not have been better for everyone if he'd just told the German guard that he was hot. He was hot. He warns himself not to think about that day but in so doing signals, 'Begin' to another barrage of one particular thought: sticky skin. He tries to replace the thought with commands such as move, smile, and speak. But then the thought that has ruined everything returns because Maggie is wearing a yellow dress. He is reminded of the baby in the basement and of her sticky skin. He clutches his trousers to feel rayon in place of her flesh. He feels the outline of a small button in his pocket. He clutches his shirt sleeves; he doesn't know what else to do.

Lil thinks Alfie looks like a decomposed moth. She releases the children from her skirt and pushes them back into the house quietly ordering them to go and play. For once, Harry is happy to do as he is bid. He takes Maggie's hand and drags her into the hallway promising to build her a den in the garden using the clothes horse and a blanket.

Lil steps out of the house, pulls the door behind her and says, 'Do you want to come inside?'

He ignores the invitation. 'I'm smiling,' he says.

She frowns because he isn't smiling and hasn't smiled in all the time he's been standing by the gate. She doesn't know what to do or what to say. She thinks she should walk to the gate and offer him her hand but she also knows that she won't.

'I'm not myself,' he says. 'I'm not right anymore.'

She waits for further information.

'I can't touch things now.'

She remembers him as a child collecting furry orange and black caterpillars in a bucket for no other reason than to see how many he could find in one day. Fifty-three. She was able to help him locate the caterpillars but she hadn't wanted to pick them up. She also remembers him burying a decomposing magpie by the railway line with his bare hands and dangling a slow worm in front of her face. She tries to think what these 'things' might be but nothing comes to mind. She finds herself saying, 'Things?' before she can stop herself.

He feels a sudden rush of heat to his head and the dreadful sensation that he's about to faint. He puts his hand on the garden wall and stares at his feet. 'People,' he says.

She wonders whether she counts as 'people'. She reminds herself that she is a person, even if she's not a very nice one, and says, 'You're home now, Alfie, that's all that matters.'

He panics because he doesn't think she's understood what he's trying to tell her. 'I'm not normal,' he says, holding out the palms of his hands as if to show her the sticky skin that covers them. He crouches down and puts his head between his knees.

She's had enough. Neither is she. Neither is she if he must know. What makes him so special? She glances at the open windows and says quietly, 'We can suit ourselves.'

'But...'

She folds her arms and waits.

'But... I'm...'

She pushes open the front door with the heel of her foot and says, 'Come inside now, Alfie. I'm putting the kettle on. We usually have a cup of tea about now.'

Part Two

The Offspring

1951 – 1991

1: The Librarians

Maggie checks to see if the coast is clear and then falls off the garden wall. She is trying to injure herself. She appraises her hands and knees with frustration; no blood. She tells herself that it's alright to say *Flippin eck* because these words aren't swear words and then mutters them in case someone overhears. Next, she skips down the road with her shoe laces undone but, even though she wants to, she doesn't fall over. She binds her ankles with her skipping rope and plays hopscotch. Auntie Joan, one of the neighbours, shells peas on her front step and shouts, 'Stop playing silly beggars with that rope, Maggie.' She wants to shout back, *It's called hopscotch, not silly beggars, Auntie Joan,* but she daren't: everybody knows that a smacked bottom from Auntie Joan is ten times worse than a splash from scalding water. She considers if she's brave enough to run full pelt into the front door but decides that she isn't. She doesn't want to break her face; she just wants a legitimate reason to knock on the door of Miss Howard and Miss Hughes' maisonette. She sits down on their joint front step and makes slits in the stem of a dandelion with her thumbnail. All she wants to do is have a quick peek inside their place. It will only take a minute. She knows they've got a piano because she's heard them playing it, but what else might they have? Now is the best opportunity she's ever had, because the two ladies are in, her parents are at work and Harry is far away fishing for roach in the gravel pits at Ham. But she's tried everything she can think of to make herself need help. She says their names: Miss Howard and Miss Hughes. She likes those names: Miss-Howard-and-Miss-Hughes. She thinks about how she used to like saying the word *village* until Miss

Howard and Miss Hughes moved in downstairs. Miss Howard is her favourite. When she's older, she's going to be just like her: she's going to dress in bright colours, wear red lipstick and laugh loudly. She sighs and considers Miss Hughes. Miss Hughes is much more like her mum to look at: grey hair, grey skin, thin straight lips. She also has glasses and wears a lot of brown coloured clothes but something Miss Hughes is, and her mum isn't, is funny. She has to be really funny to make Miss Howard laugh the way she does and funny people are most definitely the best kind of people. She wonders why her parents never laugh and why her dad had to call Miss Howard a *loud stupid bitch*. So what if he was having one of his bad days. She hates that word: *Bitch*. Sometimes, when he says things like that, she thinks she hates him. And anyway, how on earth can Miss Howard and Miss Hughes be sisters when they don't have the same surname as each other? Mum was nasty about it too. It was only a question. She thinks about a poster plastered to an end terrace wall that she passes every day on the walk to school. It's of a circus lion. He's stuck in a cage and being poked with a stick by a man with a big fat belly and a gold hoop in his ear. The first time she saw the poster, she wondered if the circus man had a baby inside him because circus people are different to normal people and can do different things. It's obvious the lion doesn't like to be poked. Her mum looked like the lion when she asked about Miss Howard and Miss Hughes. She was fierce and pinched her arm and told her to mind her own business. She said, 'Stay away from them or you'll know all about it.' Remembering this makes her wish she were a stray cat, rather than her mum's daughter. She'd spring in to Miss Howard and Miss Hughes' maisonette through an open window, stretch out on their laps, and purr like billy-o to make them want to keep her.

***

She sighs and punches her thigh because she's disappointed with herself: if only she were braver, she'd already be knocking on their door and asking for their help. She thinks about the sandwich she's been told to make herself for tea. She might suck an Oxo cube instead; it's better than jam. It's nowhere near tea-time but she may as well eat; there's nothing else to do. She trudges up the stairs and sees that she's forgotten to re-tie her shoe laces. She wonders if Harry will play cards with her when he gets home from fishing; she thinks it will depend on whether he's in a good mood. She wonders if a wish and a prayer are exactly the same thing: she wishes and prays that Harry catches the largest roach in the gravel pit and then stands on her shoe lace and falls backwards down the stairs.

**

Miss Howard applies a cold flannel to Maggie's forehead. Maggie smells flowers. Miss Hughes makes her drink a glassful of something fizzy and bitter and then feeds her a teaspoon of Cadbury's drinking chocolate. She sits on a blue velvet couch with a very sore wrist and a terrible headache and wishes she could see things more clearly: here she is, in their place at last, and her eyes have gone all funny. Miss Howard disappears and returns with a silky eiderdown that seems to have black and white birds on it. She drapes it over her. Miss Hughes then feels her wrist and peers into her eyes and down her ears and up her nose. Maggie thinks she is very gentle as her head is turned to the light so she can examine these sore parts of her body. Then Miss Hughes disappears into the kitchen and returns with a small pot that has a red lid. She tips Maggie's head to the left and applies whatever is in the pot, to the sore parts of her forehead. It is then that Maggie notices the piano in the corner of the room. The piano is covered in photo frames. A long thin thing that is the colour of a blind dog's eye and that she supposes is a vase, although there are no flowers sticking out of it, also sits on the piano. Beside the piano, a writing desk covered in sheets of lined paper is bordered by white painted shelves that are crammed with books. There are even books lying flat on top of the books that stand up. And here and there like the mole hills in the garden at the back of the maisonettes, piles of books stacked as tall as her knees sit on the black painted floor. Exhausted, she wonders if Miss Howard and Miss Hughes are librarians.

**

The two ladies talk in whispers. Maggie strains to listen. She doesn't want to go home yet. She wonders if she should pass out. She's seen her dad do it. She knows what it looks like. It was the time she thought he'd died. He turned a horrible colour, slid down the wall and lay on the floorboards with his eyes closed. She thought he looked like the letter 'L'. Her Mum pinched his ear and then he woke up. Miss Hughes glances at her and then feeds her another spoonful of drinking chocolate; she communicates in nods and smiles. Maggie begins to wonder if Miss Howard and Miss Hughes think she's a foreigner. Perhaps she ought to tell them that she speaks their language? She tries to think of a question to ask. What should she call them? Miss Howard removes the flannel from her forehead, strokes a painful spot on her skin, turns the flannel over and returns it to her forehead. She smells flowers again and decides it's time to speak. She takes a deep breath, hopes she doesn't turn red and asks, 'Are you librarians, Misses?'

Miss Howard's eyes grow large and then she laughs softly and says, 'No, Maggie, we're not.'

She is amazed: how does Miss Howard know her name? Then she congratulates herself for making Miss Howard laugh and then, though she'd rather not, she closes her eyes because she feels quite sick with them open.

***

She sits up in a very large bed and holds her hands to her head. She dreamt a rat was nibbling her brain. It is a relief to discover that her brain is still inside her head. She waits for the pain to subside and then reaches for the sides of the bed but she doesn't get anywhere close to the edges of it. It is the biggest bed she's ever seen. Every bed at home is only big enough for one person to sleep in. If her head didn't hurt, she'd roll from one side of the bed to the other and count the number of times she was on her front and then her back to see how many eight-year-olds could fit in it. She thinks it might be as many as seven as long as they were skinny like her. Carefully, she lies back down and imagines that she is lying in the centre of an island. She smells flowers and imagines her island is covered in them. She likes the idea of being marooned on this island forever. She slowly surveys the room. She thinks Miss Howard's bedroom is the brightest room she's ever seen. Every wall is painted a different colour: blue, orange, yellow and beige. The yellow wall is her favourite because she's not allowed to have anything yellow at home. She can't tell what's supposed to be happening in the pictures that hang on it. She wonders if Miss Howard has nieces and nephews and if they painted the pictures for her, or if her eyes are still not working properly. They certainly look like the work of children. She wishes she was Miss Howard's niece and that it was her work on the wall. She could paint a better picture than that. If Miss Howard was her aunt, she could stay with her in the holidays like Patsy gets to do with her Auntie Madge in Chertsey. Why couldn't she have had an aunt? If only her mum's sister, she can't remember her name, hadn't died of scarlet fever as a baby. But then again, if she'd turned out like her mum, it wouldn't be worth it. She thinks about Uncle Louis. It was a shame he got killed in the war because he'd have probably got married but he might have turned out just as horrible as her dad. If Miss Howard and Miss Hughes were to adopt her, she wouldn't care about not having an aunt. The feeling that they probably won't makes her turn away from the yellow wall. She doesn't want to look at the pictures anymore. She doesn't want to think about Miss Howard's real relatives. She sniffs the pillow and finds that it smells the same as Miss Howard. She sees a beige coloured nightie neatly folded on the pillow next to her. She spies a long grey hair on the silky material. She rolls on to her other side, closes her eyes and pretends that the room and the bed are hers.

***

She needs a wee but she doesn't want to go outside to use the toilet in case they don't let her back in again. She looks under Miss Howard's bed but can't see a bucket. Perhaps Miss Hughes has a bucket in her bedroom? She decides to check. The bay window tells her that Miss Howard, just like her parents, has the front bedroom. This means that Miss Hughes must have the room next door. Her parents call it the second bedroom; it is the room she has to share with Harry and it is the darkest room in the house. She frees herself of a white sheet and a yellow blanket, slides out of Miss Howard's cavernous bed and delights in the feel of the thick orange rug beneath her feet. She catches sight of her forehead in the mirror on the wall. She stands on tiptoes for the full picture and realizes that the cream Miss Hughes' rubbed on her sore skin was yellow. Without hesitation, she licks her finger and wipes it off even though to do so makes her skin burn and her eyes water. She doesn't want to think about the splinters that are now visible under her skin. She spots a bottle of perfume on a small bedside table. She picks it up and reads the label: 'Joy'. She sniffs the nozzle. It's this that makes Miss Howard smell of flowers. She sprays some on her wrist and then licks it; it tastes nothing like it smells. She screws up her face and tiptoes to the door. She can hear the two ladies talking quietly in the sitting room at the bottom of the hall. She turns right and peers through a crack in the door to view Miss Hughes' bedroom. She listens to the sound of her own breathing and tries to make sense of the room. But what she discovers doesn't make sense at all because not only is there no bucket in Miss Hughes' bedroom, there is also no bed.

2: All the Same

'That's Mrs Edwards on the stairs,' says Edith Hughes lowering her copy of *The Lancet*.

Eveline Howard plays a game of Patience upon the desk on the other side of the room. She looks up from her cards and sighs, 'Yes.'

'I'll take Maggie home,' says Edith.

'But it seems such a shame to wake her,' says Eveline.

'I imagine Mrs Edwards will want to know where she's got to.'

'What an imagination you have,' smiles Eveline sadly. She crosses the room and joins Edith on the couch. She taps Edith's thigh and says, 'What if I nipped upstairs and told her about Maggie's fall? I could promise to return her once she wakes.'

'What an imagination *you* have, Eveline.'

'As a *doctor*, you could insist,' she says, stroking Edith's cheek like she might the cheek of a rabbit or a kitten. 'You could explain to her mother that she's hurt her head and she shouldn't be moved for the present.'

Edith raises her eyebrows.

'Just a little while longer,' pleads Eveline.

'Alright, my love,' says Edith capturing her hand. 'Finish your game and then I'll consult with her mother.'

***

Maggie loves the names Eveline and Edith and the fact that the two ladies have the same initials as each other; it's as if they are twins. Everybody knows that twins are very special and have to do everything together. She uses her hands to secure her head, and tiptoes back to their bedroom with an excitement in her tummy that ordinarily only ever visits that region on Christmas Eve or the morning of her birthday. Slowly she climbs into the bed on Miss Howard's side but takes up Miss Hughes' pillow with the silky nightie on top and hugs it to her bony chest. The grey hair on the nightie drifts across her chin and tickles the spot that in springs gone by, her friends jabbed with buttercups to check that from one year to the next, she still liked butter. Who could go off butter? She pulls the long strand free and lets it stray to her hip. She's starting to think that Miss Howard and Miss Hughes might like to keep her forever. She considers being their daughter: Miss Howard would teach her how to play the piano. She thinks of her current mum, 'Lil'. It feels good to call her Lil. Lil once told her that only girls who had a piano could go to grammar school. If she lives with Miss Howard, she'll be able to go to grammar school and then, when she's older, she might become a doctor like Miss Hughes because everybody knows that you can do jobs like that once you've been to grammar school. And she'll have the second bedroom if she lives with them, and she'll have it all to herself. No more sharing with grumpy Harry or fighting for space with the bits of furniture that Alfie collects and dumps behind their bedroom door. *Flippin eck*, it feels better than getting a packet of sweets to say 'Alfie'. Why did there need to be dads anyway? They weren't very nice and they didn't like children. And she didn't like *them* either. The second thing she's going to do is call everybody she loves, 'my love', and then she's going to ask Miss Howard and Miss Hughes to paint every one of her walls sunflower yellow, and then she's going to ask them to buy her a yellow dress and knit her a cardigan to match and she's going to wear this outfit outside where Alfie can see and she isn't going to care what happens to him when he does.

'Please let my loves adopt me,' she wishes and prays into Miss Hughes' silky nightie, 'double, triple, please…'

***

Lil stares at Edith's outstretched hand as if it is bloody. 'I know who, and what you are,' she says, plunging her hands into her housecoat. Edith slowly withdraws her hand and says pleasantly, 'Of course you do, Mrs Edwards, of that I have no doubt.'

Lil stiffens. She tries to see herself as a gigantic piece of granite that nobody can move, or damage, or do anything about. 'What do you want?' she asks savagely.

'Maggie fell down the stairs this afternoon and bumped her head. She has concussion, a sprained wrist, some bruising and a few splinters. I treated her for these injuries and then put her to bed.'

Lil glances over her shoulder at the door to the second bedroom.

'With us,' says Edith. 'Concussion should be monitored.'

'I want her home,' says Lil with flared nostrils. 'At once.'

'She's sleeping.'

'Is she indeed?'

'It would best if she was left to do so.'

Lil glares at Edith and says, 'All the same…'

Edith raises her eyebrows and says, 'Interesting choice of words, Mrs Edwards.'

Lil glares at her and spits, 'Now that I'm home, she can sleep in her own bed.'

'You'd like me to wake her?'

'I can look after her just as well as you can.'

'Very well,' says Edith with a wry smile. 'Perhaps you'd like to come and fetch her?'

'No,' says Lil, feeling her granite legs crumble. 'I most certainly would not.'

1955

3: Spam

Harry and Maggie take it in turns to push the old utility pram back from the coal merchants because Maggie insists that taking turns is what they have to do to make the activity fair. Harry would prefer to do all the pushing because Maggie can't push in a straight line, and it isn't funny when the wheels run over his feet, particularly when his toes are already sore from being crammed into shoes that are too small for him. And using a pram to transport a hundred weight sack of coal is embarrassing. And the fact that he's in the midst of a growth spurt, and towering over the pram handle and having to walk down the road bent-legged just so that he can reach the handle with his fingertips, makes it worse. His trouser bottoms swing above his ankles and the cuffs of his long-sleeved shirt are a good three inches above where they should be; he's already been accused of waiting for the Thames to flood by a boy with impetigo round his nose who was walking on the opposite side of the road smoking a rollie. (He suspects the boy was trying to start a fight but because Harry knows that impetigo is highly contagious, and also that he isn't much of a fighter, he said nothing, just pretended the sack of coal needed his attention, ministered to it with all the care of a new mother adjusting the position of her new baby, and carried on.) What he doesn't understand is why Mum won't allow him to borrow a wheelbarrow off the neighbour; it's not as if a trip to the coal merchants is going to wear it out. And he'd look after it, and he wouldn't lose it, and he doesn't think the neighbour would mind. He wishes they could afford the delivery charge or that they could afford to buy more than one sack of coal at a time because then the coal merchant would deliver it for free. He wonders if his height prevents the coal merchant from taking pity on them and scrapping the delivery charge altogether. Regardless, it's a trek he could do without and being forced to take Maggie along on the job adds insult to injury. She looks a sight in those old school shorts of his that she reckons she found down the side of *her* bed? and that are far too big for her and that he doubts Mum knows she's wearing because Mum wouldn't approve of her wearing shorts, and definitely not shorts with a fly. And why she went and cut her fringe with the nail scissors he'll never know: she looks like the kitchen window with its wonky blind. And she never stops yacking even though earlier on, before school, she reckoned she couldn't find her voice and could only whisper. Not that Mum was having any of it. Lost her voice his eye: it's one bloody question after another with her and all of them are pointless: 'Which do you prefer, Harry, Jelly Babies or Winegums?'

'Neither,' he says.

'How come?'

He shrugs. She sighs. They walk past the house with the old bathtub in the front garden. Maggie stops pushing the pram and peers over the garden wall to check that the tub's still there. The tub's been there for years. It's become something of a landmark. She risks peering beyond the bathtub to the window of the sitting room: sometimes a horse is parked inside, but it's not there today. Harry seizes the pram and waddles up the road like a duck on the run from a ferret. Once Maggie realises that her turn has been cut short, she runs after him shouting, 'Hey, I'm still pushing, Harry.'

He removes his pointers from the pram handle without saying a word because it's easier than listening to Maggie whine.

'Do you want to get married?' she asks.

'Of course I do,' says Harry with a scratch of his ear. He wonders if he's got a spot down it or if it's just Maggie's questions that make it ache. 'Everybody does, eventually,' he adds.

'Why do they?'

'Because it's what happens.'

'Do you have to get married?'

'If you don't want to starve to death you do,' he says.

'What if you didn't want to?' she asks.

He picks his ear and ignores her.

'What if you didn't want to, Harry?' she says more urgently.

He sighs. 'Why wouldn't you want to?'

She shrugs and turns red. First the P.E teacher talked to all the girls about periods (and any girl that sniggered got a penalty and was in disgrace), then the biology teacher did a lesson on the reproduction of rabbits. Now she knows that girls need periods to get babies and worse than this – having pieced a number of things together from the playground talks – she knows that girls also need the other thing – the thing she can't bring herself to say – that begins with the letter 'P' and is on boys, and girls will have to know all about it the minute they get married. She thinks about the word *penetration* because the biology teacher said that this was what the buck had to do to the doe. Esme, the much older sister of a girl in Maggie's year, gleefully pointed out that this *penetration business* was exactly the same as what the human man did to the human woman. Before the rabbit lesson, the use of the word *penetration* was limited to history lessons: *Today, class, we shall consider the causes and consequences of the Norman* **penetration** *into Wales and Scotland*. But now… If only she'd been off school sick on the days of the *period* and *penetration* lessons. She wonders why all the words she doesn't like begin with the letter 'P'?

'My turn now,' Harry says, trying to take over the pram.

'I'll just push to the end of the road,' she says.

'Just to the end and then I'm pushing it the rest of the way home,' he says deepening his voice to add some weight to what he says.

Reluctantly she agrees and then says, 'I saw people kissing at Chiswick Baths yesterday… their tongues touched and went inside each other's mouths.'

'So?'

'You don't want to do that with someone, do you? Cos I definitely don't.'

Harry supresses a smile: it's exactly what he wants to do with someone just as soon as he gets a chance but, for Maggie's benefit, he says, 'No, of course I don't.'

'But it's what you have to do it if you get married.'

Suddenly, Harry cottons on to the fact that Maggie is leading him into a discussion on the facts of life; he doesn't want to discuss this with his twelve-year-old sister. 'Alright, alright, Maggie,' he says, 'talk about something else, will you?'

'Their tongues looked like spam, Harry,' she blurts out.

'Crikey, sis, how long was you gawping at them for?'

'Until they got told off by the man,' says Maggie. 'They had to leave the baths. It's called heavy petting what they were doing.'

'Do me a favour, sis, and don't look next time, will you? And don't say anything about this to Mum, and definitely don't repeat 'heavy petting' when she's around, not if you want to go swimming again.'

'I don't want to go swimming again.'

'Yes, you do.'

'Do you think…?'

'No more questions,' he says. 'I thought your throat was sore?'

'It's better now. Just one more, Harry. I promise this one will be the last one, okay?'

He sighs. 'Last one then but after that, you're not allowed to talk to me for the rest of the way home.'

She weighs up the deal, nods, and then says, 'Do you think tongues taste like spam?'

'Hmm… Do I think tongues taste like spam…?'

'Do you, Harry?'

'Well…,' he says, 'that's a very good question, sis.'

She smiles to herself.

He gives the question some further consideration and then says, 'I blooming hope so, I like spam.'

Maggie says, 'Hmm,' and then adds, 'I like spam too, but even if they do taste like it, I still don't want to get married.'

1962

4: Fishing

Harry had met Astrid on an Angling club excursion to Mapledurham one Sunday afternoon. He'd been eighteen and so had she. Usually, Bill, Astrid's father, would take Sille, Astrid's mother, on these trips because she liked to sketch the river and had a thing for kingfishers. But the ligation and stripping of her varicose veins had kept her from the riverbank and her hobby that day. Astrid, with nothing better to do, had gone in her place. When she'd first appeared on the coach, Harry thought she must have misread the destination board, but then Bill had got on and said, 'Everyone, this is my daughter, Astrid,' as if she'd been nothing to look at. Harry had stared at Astrid all the way to Oxfordshire. Even if she'd been wearing waders and a fisherman's jumper he'd have stared: the tight-fitting dress and stiletto heels had nothing to do with it.

All that day, Harry hadn't been able to concentrate on the fish. He'd never been so eager to talk baits or river speed with Bill. He'd wished the stretch of river wasn't so long, or that he and Bill had been given neighbouring beats. He'd wandered along the river bank on the pretext of asking Bill whether he'd had any success. By happy accident, he'd found Astrid before he'd found Bill. She'd been returning Bill's pinkies to the cool box: it had been a spectacular sight. When Astrid had looked up and had said, 'hello,' he'd smiled and had then walked straight into Bill's rod rest.

***

Now, two years later, Harry wears the same waders and stands in the middle of the same river while Astrid, now pregnant, watches him from a stripy camp chair.

'I forgot to tell you this, Harry, but the other day, a man told me that I'm expecting a girl,' says Astrid.

Harry says, 'Mmhmm.'

'I like the name Saskia,' she says, tearing a lump of bread from the loaf in the bait bag.

'Mmhmm.'

'He was Lithuanian.'

'Mmhmm... Who was?'

'The man who said I'm expecting a girl. He was on the Tube.'

'Mmhmm.'

'He was very old.'

'Yeah?'

'And really short.'

'Right.'

'Massive hands.'

'Did you say Lithuanian?'

'Yes.'

'Oh.'

'They're very knowing, aren't they?'

'Who?'

'Foreigners.'

'Are they?'

'I think so because he said if a lady looks ugly when she's expecting, she's going to have a boy, but if she looks beautiful, she's going to have a girl. He said I was beautiful.'

'Hmm.'

Astrid narrows her eyes and says, 'What?'

'What happens to ugly women when *they're* expecting then?'

'Well, I don't know,' says Astrid. 'All I know is what *he* said: "Ugly face: boy. Beautiful face: girl."'

Harry smiles at her Lithuanian accent.

'Anyway, I agree with him,' she adds. 'I think *I am* having a girl.'

Harry feels a pull on his rod and says, 'I've already told you, I don't mind what we have as long as...'

Astrid cuts him off because she's bored of that *as long as it's healthy* talk: that goes without saying. 'So what do you think about Saskia?'

'For what?' asks Harry, slowly reeling in the line.

'What do you think?'

'The baby?'

'Yes, for the baby.'

'Saskia?'

'Yes.'

'It's different.'

'Y-e-s... and...'

'Chuck us the landing net, will you?'

'And what about Saskia?' she asks, waddling over to the net.

'Nah,' says Harry. 'It wasn't a fish. It was just a bloody reed. Sit back down, love.'

1962

5: Baby Blues

'Whose baby's that then?' Astrid asks Lil.

'It's your baby, Astrid,' answers Maggie. 'Yours and Harry's, remember?'

'Do you know something? You're a shocking secretary. I'm not even married. If you're not careful, I'll be forced to give you your marching orders. My baby indeed...'

Astrid leans over the fireplace in her and Harry's flat, and paints her nails pink, not caring that the varnish has dripped onto the mantelpiece or that she's forgotten to paint either of her thumbs, that she has grass stains on her cherished white stilettos, or wears a salad-green skirt that won't fasten at the waist, or that her blouse is damp with breast milk. Harry stands at the kitchen window cooling a bottle of formula for their baby in a jug of tepid water and watching for a new blue Ford Anglia on the road outside. He visualizes a street map in the glove box and a black bag on the back seat that contains miracle cures or failing that, sedatives. He tells himself that help knows the way and is coming fast. Maggie thinks about the new girl at *Foyles*, and then, how she might use this palaver with Astrid and the baby as a legitimate reason for declaring that marriage isn't for her. She wonders if her mum will buy it. She hopes that Astrid won't insist on painting her nails, too. She wonders why she has to be the secretary. She decides that as bosses go, Astrid is worse than Miss Foyle.

Lil secures her screaming grandson's terry towelling nappy with a pale-pink pin – Astrid was convinced she was having a girl – buttons his white babygro, props him on her shoulder and wonders if Alfie is following her advice and having a nap at home. She thinks about the bruises she glimpsed on his arms that morning: ugly purple things that reminded her of rotting plums and that he was very careful to hide from view with a long-sleeved shirt. She wonders why, seventeen years since returning home from Germany, his nightmares should get worse rather than better. His recent intention to buy a gun concerns her. She keeps telling him that there are aren't any Nazis in Chiswick, but he doesn't seem to believe her.

'I haven't got a baby,' says Astrid, popping a liquorice allsort into her mouth. 'Shut that fucking baby up, Mrs Edwards,' she shouts at Lil, spitting shards of yellow coconut roll on to her chin.

Maggie looks from Astrid to her mother. Harry pretends that he didn't hear his wife just swear at his mother and checks his watch. The baby wails louder and Lil wishes she could slap Astrid and be done with it. She rubs her grandson's back and takes him to the kitchen knowing a bottle is what he's after.

'Is it ready?' she asks Harry.

'She swore at the doctor,' he says, handing her the bottle. 'She burst into his room, effing and blinding, demanding to know who he thought he was for keeping her waiting. Everybody in the waiting room heard her, Mum. *Now*, she thinks *she's* some Lady or other, *Maggie's* her bloody secretary and *we're* the sodding servants. As for him,' he says, pointing at his son, 'she has no idea who he is.'

Lil puts the teat in her grandson's mouth and the way he goes to work on it tells her that he's starving. She wonders when he was last fed. 'Never mind all that now, Harry. Let's just see what this doctor has to say.'

'I thought he'd be here by now,' he says, returning to his vigil at the window and resuming his old boyhood habit of biting his nails. 'I wish she'd stop saying that word. She's never said it before. She sounds...' He wants to say ugly but he can't bring himself to call her this. 'She sounds strange,' he says.

'We all have our moments, Harry, believe me.'

'Well, she's having plenty of them, isn't she?'

Right on cue, Astrid shouts, 'Come on, everybody, let's get dolled up and go shopping. I've won the fucking pools. We can buy whatever we bloody well want.' Then she looks at the nail polish that she's just swept onto the carpet and says to Maggie, 'Clear that up, secretary bird.'

***

'Ants?' says the psychiatrist, trying to take the doubt out of the question. He doesn't think the round cane chair in which he sits was designed for tall people. He wonders if the chair's design expresses some degree of latent sadism on the part of the designer. Where does the husband sit? He spots a tired but upright armless chair at the back of the room and wishes he'd perched there instead.

'Yes, that baby was crawling with ants,' says Astrid, pacing up and down in front of him on a small Chinese rush mat. The heel of her right stiletto catches on a fibre. She frees it by kicking the entire shoe off her dirty bare foot. It lands between the psychiatrist's black winkle pickers. It has to be a gauntlet. He picks it up and hands it back to her. She takes off the other stiletto and tosses the pair onto the unlit coal in the hearth.

'In the hospital?' he says, after a time.

'Yes.'

'Then what happened to the baby?'

'They poured boiling water on it.'

'Who did, Astrid?'

'The nurses,' she says, tutting impatiently.

'Why do you think they did that?'

'How the bloody hell should I know? I'm not a fucking nurse, am I?' She rubs her face in irritation.

He takes a small notebook from the inside pocket of his jacket.

'Do you want my particulars?' she laughs. She thinks he's too young and too handsome to be a detective. He looks like one of the male models in *Woman*. He laughs easily and she sees that he's got straight teeth. Even though he doesn't sound Scottish, she starts to wonder if he's Sean Connery incognito and starts fussing with her blond up-do.

'It would be helpful to know your full name,' he says. 'I should really make a note of who I've spoken with, you see.'

'You don't know who I am?' she says, sashaying over to the empty book case. She takes a cigarette from a packet on the second shelf. She doesn't have anything to light it with but she puts it between her lips and blows imaginary smoke in his direction.

He smiles kindly and says, 'I've got a poor memory.'

'I should think that's a fucking problem in your line of work.'

'Yes, it can be.'

'Lady Astrid Rawlings,' she says, drawing on her unlit cigarette.

He scribbles her name on his notepad. 'Is it alright if I call you Astrid?'

'Yes, if you must,' she says, lifting up the rush mat. 'Everybody else seems to be.'

'Thank you.'

She snaps her cigarette in two, crouches down to a pencil-length gap in the floorboards and posts the two bits through the hole. 'That will teach the fat cow downstairs to earwig on my conversations, won't it?'

'I should think it will,' says the psychiatrist, shifting to the edge of his seat for a better view.

'I hope my ciggie burns your fucking place down,' she shouts through the hole.

'Why would you like to set your neighbour's flat on fire, Astrid?'

'Because she ate my rabbit.'

'Oh.'

'Yes, you might well say "Oh", Detective. She had him for her tea. One day he was in his hutch, and the next day he was in her fat gut.'

'I'm not a detective, Astrid, I'm a doctor.'

She looks at him as if he is defective and then says, 'You should arrest her for butchering Peter.'

He writes *Detective* on his notepad and then says, 'Peter?'

'My rabbit.'

'Ah, Peter Rabbit.'

'Yes, except my Peter was white all over and had red eyes.'

He writes *Peter Rabbit* but confuses Beatrix Potter with Lewis Carroll and thinks of Alice. 'When did this happen, Astrid?'

She frowns and starts to count her fingers. After an age she says, 'Yesterday,' and turns her hands into fists.

'That must have been very upsetting for you.'

'It was,' she shouts at the gap, and then, 'You'll pinch anything, won't you, Mrs Bush?' She stands and smooths her skirt. Then she turns to him and warns, 'I hope you haven't left anything in the porch, Detective, because she'll have it from you if you have.'

'It's alright, Astrid, I haven't.'

'Anything at all: coal, RABBITS, bog-roll, that baby if you let her.'

'Tell me, Astrid, why have you been in hospital recently?'

'I've been having a rest,' she says, uncertainly.

'Why have you needed to rest?'

'Because I've been fucking tired, why do you think?'

'I see... I see... I'm sorry; I don't mean to upset you.'

'I'm going shopping,' she says, brightly, 'for some new shoes. I want some white stilettos.'

They both glance at the hearth. 'Is this going to take much longer?' she demands.

'Do you know why I'm here?'

'Of course I bloody well do.'

'Why am I here, Astrid?'

'To take that awful baby away,' she says, nodding at the closed door.

'Could you remind me who the baby belongs to, do you think? I'm afraid I'm in a bit of a muddle today.'

She rolls her eyes, sighs and says, 'I have absolutely no idea but he's not my baby and I don't want him here. If you don't know where he lives, you'll have to take him back to the hospital or to the police station. All he does is scream all day and I can't stand one more minute of it.'

'Do you know if the baby has a name?'

'If he does, I don't know what it is. You might try asking my secretary. She might know, but then again, she might not. She's not terribly good at her job. Between you and me, I'm thinking of giving her the old heave ho. I'm perfectly within my rights. She's very slack you know.'

'Oh, dear,' he says rising to his feet. He resists the urge to stretch and massage his shoulders. 'I'll just have a quick word with your...' he pauses, hoping she'll fill in the gap.

She takes the bait and tuts, 'Staff.'

He nods and adds, 'If that's alright with you, Astrid?'

'Yes, but don't keep them long, they've got work to do. I'm going to the shops, you know, and my man will have to drive me.'

***

In the kitchen, and in whispers, and after he's stepped in soggy kibble, the psychiatrist tells Harry, Lil and Maggie that he is going to section Astrid. It's a galley kitchen and they all stand in a line as if they're waiting for some sort of uniform inspection. Lil jigs the baby in her arms. He sighs with each bounce and his grey eyes open and close like a dolly's until he is too tired to fight the sleep. Harry stares at the psychiatrist as if he is God, and Maggie ducks out of the kitchen every now and then to the crack in the lounge room door to check that Astrid isn't opening any windows, or hasn't found the lighter down the back of the upright chair, or isn't preparing Maggie's P45 on the newly painted walls.

'Do you have a car, Mr Edwards?'

'No,' says Harry, as if this fact means that Astrid won't get treatment.

'Not to worry, Mr Edwards, not to worry, we'll use mine, but we might have to say that yours has gone to the garage or something of that nature because Mrs Edwards thinks that you do have a car. You see, I'd like to get Mrs Edwards to the hospital without any fuss, but since she's very keen to go shopping and doesn't comprehend that she is extremely unwell I'm afraid it's going to involve telling a few white lies.'

Harry glances at Maggie and Maggie's mouth falls open in protest at the implied suggestion that she's an expert at this. Lil thinks the psychiatrist has trouble getting to the point and, resisting the urge to dismiss whatever comes out of his young posh mouth, says firmly, 'Whatever it takes, Doctor.'

He thanks her and then says, 'One more thing, Mr Edwards: who lives in the flat beneath yours?'

'It's empty,' says Harry.

'You're sure?'

'It's been empty for months.'

'I see, I see. Oh, and just one other thing: do you know a Mrs Bush?'

'Mrs Bush?' says Harry and tries to think. 'No, Doctor, the name doesn't ring a bell.'

***

Harry and Maggie sit either side of Astrid on a bench that is nailed to the floor, and in a lofty room that offers no stimulus. Light floods in through the barred Victorian windows and bounces off the crumbling plaster. Hairy brown carpet covers the floor in squares. Painted pipes traverse the walls like veins. The room smells as if it is trying to dry in the sun. In the distance, feet can be heard squeaking down polished corridors and doors being locked and unlocked. Maggie watches the dust motes and thinks about their source: dead skin. Then Astrid scratches her arms and Maggie closes her eyes. Even with her eyes shut she sees particles of Astrid floating in the room and mixing with all the others. She takes shallow breaths and rests her hands on her knotted stomach. So far, she decides, the lies haven't been as white as she would have liked. She wants to bundle Astrid out of the hospital. She tells herself that a decent night's sleep is all she needs because this is the sort of thing they say in films. She watches Harry puts his hand on Astrid's thigh. Astrid flicks it off and calls him a sex pest. He shoves his nails in his mouth and stares at the door. When the ward sister enters the room, Harry puts his head in his hands and Maggie hears her own head beat as if her brain has taken over the pumping of her blood. Astrid expresses her frustration at being kept waiting and then orders the sister to bring her a cup of tea and a custard slice. She invites Harry and Maggie to order whatever they'd like, too. 'My treat,' she says, benevolently. They both look at the sister as if they've been offered fish and chips on top of a ten-course meal.

'Before I organise the refreshments, Mrs Edwards,' says the sister helpfully, 'I'd like to give you something to make you feel better.'

'Have I been unwell then, Nurse?'

'Well, you've been very tired, Mrs Edwards.'

Astrid turns to Maggie. 'Have I?'

The sister nods at Maggie and Maggie says, 'Yes.'

'So it's a vitamin jab you're giving me, is it?' she asks. She's read about vitamin jabs in *Woman;* some doctor with a funny name like Doctor MakeLove gives them to all the big names in Hollywood and beyond to keep them going. She thinks of President Kennedy and Marilyn Monroe; she forgets that Marilyn Monroe has recently died.

She likes the idea of getting star treatment. She begins to wonder if she's a starlet; she knows she's very pretty.

'That's right, Mrs Edwards,' says the sister, helping her off the bench. 'Vitamins.'

'Do you know who I am then?' she asks, hopefully.

'Yes, Mrs Edwards, of course I do.'

Astrid beams. 'Can secretary bird come with me?'

Maggie doesn't want to go with her. 'What about Harry?' she says. 'Shouldn't he go?'

'The fucking driver?' Astrid says shrilly. 'Of course he shouldn't. He can wait for us outside.' She turns to Harry and with a wave of her hand says, 'Go and warm the car up; once I've had my vitamin injection, I want to visit the boutiques.'

Harry knows there are tears coming but he can't help it. He wants to kiss his wife goodbye, but he doesn't know where she's gone. He feels as if she left him without saying when she was coming back. He turns away from her to face the barred window. He hates the aristocracy and their bloody titles. Why did she want to be like them?

'Come on then,' says the sister, pushing open the door. Astrid exits the room with the air of a film star on the red carpet and Maggie follows behind with the despair of a child evacuee on the station platform.

***

Maggie stands in the corner of a room that is no bigger than the box room she sleeps in at home. The walls of the room are blancmange pink. She's never been able to eat blancmange without retching. She imagines Astrid being force-fed blancmange and wretches behind her hands. The sister retrieves a kidney dish containing a syringe and a bottle of transparent fluid from a small shelf. Holding the syringe up to the ceiling, she draws Astrid a hefty dose of God knows what. Astrid lies on her front on the bed with the waist band of her skirt pulled down. Maggie spies angry stretch marks on her flaccid skin and looks away. She decides to notice the architecture. The ceiling in this room is much lower than that in the waiting room and the only window is in the roof. She is reminded of a prison cell. She worries that Astrid will be treated as if she's done something wrong. She shuffles out of the corner to stand beside Astrid's head. Astrid holds out her hand and Maggie clasps it between her two.

'I don't like jabs,' says Astrid.

'No,' says Maggie.

'You won't feel a thing, Mrs Edwards,' lies the sister.

'I can smell dinner,' says Astrid. 'I only want a custard slice, Nurse. I'm not stopping for that bloody stink.'

'Yes, Mrs Edwards,' says the sister, swabbing her bottom with alcohol. 'I know.'

'Do you eat it?'

'Yes, Mrs Edwards, now lie still.'

'I'm used to better.'

The sister grabs a handful of Astrid's pregnancy fat and darts it.

'Fuck a duck,' shouts Astrid.

The sister raises her eyebrows; she's heard a lot in her nursing career but never that. 'All finished,' she says, giving the injected area a brisk rub. She lays the syringe in the kidney dish and leaves it on the shelf.

'How often does Elizabeth have this done, secretary bird?'

'Elizabeth?' says Maggie.

'Taylor,' snaps Astrid. 'What's wrong with everybody today? How often does Elizabeth Taylor have a vitamin jab?'

'I don't know.'

'What do you mean, you don't know?'

'I mean, I don't remember.'

'Bloody hell.'

'I'm sorry, Astrid.'

'Never mind; let's just hope I don't have to have it done too often. I'd hate to suffer a prick like that on a regular basis.'

Maggie's face darkens at an unwelcome mental image.

'I don't suppose you've checked the price of these jabs, have you?' she adds.

Maggie turns to the sister for help.

'The first one is free, Mrs Edwards, so don't worry about that,' she says.

Astrid checks this with Maggie. 'Free?'

Maggie nods weakly.

'Well, it doesn't matter anyway; I'm rich now.'

'I think Maggie needs to visit the ladies, Mrs Edwards,' says the sister, taking a folded cellular blanket from the bottom of the bed.

'Do you?' says Astrid, wondering if her secretary was holding her Union Jack in public.

Maggie nods and looks flustered. Astrid takes her expression to mean she's busting. 'Oh my sainted aunts she's about to wet herself,' she declares.

'Come on then,' says the sister, seizing the opportunity for a fuss-free exit.

'You will come back after you've piddled though, won't you?' says Astrid pouting.

'Yes,' says Maggie.

'You won't leave me?'

Maggie shakes her head.

'You're just going to have a little rest, Mrs Edwards,' confirms the sister, shaking out the blanket. 'Once you've had that, I'll get you that cup of tea.'

'Don't forget the custard slice.'

'I'll see what we've got,' she says, covering her with the blanket. 'I'll show you to the Ladies,' she says to Maggie, as she retrieves the kidney dish from the shelf.

Reluctantly, Maggie pulls her hand free of Astrid's.

Astrid tucks her hand under the blanket and yawns loudly. 'See you in a minute, secretary bird,' she says. 'I'm just going to rest my eyes.'

6: Straight-Forward

Lil's new kitchen wasn't her choice, but leaving Alfie to get on with it was. But when it was finished, she did wish it didn't look like the public swimming baths. Alfie blamed the colour scheme on their new appliance. 'I painted the walls to match the fridge.'

'Not everything has to match,' she muttered.

'What do you know about it?' he replied. 'Last time I shitting looked, I painted and decorated for a living, not you.'

Lil stiffened.

'Well,' he continued, 'it's not as if I tell you how to go about cleaning houses, is it?'

Lil hated to be reminded that she was just a cleaner: before Alfie ruined her life, she'd worked in an office where she'd typed sixty-five words per minute and written in shorthand and had worn a suit to work. She hadn't always scrubbed the insides of other people's toilets, or spent every day in a housecoat. If it hadn't been for Alfie, she could have been really important by now in the office world. She could have been a supervisor. She could have been like Miss Whyte. 'Out of my kitchen,' she spat and allowed her shooing fingers to get dangerously close to his chest.

'You chose the fridge,' mumbled Alfie as he retreated.

It was the first time in Lil's life that she'd owned a fridge. It was also the first time she'd lived in a two-storey house – excluding the years she had lived with Alfie's parents – and the first time she had had the comfort of an indoor toilet and fixed bath. But now, as she leans against her new fridge with her grandson in her arms, she contemplates the irony that the family business booms as the family itself falls to pieces. She wonders how long it will take the doctors to sort out Astrid. She thinks of Alfie and all the years he's been difficult and strange, and of Nell: the telegram proclaiming Louis' death silenced her for the rest of her life. But this was different, Astrid wanted a baby. She hadn't gone cuckoo because she'd seen something terrible or lost someone she loved. Surely it wouldn't take the doctors long to fix her? She wonders if her family is cursed and if it's down to her and what she is. 'We can't go on calling you Baby,' she says, changing the subject. 'You need a proper name.' She wants to think of names but can only think of one: Geoffrey. 'Perhaps we should leave that to your dad,' she says, emphatically. She checks that Alfie has set the camp-bed up for Harry in the front room, lets Astrid's cat outside to explore its new surroundings, and then carries the baby upstairs. She goes to Alfie's bedroom, a room she normally avoids, and lays the baby on his bed. She thinks the baby must be dreaming about milk because his mouth moves up and down as if he's at the breast. She removes a drawer from the chest and empties it of Alfie's socks. Then she stands on tiptoes and, ignoring the dust, retrieves a battered cardboard box from the top of the wardrobe. The box contains the blanket that Nell knitted Louis before she knew he'd been killed in Westkapelle. After the arrival of the telegram, Nell had put the blanket away and then done the same with her mind. Now, Lil folds Louis' blanket to the size of the drawer and puts the baby down to sleep.

***

The baby's face makes Lil ponder the idea of old souls and reincarnation but he looks too sharp to be Fred. She doesn't let herself consider any other candidates. Instead, she decides that she'd only want to come back as somebody else if she could retain the knowledge she'd gained as herself, in this awful life. She doesn't like the thought of making the same mistakes twice. Her reincarnated self should either want to get married and have children, or know not to make rash decisions at bus stops. She thinks of Maggie. Wouldn't the first version be easier in the long run? How much more straightforward her own life would have been if she hadn't met Margaret. The baby sighs in his sleep and smacks his lips. He doesn't seem to look like any of them and she thinks this is a good thing even though everybody says the

Edwards' are a good-looking bunch. She gently rubs his tummy and decides to take Maggie's future in to her own hands. She picks up the makeshift cot with her grandson inside, and sets them up in Maggie's room. Maggie just has to fall in love with a different life before someone like Margaret comes along and ruins her chances.

7: In Memoriam

Maggie had suggested names for the baby, but Lil couldn't, and Harry wouldn't. He insisted that Astrid would recover, choose a name she loved, and go with him to register their son's birth within the forty-two days that the Birth and Deaths Registration Act of 1953 allowed.

But now, the baby is forty-one days old and remains nameless. Early that morning, before Harry and Alfie could don their overalls and slink off out of it to paint and paper the walls of the wealthy, Lil had put her foot down. Yet, even as Harry had stood at the front door, and had watched her tuck into his breast pocket the piece of paper that contained all the information the registrar would require, he'd still counted on getting a last-minute reprieve: Astrid dinging the doorbell perhaps, or even just a message from the hospital to say that she'd been discharged and was awaiting collection or already on her way home. He'd lingered at the door to give these fantasies more time to materialize, but then his mum had shooed him out the house as if he was a stray and his dad had stood at his back and, without really meaning to, had blocked the line of retreat. 'Don't come back, without a name for my grandson,' she'd called after them, and the baby had wailed as if to say, *hear, hear*.

Now, Harry walks to the register office as if he's off to register a death. He wishes his mind was a list of names. He thinks of the men he knows, but he doesn't want his son to be Roger or Vince or Del, and he isn't enough of a narcissist to name him after himself. What he does know of Astrid's wishes is no help whatsoever: he can't call a boy Saskia. He sees himself standing mute before the registrar and wonders what the penalty is for failing to register a birth within forty-two days. Then he decides it doesn't matter; he already feels as if he's doing time.

Alfie keeps to the kerb and watches the ground with his fedora pulled down low over his eyes and his gloved hands safe in his pockets because this sort of expedition is fraught with danger: people meet on the street and when they do, they shake hands. Sometimes, they go further than this and with their free hand grasp his forearm or pat his back, or rest the bloody thing on his shoulder, and get in his face and it's all he can do not to piss his trousers, or vomit all over his shoes, or fall down on them like a whacked skittle. Alfie keeps to the kerb and watches the ground so that he won't meet people, and by extension, won't have to touch or be touched by them.

When they reach the steps of the register office, Harry finds he can't walk through the large red door and doesn't care that his distress is witnessed by strangers, because it's just occurred to him that Lady Astrid might have the constitution of Queen Victoria and endure and endure. Alfie flinches as Harry forgets himself and lunges at him; he wants to be comforted, reassured, reminded of the marvels of modern medicine etc. etc. but Alfie isn't the person to do it. As Harry holds on to the lapels of his dad's jacket and weeps into the wool, Alfie stands still like a snared animal with upturned palms and his head thrown back to avoid Harry's head on his face. Silently, he waits for the ordeal to be over and seconds later, it is. Harry transfers the slip of paper into his dad's breast pocket, and walks off without a backwards glance and Alfie, whiter than heaven in snowfall, enters the register office, confirms his eligibility to register the birth of his grandson, says the first two names that enter his head, and thinks: *That's the little fella with a name at last.*

8: An Outing

Astrid knows that the baby sitting on her lap is her baby. What she doesn't know is when she's going to *feel* that the baby sitting on her lap is her baby. This is the third time she's been allowed to leave the hospital to spend an afternoon with him: how many afternoons will it take before she starts to feel like his mum? It's a question she wants to ask the doctors but she knows she won't because if she admits to this deficiency of maternal feelings, they'll never let her go. 'One day at a time,' the doctors keep saying, but the days have added up to months and the months nearly a year.

Harry doesn't like the way Astrid keeps staring into space; he worries she's on a one-way ticket to that place he's yet to fathom. He wishes he could see inside her head, then worries about what he might, or might not for that matter, see there. When he heard the rain strike the guttering of his parent's house in the minutes before it was time for him and the baby to leave for the hospital, he agreed with his mum that a café would have to replace a walk in the park. In a bid to put some fat on her bones, he ordered a plate of sausage and chips for Astrid, but she hasn't touched them and she's barely said a word since they sat down at the table. He wishes he could stop himself from remarking on the rain and fiddling with the lid of the tomato ketchup bottle.

Meanwhile, Maggie's premenstrual and already missing the baby. It's a paralysing combination that stops her from making the most of her afternoon off. Since Lil is not there to prevent it, there's danger of her spending the hours until the baby's return perched on the windowsill watching the rain, waiting for Harry to amble into view pushing the Silver Cross. There is much she could be doing such as mashing the baby's tea; washing his nappies; changing his cot bedding; pressing his Babygros, or recording the long and ever lengthening list of his firsts in the baby book she bought him when they were last at WHSmiths, but all she wants to do is sit and wait for him to come back to her. So, armed with a Farley's rusk and a mug of tepid Camp coffee, that's exactly what she does.

On the wall beside the café's hat and coat stand is a mirror that shows Astrid precisely how awful she looks without make-up and freshly washed hair. Her hair dangles from her head in dull clumps like pond weed and the colour of her face – yellowish, with brown rings circling her eyes – puts her in mind of the ferrets housed in the car-park of Harry's favourite boozer. She remembers that before the pub had ferrets, they had penguins that stank to high heaven. Harry said that people came from all over London to see them, but whenever she went there with him for a drink, which was rarely because of the smell, she only ever saw the same old faces. Then the penguins were eaten by the foxes and shortly after that the ferrets arrived. It seems like years since they last went to the pub for a drink but it couldn't have been that long ago because it was just before the baby arrived. They'd been to the doctors' beforehand for her final routine appointment. The doctor measured her bump with a seamstress' tape measure and mentioned that the baby might be too big for her pelvis, but only briefly as if no sooner had it he said it he'd decided that this wasn't actually the case or that, if it was, it didn't really matter. At the pub, Harry had made her put her feet up on a bar stool to relieve her swollen ankles, but there was nothing he could do about her aching ribs and she'd already taken two Paracetamol for her headache. The barmaid went overboard with the ice in her lemonade and the glass seemed to taste of bleach. They'd run out of salt-and-vinegar crisps and the pork scratchings Harry bought as a substitute were soft and made her feel bilious. Now it seems entirely plausible to her that they won't ever go to that pub for a drink again and she doesn't mind.

In the café, she picks up her glass of orange squash and takes a sip while the baby sucks on the knoll of a Marlborough bun and bounces on her lap. Another glance in the mirror and Astrid's asking herself what in the world the doctors thought they were doing letting her out looking like this: who really was the maddest of them all?

Two old men sitting in the café bay window discuss a blocked drain over their mugs of tea, bowls of Oxtail soup and thickly buttered slices of Mother's Pride. Harry swallows the last mouthful of his bacon sarnie and wonders whether he should tell them how to unblock it. He can either advise the old boys to pour caustic soda down the plughole or talk to Astrid about the hospital and ask her how the recent visit with her parents went.

'I've given it a good poke with a coat hanger,' says the man with the blocked drain.

Harry removes a piece of bacon from a wisdom tooth and considers this: if the blockage is not too severe a coat hanger can sometimes be enough to dislodge it but it really depends on...

'Stick some caustic soda down it,' instructs the friend just as Harry is twisting in his chair to advise the same. Foiled, he twists back to see Astrid frowning at him with her chin resting on top of the baby's head. Remembering he's already used his serviette to mop a glob of sick from the baby's chin, he wipes his mouth on the back of his hand, takes a breath large enough to make him hiccup, and then asks, 'How did the visit with your parents go?'

Astrid thinks about this but she's too tired to show Harry the facial expression that shows she's thinking about it. Mor just kept repeating, as she did every visit, the same old empty words: this *post-partum-whatdoyoucallit, darling,* won't last forever. While her dad just sat as far away from her bed as he could get, and swapped *The Daily Mirror* for *The Times* so he could hide from her hideous appearance and didn't have to comment on her abnormal hormone levels. Reminded of the hospital and the lack of progress she's sure she's making, she returns the baby to his pram and then asks Harry, 'When have I got to be back?'

Harry looks at his watch: not yet is the answer, but he reaches for his coat anyway.

9: The Check-Up

Maggie is about to drop in on Astrid and the baby while Harry is at work. As she walks to their flat, she thinks about nappy rash, sore gums and infected eyes. She pictures dirty bottles kicking around the floor and bowls of unsuitable food left to fester in the warm. She imagines him malnourished and distressed. She thinks about dysentery and choking. She imagines Astrid leaving him outside a shop in his pram, and forgetting to take him home with her and then an unshaven man with dirty fingernails wheeling him away to use him as an ashtray and other things beside that make her say out loud, 'No'. She imagines him thinking she abandoned him and begins a walking-trot along the paving slabs. Her marmite and tomato sandwich gives her a stitch. Her thoughts make her nauseous. By the time she gets to the flat, she knows she should have worn a summer dress and sandals. She finds his pram outside. She picks up his pram blanket and finds that it smells different. She wonders what washing powder Astrid is using and what harm it might be doing to the baby's sensitive skin. She puts her ear to the front door and rests her free hand on the pram handle. She can't hear him crying. She wipes her face on her shirt sleeve and takes a deep breath. She's going to pretend that she forgot to give Astrid the box of Ashton and Parsons Infant Powders. She's going to thrust the box at her, claim she was passing, and insist that they really do soothe the baby's gums. She knows Harry asked her to stay away for a while, but he never specified how long, and it's been ten days. She rings the doorbell and steels herself.

***

Astrid offers Maggie a piece of home-made shortbread. The baby sits on her hip as she makes tea and arranges her shortbread fingers on a gilt plate that was a wedding present from a Godmother she doesn't know. 'Harry's favourite,' she says. 'I thought he could do with a bit of feeding up.'

Maggie accepts a biscuit and realises that she's still looking for signs of child neglect when there are none. She smiles at the baby in his pressed stripey shirt and pale blue shorts. She doesn't recognise one item of what he wears. The baby returns her smile but pats Astrid's cheek with his plump starfish hands. 'He likes to be carried,' Maggie announces.

Her mum had told her to stop carrying him everywhere. She said she was making a rod for Astrid's back and that Astrid wouldn't thank her for it when she got out of hospital. Maggie remembers paying no heed to her; the baby was hers to look after. Wasn't that what she said?

'LJ likes to shuffle round on his bottom now,' says Astrid.

Astrid wonders when Maggie and the rest of the family are going to stop calling LJ 'Baby'. She wishes she hadn't been so convinced that he was going to be a girl. She wonders if her insistence was a sign that something was already starting to go wrong in her head. It seems ridiculous to her now that she didn't pick out any boys' names. When Harry had told her what he'd named their son, she'd cried.

'I didn't know what to call him,' he'd said, worrying that her distress over the baby's name might stall her recovery. Then he'd lied. 'I stood in the register office and said the first two names that came in to my head. You never mentioned any boys' names when you were expecting him. I just picked some names, Astrid. You know I'm no good at that sort of thing. Please don't get upset.'

Then, when Astrid was discharged from hospital, she'd discovered that they weren't even calling her son by the name Harry had picked for him; they were calling him 'Baby.'

'He was "Baby" for so long that we just got in to the habit of calling him that,' a stung Maggie had explained. She'd thought Astrid had a cheek. She'd wondered if the psychiatrists had discharged her too soon.

When Astrid held LJ for the first time, knowing she was his mother and he was her son, she thought: Stefan Harry Edwards, but nobody else knows this. In the end, the only say she had in his name was that, from then on, he was to be known by his initials, 'LJ.' She told herself that it was something.

Now, LJ and Astrid sit on the rush mat beside a wooden peg puzzle. Maggie abandons her chair to sit with them. Astrid's hands tighten around LJ's pudgy tummy. Maggie breathes in his scent; like the blanket, he smells different too. She notices a new patch of cradle cap on his scalp and frowns: she'd have stopped off at the chemists and bought a bottle of olive oil if she'd known. Astrid sees her staring at LJ's crusty scalp and says, 'LJ can say "Mum" now, can't you, LJ?'

Maggie catches his fleshy hand and says, 'Can you? Say "Mum" then. Go on, Baby, say "Mum". She takes objection to a cat hair on his hand, pulls it off and wipes it on her trousers.

LJ retracts his hand as if her skin is coated in golden syrup or mud. She strokes his bare arm and says, 'What about Mag-ee?'

LJ looks at her quizzically and then turns his drooling mouth on Astrid's chin.

'Can you say, Ma-gee?' She bends down and draws level with his head. Then she blows a raspberry in the crease of his neck with an exaggerated intake of breath to signal her intention. He used to love her raspberry kisses and grasping the memory of what is to come, duly lets out a squeal of delight before launching the back of his bald little head at Astrid's bony chest. Astrid loses her balance and, without the restraint of both her hands around his tummy, LJ lollops to one side and raises his arms to Maggie.

'Baby overboard,' she exclaims delightedly, and puts her hands beneath his armpits as if she is going to lift him from Astrid's lap. Astrid rights herself and Maggie catches the expression on her face. She removes her hands from his armpits. Astrid restores hers around his tummy. Maggie folds her arms. 'Saved you, LJ,' she says, and then bursts into tears.

10: Walnuts

Lil is at the kitchen sink slicing young runner beans from the garden. She has a leg of lamb in the oven and her family to lunch to celebrate LJ's first birthday. Maggie and Harry stand close together at the kitchen table waiting for their dad to show them his new gun while Astrid helps LJ with a new shape sorter on the sitting room floor.

Alfie assembles the gun on the kitchen table with the solemnity of someone laying out the dead. 'It's an Aguirre and Aranzabal '117 sporting shotgun, with a hammerless triple bolting system,' he says. 'Do you see the two triggers?'

Maggie is uninterested but nods like an obedient child. (She'd rather spend this time telling everybody about her decision to attend university to become a social worker. She's starting in October and can't wait for the distraction.) Lil bastes the meat and pretends not to listen to Alfie. Harry smiles at his dad's pronunciation of Aguirre and Aranzabal one minute, and worries about Astrid's state of mind the next.

'You can see the quality in the case. Real Spanish leather,' says Alfie.

'Is Astrid alright, do you think?' whispers Harry in Maggie's ear.

Alfie pauses and stares at the leather gun case: he's forgotten what he was going to say next.

Even though Maggie wonders the same she tells Harry, 'Yes, I do.'

Lil sees that Astrid has now taken LJ to the garden. 'I know what you two are whispering about,' she says. 'Stop fretting, Harry. Astrid's in the garden, I can see her from here. And, before you ask, LJ looks happy enough.'

Harry leaps over to Lil's side. Maggie forces herself to stay put. He wipes the smeared kitchen window with the cuff of his shirt and peers out. 'I didn't know she wanted to go out,' he says. 'I can't see them. I better go out.'

Maggie turns to the kitchen window.

'She's just gone behind the hedge,' says Lil. 'Stop it now, Harry. She's probably gone to pick some mint. I expect she heard me say that I had yet to make my mint sauce. I'm very behind today. Hurry up and have a look at that gun so I can have my table back will you?'

Reluctantly, Harry does as he is asked. Alfie thrusts the gun in his face and says, 'Look at the engraving on that; it's handcrafted.' Harry steps back from the gun and Maggie makes a big show of inspecting the engraving.

'What's the gun all about, Dad?' asks Harry.

Alfie looks confused; he can't remember.

'He's thinking of taking up shooting,' says Lil. What she doesn't say is: *He thinks we're surrounded by Nazis.*

'Shooting?'

'It's got to be more interesting than golf,' she retorts.

'Was golf the alternative, then?' He can't picture his dad doing either.

'We can't have lunch until the table's cleared,' she snaps.

'Is it really handcrafted, Dad?' says Maggie charitably.

Alfie takes Maggie's comment to mean that she doesn't believe him. 'I'll show you a picture of the engravers,' he says.

'No need, Dad,' says Maggie, nearly patting his arm. She looks at her hand as if it's a liability and then cages it in her pocket.

'The catalogue's in the bedroom,' he says, leaving the kitchen with the gun in his hand.

Harry rolls his eyes and Lil notices. She thinks her own eyeballs got tired of rolling a long time ago. She gives him a withering look even though she feels the same as he does about it all. Harry seizes his chance to be with Astrid and legs it to the garden. Maggie wishes she could go with him, but not to check on Astrid. Alfie returns to the kitchen with a well-thumbed shotgun catalogue for 1962 tucked under his arm. He doesn't notice Harry's absence. The gun goes back on the kitchen table and the catalogue is opened. He shows Maggie a grainy photograph of some men in overalls. They are bent over engraving machines. 'Hand Engraving Room,' he reads. Maggie peers at the catalogue from a distance. Then Alfie tosses it on the table and picks up the gun. 'Look at the engraving on that,' he says, and they start all over again.

'Craftsmen,' she declares.

'Yes,' says Alfie, sounding like a father whose child has just solved the Friedmann equations. 'It's a 12-bore shotgun with twenty-eight-inch barrels. I thought they'd have used beech for the stock but it says in the catalogue that the stock's made of walnut.'

'That reminds me, Alfie, I haven't pickled any walnuts yet,' says Lil. 'I'll have to get on and do that for you if you want some by Christmas.'

'Yes, Lil, I must have my pickled walnuts, mustn't I?' he says.

'Yes, Alfie, you must.'

Maggie thinks that the shotgun and her mother's pickled walnuts are the only things her dad loves.

1967

11: The Birth of Need

Astrid isn't sure her conscience will allow her to do more than leave Harry's condoms baking in the sun during the hours that he is at work with Alfie, painting and decorating. In terms of liability, she thinks there's a gulf between accidentally leaving a condom on the sunny bedroom window sill while putting away her husband's clean socks and pants, and going to her sewing box, selecting her sharpest needle and transforming the offending item into a colander. She wonders if it's wrong to hope that at least one employee on the production line at the London Rubber Company has a lust for sabotage: after all, one little prick is all it would take.

She notices she's paired two odd socks together and then thinks of Babs, her next-door neighbour. Last month, during one of their weekly coffee mornings, Babs blamed her youngest child on a 'dodgy dick sock'. 'That one,' she'd said, nodding at two-year old Douglas, 'was an accident. It must have been a dodgy dick sock because I know I put the thing on right. Be warned,' she'd added, 'if it can happen to me, it can happen to you.'

But Astrid doubts a faulty condom was responsible for Douglas. Secretly, she wonders if Babs' long and pointed fingernails are to blame; that Trevor's condom split because Babs' raked it with her talons. But in her own marriage, the donning of the condom has always been one of Harry's jobs, like putting out the bin, or tightening the kitchen tap, or re-grouting the bathroom tiles. She wonders if she should offer to do it, and then if he would he let her. She pictures herself dressing Harry's penis in the manner of the cat roughing up the cat post. But then she considers her own fingernails; unlike Babs' they're short and round. Even if she wants to grow them long, and then sharpen them on Harry's post, the constant washing-up and daily hand-washing that housewifery demands keeps them brittle and blunt. She puts Babs' long nails down to the fact that she isn't particularly house-proud and her children are invariably grubby, and then turns to Trevor's appendage. Hot-faced, she considers whether Douglas was actually the consequence of an over-stuffed French letter. She thinks about *The Dam Busters,* a film her dad took her to see when she was a teenager. *God it was boring.* But what if Harry's missile lacked the capacity and the clout to breach the dam? She sighs, as Barnes Wallis might have done when his bouncing bomb failed its first test in the waters off the beaches of Kent, and wonders if it's possible to buy small-sized condoms. Then she sighs for a second time: as if there was any chance of her buying such a thing, she was bound to know the girl behind the counter in the chemist. Perhaps it's time they moved out of Chiswick. She finishes putting away Harry's underwear and does as much as she dare do for now; she moves his condoms along the window sill to keep pace with the dying June sun and prays for an accident.

***

The next day, Harry falls off his ladder while sanding down a Georgian sash window and slips a disc. He spends the next six weeks on the floor of the lounge growing a beard and urinating into empty milk bottles. The nearest Astrid gets to the family allowance is during week four of his convalescence when his back goes into spasm at the same time as he's trying to have a wee. To save the carpet from a urine stain, Astrid throws herself on his penis with the selflessness of a soldier on a stick grenade, and wonders why they have to make the neck of the milk bottles so narrow.

***

Even in a dream, Astrid finds waste upsetting.

Dressed in a Victorian nightdress with white tap shoes on her feet and lips that look like two fat slugs covered in salt, she floats into the kitchen. She opens the cupboard where the Schwartz spice rack lives and discovers that each of the jars contain wallpaper paste. Gone are the nutmeg, mace, cloves, and the like. A disembodied voice that sounds a bit like a psychiatrist wants to know how many recipes call for cardamom pods in her copy of the *Constance Spry Cookery Book*. But she doesn't know off the top of her head. *Turmeric?* it asks. She doesn't know. *Spell Asafoetida*, it demands with menace. A fountain pen then appears in her right hand even though she's left-handed, and a blue leaf of Basildon Bond pops out of the toaster in pristine condition. When she plucks the paper from the toaster she finds, in her own neat script, the following already written there: *In future, Harry, don't use my spice jars to store your left-over wallpaper paste, with all my love, Astrid.* The disembodied voice hoots before another leaf of Basildon Bond, this time creased and stained with tea rings, pops out of the toaster. In Harry's untidy writing it reads: *What can I say, Astrid? It's not my wallpaper paste, it's my sperm. Where else am I supposed to keep the bloody stuff? Lots of love, Harry.* She does a shuffle ball change in irritation before the disembodied voice suggests that she open the jars and help herself to Harry's sperm. *Yes,* she says, *yes, I'll just help myself.* She lines up the jars on the kitchen side and, one by one, tries to unscrew the caps, but none of them will open. She wraps a jar in the skirt of her nightdress and twists, but the cap doesn't budge. Then the kitchen ceiling opens up and a waterfall of hot suds thunders onto the black tiled floor. She thrusts a jar into the water to loosen the cap but the sperm evaporates in the heat. Horrified, she watches the frothy water creep over her tap shoes and up her shins before realising that the contents of each jar are going to suffer the same fate as the Turmeric and the Asafoetida: they are going to spoil in the cupboard. The disembodied voice begins to sing *I'm singing in the rain*, and before she knows it, she's tapping a four-beat shuffle waist deep in water.

1967

12: A Quick Look at the Lesbians

Frankie crossly yanks and knots her tie and tries to keep her temper under control. God, for the first time in a long time, she wants to punch something. She told Maggie they were going to have a quiet night in. She made it very clear to Maggie that that was what they were going to do. Cuddle on the sofa, she said, and watch T.V. And besides all that, Maggie knows she's fed up with The Gateways Club and Gina, the proprietor, dictating what can and can't be debated in the bar. That was the problem with The Gates, it was *for* lesbians but it wasn't run by one. Frankie couldn't leave her politics at the door any more than she could leave her vagina there. That Maggie doesn't seem to care about this, *and* that she seems to think that it's okay to piss their money down Gina's carsey every Friday night, makes her have to punch the mirror. What does she see in that place? It's a cellar for God's sake; a small, dark and dingy cellar that looks as if it's been gutted by fire. She may as well spend her evening sweating in a coal bunker. That she now has to go there and drag Maggie out of the poxy place makes her punch the mirror again.

***

Nobody could say that it was love at first sight the first time Maggie clapped eyes on Frankie. The woman Maggie fantasized about before she dropped off to sleep didn't wear a suit and tie on a night out or a heavy square signet ring on her right ring finger, and she didn't go to the barbers for a short back and sides. The woman Maggie envisioned loving had tits, curves, a dress or three in the wardrobe, and she plucked her eyebrows. What's more, she favoured hairspray over Brylcreem and wore a bra instead of a vest. When Maggie felt Frankie watching her at The Gates, she thought she was being eyed up by a bloke. (This was before Gina had implemented the women-only policy at the club.) In fact, Maggie had been about to tell Frankie that if she wanted to be ogled by a bloke, she'd have gone for a bop at her local boozer and saved herself the bus fare to Chelsea. But, before she could open her gob and give her admirer what-for, Frankie smiled and said hello and Maggie, for some inexplicable reason, just melted on the spot.

***

Ordinarily, Frankie doesn't take her beloved dove-grey *Norton Dominator 99* motorcycle out on wet roads. Riding in the rain is dangerous. Maggie knows that. On a wet road, Frankie's ability to control the *Dominator* is reduced by at least fifty percent. Maggie knows that too. And, hadn't she'd been massaging Maggie's foot when that newsreader reported that the number of people killed in traffic collisions on British roads in 1966 was the highest recorded number in peacetime? It was only a bloody year ago. It was eight thousand odd deaths, for God's sake. And, as she rubbed Johnsons' baby oil in to Maggie's calloused little piggy, didn't Frankie tell her that most of those accidents had *no doubt probably* happened on wet roads, and furthermore that most of those that had snuffed it had *no doubt probably* been motorcyclists? It's as if Maggie wants the *Dominator* to skid off the road. It's as if Maggie wants a lamppost to knock her bloody block off. Clearly, it's because Maggie's *no doubt probably* seeing some other bird behind her back. That's why she's stuck two fingers up at the quiet night in. She's seizing the opportunity to meet some little slapper who *no doubt probably* shags anything in a skirt. God, the thought makes Frankie have to run a red light; have to twist the Dominator's throttle; have to kick the death-trap up a gear.

***

Maggie moved in with Frankie two weeks after they first met. Frankie said she couldn't live another day without Maggie and Maggie decided that she couldn't live another day with her parents. She told her mum that her new job as a social worker came with accommodation in Ealing. She said she would stop by now and then; she did not give them her new address. Maggie soon learned that Frankie was a bit of an oxymoron in so much as she was a gardener with no shed, a gardener without so much as a lean-to in which to store the tools of her trade. Consequently, her flat, which was more of a bedsit than a flat, was actually more of a shed than a bedsit. As well as harbouring Frankie, Maggie, and Frankie's gardening tools, Frankie's 'shed' also harboured a fair to middling sized mice infestation. Maggie didn't like mice. Frankie asked the landlord to get rid of them. The landlord didn't want to. He said to Frankie, 'Come on, Frank-me-old-son, what are you: a man or a mouse? You get rid of 'em, mate.' Frankie didn't, partly because she was neither man nor mouse and partly because she couldn't be arsed. One morning, Maggie discovered that her favourite dress – a velvet number with lace cuffs and a lace collar – had been blemished by mouse poo *and* Frankie's lapping compound. Frankie's response, Maggie decided, was typical of a man: it was passive-aggressively non-existent. Secretly, Maggie started saving for her own place. What with her dad and now Frankie, she'd had enough of living with men.

1968

13: Spaceships

LJ sits in the bright orange swivel chair that doubles up as a lunar module when he's bored. The chair/lunar module belongs to Assumpta, his childminder. Hanging on the wall of her house above this chair is a black-and-white photo of a man Assumpta calls the Holy Father. The Holy Father has scary eyes that follow him all around her lounge. He takes lazy pot shots at him with his Colt Peacemaker while Assumpta ponders a recipe for Baked Alaska and absent-mindedly strokes the mole that she privately regards as her very own stigmata.

At first, going home with Auntie Assumpta after school on Wednesdays so that his mum could sell lots of ladies a special cream for their faces, in a shop with a big escalator and a cafe that sold cockles even though it was nowhere near the seaside, was quite good. Her biggest boy, Gerard, owned a penknife. On the walk home from school, they often collected sticks and then, in the garden if it wasn't raining or in the stinky garage if it was, they sharpened the sticks into arrows and threw them at Gerard's younger brothers and sisters. An arrow in the head scored ten and anything below that, five. But then Gerard sharpened the knife without telling his mum, and LJ nearly chopped his finger off and had to have a big bit of it sewn back on at the doctors, and Auntie Assumpta took the penknife away and locked it in the shed, and Gerard got slapped legs after shouting that he would never ever play with stupid LJ again. Then Wednesdays went from being quite good to worse than rubbish.

Now, LJ does a head stand off the swivel chair because he likes being upside down and reluctantly thinks about what Neil Baldwin said at play-time: *if your sick's green, you're going to die; when you die, you don't go to heaven, you go in the ground and get eaten by worms; all of your blood can come out of your mouth when you're old and just coming out of the paper shop.* Why did Neil have to find him in the concrete tunnel and tell him all that stuff? He wonders if it's possible to keep sick and blood inside even when it really wants to come out. He decides to tell his dad about heaven and the worms on the way home from Auntie Assumpta's house, and tell his mum the stuff about the green sick and what can happen to old people in the paper shop when she gets home from work because she knows more about sick than his dad.

***

'What happens when you die, Dad?' LJ asks.

'That's a funny old question, son.'

'Why is it?'

'It just is.'

'But what happens?'

'How should I know?'

'You must know.'

'No one really knows until they pop their clogs, do they?'

'Until they what?'

'Die. It means die.'

'What's a clog?'

'It doesn't matter.'

'Why did you say it, if you don't know?'

'Because I do know, LJ, that's why. It's a type of shoe… a wooden shoe… they wear them in Holland. They look bloody uncomfortable to me.'

'I don't really get what a shoe has to do with a dead person.'

'Neither do I, son.'

'You don't know much, do you, Dad?'

'I know enough, L.'

'But you don't know anything about heaven.'

'Heaven?'

'Hmm… heaven.'

'What do you know about it then, clever clogs?'

126

'It's where you go when you die.'

'If you know that, why are you asking me?'

He pictures himself being eaten by worms and his tummy and his mouth do the thing they do when he's about to be sick. Then he feels something very hot in his throat. It tastes like banana but he worries that it's green. He pictures grass in his throat and cries out 'Dad.'

'Gordon Bennett,' says his dad taken aback by the panic in his child's voice. He picks him up and says, 'Whatever is the matter?'

He swallows hard and then tells him.

'Well how does he know that?' He bounces him up and down on his arm and adds, 'Has this Neil fella ever popped *his* clogs?'

He shakes his head; the shoulder of his dad's donkey jacket feels like a cold conker against his cheek.

'Well then.'

'He said that heaven and God weren't real and that was why you end up being food for worms.'

'Did he now?'

'God is real, isn't he?'

'I don't know, LJ, but I can tell you this for nothing, neither does that little...'

He starts to wonder if angels are made up too; Assumpta once said that God made them from His own special type of play-dough. But making people from play-dough was hard. He could only make flat things with it or snakes or... worms. He sighs. Now he won't be able to do play-dough anymore because it will remind him to worry about all of this stuff.

'Want to go on my shoulders, son?'

He shakes his head, buries his face in the collar of his dad's jacket then lifts his head again because the collar feels like his mum's prickly hair brush. 'But, do you think Morfar's feeding the worms?'

Morfar was Astrid's late father, Bill. He died a few months before. It was on the day of the Grand National when a car hit him as he hurried to put a bet on *Go-Pontinental*.

'No, LJ, I don't.'

'But, do you just think that, or do you actually know that?'

'I know Morfar's not feeding any worms, okay?'

'How do you know?'

'I just do.'

'You don't know, do you?'

'Yes I do, L, because I know that he's nowhere near any worms.'

'Where is he then?'

'In a pot.'

'A pot? What sort of pot?'

'A special one.'

'It must be big.'

'Not really.'

'Well how big is it?'

'Hells bells, L.'

'How big is it, Dad?'

'You know that bucket you got at the seaside?'

'The red one with the yellow handle?'

'I'll take your word for it, son, but that's about the size of it.'

'That's a bit funny; I don't really get how Morfar fitted inside my bucket.'

'He turned into dust and then went inside.'

'How?'

'What did you get in that Jamboree bag?'

'What Jamboree bag?'

'The one Auntie Maggie gave you on Sunday.'

'Can't remember.'

'Can't remember?'

'I can't remember everything you know, Daddy.'

'I bet you got some milk bottles.'

LJ sighs. 'If you must know, I got a toffee chew and some spaceships.'

'I like those spaceships, I do. Did you save one for me?'

'No, I ate them all because Auntie Maggie said I could. So, how did Morfar turn into dust?'

1969

14: The Progress of Need

When Astrid's mother, Sille, had announced her intention to leave Kent and return to her native Denmark, Astrid had suggested a farewell party, not a slide-show. She finds viewing the slides her late father took of LJ during the months that she was in hospital distressing. She doesn't know the baby in them. She cannot say when and where each image was captured. She has no idea how many months old the baby is in each, and she cannot explain to those gathered around the white bedsheet projector screen the reasons for any one of the expressions on his face. Her baby was born ten months old. All these slides do is force her to think about where she was and what she was doing at the time each was taken; she finds the possibilities both finite and painful and wonders if she should make a start on the washing-up.

Seven-year-old LJ doesn't like all the attention he's getting, all the *Oohs* and the *Aahs*; it was fine while there were still chocolate biscuits on the plate but now… he licks his finger and cleans his shoe. When will they go to the park? Mormor's park has a witch's hat and a rocking horse and Auntie Maggie promised to take him after lunch. When is she going to stop eating those round pastry things with the chopped-up slugs inside and get her shoes on? If she doesn't hurry up, it will be time to go home soon.

Lil wants to tell LJ he'll get worms if he carries on putting dirt in his mouth but why does she always have to be the Nanny that tells him off? Sille-by-name-Sille-by-nature lets him get away with murder. But it's only to salve her guilty conscience. Fancy flouncing off to Denmark; her place was with her daughter and grandson. Beneath those fancy clothes was a selfish woman. She wishes she'd feigned a migraine; it wasn't hard to do. All she had to say was, *My eyesight's gone and I'm off to bed till it returns.* Alfie had wriggled out of the party by arranging to fish at Shiplake with his angling club. If she'd feigned a migraine and stayed at home, she would have had the entire day to herself. She could have watched the figure skating and finished that box of Maltesers.

Maggie loves Sille's glamour, accent, and husky voice; that she dresses like a young woman instead of an old one. She likes the casual way Sille wears her feather boa and that she indiscriminately pets the cheeks of her guests and calls them all *darling*. She feels as if she's scoffing mushroom vol-au-vents in the company of a Danish Brigitte Bardot. She thinks: *Lucky Astrid.* She glances at her own mum and hopes that whatever she's due to inherit from her operates like baldness and skips a generation.

Harry stares at a purple stain on the make-shift screen because he knows Astrid is waiting for him to look at her. Staring at the bright purple stain is better than being begged for another baby. He suspects this supposed impromptu slide show was nothing of the sort. He imagines his wife and his mother-in-law plotting emotional blackmail during their weekly phone call: *I know, let's have a slide-show of LJ as a baby. Once Harry is reminded of how gorgeous LJ was, he'll be as desperate as you for another…Yes, let's invite lots of people to the slide-show, he'll find it hard to say no in front of others when I beg him for a second baby.* He thinks the stain on the bed sheet must be gentian violet: a doctor sprayed some in his mouth once.

'Wasn't LJ a beautiful baby?' exclaims Sille's neighbour.

Harry eyes her suspiciously.

'Will you have more?' she asks.

Nosey Parker, thinks Lil.

Here we go, thinks Harry.

A baby brother might be alright, thinks LJ, *but a baby sister would be rubbish. A tortoise would be better: I can paint the hexagons on its shell.*

'No,' says Harry.

'Oh, but you must…' says the neighbour.

Astrid looks at the neighbour as if she's the patron saint of motherhood.

'…to make up for all the ugly little buggers you see running around,' she continues.

The room erupts but Maggie laughs loudest because it's the first time she's been able to laugh properly in three years. And it is only possible because two days before this one, she finally got shot of Frankie.

Lil wishes Maggie didn't laugh like that; she sounds like a workman. And why does she never sit with her legs crossed?

Harry smiles at LJ and says, 'I'm happy with the one we've got, thank you.'

'Quality, not quantity,' says a stranger with a beery moustache.

Harry hasn't heard this phrase before, but he likes it. He stares at Astrid and says, 'Exactly.'

It's this sort of moment that makes Astrid wish she'd married somebody else. Why did she have to fall in love with a man who was satisfied with one child?

'There's *min guldklump* with Morfar at Bell Wharf beach,' declares Sille with a clap.

'What's that in English?' mutters Lil, louder than she intends.

'Sorry, Lillian,' says Sille. 'I forget that none of you speaks Danish. I call LJ my little gold nugget.'

Lil snorts without making a sound. She stares at the slide of LJ being dipped in the sea by his other granddad with twitching lips; as far as she's concerned, Bill's beach attire is pornographic.

'I like the sea,' says LJ, 'so why am I crying in that picture, Mummy?'

Astrid rises from her chair. 'Ask Mormor or Daddy,' she squeaks. 'I've got to wash-up.'

***

When did Gunnersbury Park become the meeting place of the pregnant? That's what Astrid wants to know. The smug and the smocked are everywhere. She's counted seven pregnant women in a matter of minutes. This is what she'll tell Harry when he gets in from work: *I saw seven pregnant women today. And one of the women was towing along two other children, AND, had at least one other at school because the woman was discussing with her friend, also pregnant and with a toddler by the way, the extent to which the school toilet roll was more tracing paper than tissue and spread poo on Wendy's bottom rather than wiped it off. In total, that woman has at least three children plus one on the way; that makes four children altogether, Harry, four. And, since the woman's friend had an opinion about the school toilet roll, it means she has at least two children plus one on the way. That makes three children, Harry.* She won't mention the pregnant woman with the St. Bernard who appeared to have no other children because, overall, this anomaly doesn't alter the fact that Harry's refusal to procreate is unnatural. She's a young married woman; she's supposed to reproduce. She thinks these women are having her share of all the available children out there; it makes her want to scream and cry at the same time. How many more times does she have to tell him? She only wants one more child. One more child and she'd be happy.

Stomach cramps make her sit on the bench by Potomac pond. Her head swims as if she's bleeding to death. On the walk to school, LJ had wondered what the word of the day would be in his class. He'd guessed it might have something to do with Easter. He'd come up with the word 'Resurrection.' She hadn't thought to be impressed by this because she was too busy deciding on her own word of the day. She came up with the word 'Gush.' A woman creeps out of a nearby bush and twists and turns to check her denim flares for splashes. When she notices Astrid, she says, 'Baby was pressing on my bladder.' Astrid can tell by the way the woman says it that she's expected to understand, so she nods even though she can't remember what this actually feels like. Then she turns to the two ducks squabbling on the pond because she doesn't want to count anymore children today and contemplates a future in which she never gets to hold and care for a newborn baby of her own. She tells herself that this future mustn't happen but she doesn't know what else she can do to prevent it. Before all this, she would never have described Harry as stubborn. *Why can't he just give in?*

Across the water, a man is jogging. He's doing laps of the pond. He's already jogged past her twice but she didn't notice him then. Now, she watches him drop to the ground and do twenty press-ups. He seems to find press-ups easy. She doubts Harry could do five. Next, the jogger does twenty burpees, or as LJ calls them at gymnastics club, bird peas. If this jogger wasn't so tall and beefy, she'd think it was Keith, the boy she courted as a school girl.

She thinks about Keith and remembers that he enjoyed throwing a javelin but wasn't selected to represent the school because he couldn't throw it as far as a boy named Joey; that he had teeth such as an archaeologist might expect to find on a dig, but was one of the best-looking boys in the school with his mouth shut; that he didn't like her talking to any of the other boys even if they were just passing the time of day with her; that he said all boys were moody, that it wasn't just him; that he insisted their relationship was as good as it gets and that she should be grateful to him for choosing her.

A menstrual cramp makes her double over. As she waits for the pain to pass, she watches a beetle scuttle beneath the sole of her shoe. She moves her foot and it's nowhere to be seen.

'Hello, Astrid. It is you, isn't it?'

Astrid looks up. It's the jogger with his hands on his track-suited hips. Then she corrects herself: It isn't the jogger at all, it's actually Keith, and he's had his teeth fixed.

***

Harry and Astrid are having a row. She claims it's about Harry and LJ's 'indoor bonfire' conversation, but they both know that it isn't.

'You've given him nightmares,' she seethes. 'Why did you tell him about crematoriums?'

'Because he was worried about being buried and eaten by worms,' says Harry.

'And being burnt to smithereens on an indoor bonfire's better, is it? How stupid can you get?'

'He wanted to know, Astrid. I tried to change the subject but he wasn't having it. You know what he's like: you can't just fob him off.'

'All I know is that, every night since your little *Jackanory* about the crematorium, I've had to keep getting up to him. Look at the state of me, I'm exhausted.'

'And you want another baby?'

'I'll pretend you didn't say that.'

'Why will you pretend I didn't say that?'

'Alright, try this for size: I can't believe you just said that?'

'Why? It's all *you* talk about. You're not angry because LJ's having nightmares, you're angry because I won't agree to another baby. You're obsessed.'

'You think you can stop me from having another baby?'

'All I can say, Astrid, is that *I* don't want another baby. I'm not going through all that again.'

'Selfish, Harry, that's what you are. All the things I do for you, but you won't do this for me.'

'I'm sorry.'

'Is that all you can say?'

'I don't know what else *to* say.'

'Well, it's alright for you, isn't it? Your body leaves you in peace, but every month my body reminds me that I'm not pregnant when there's no reason, no reason at all, that I shouldn't be. It's unbearable, Harry, please do this for me, please...' she cries.

'Alright then, say we have another baby and it all goes tits up again. Who'll look after the baby this time? And, let's not forget LJ. Who's going to look after the two kids? Maggie won't give up the job she's got now, not this time, I can tell you that for nothing, and Mum has to look after the old man. Now that your mum has pissed off to Denmark, there's no one, Astrid, not one single person.'

'Don't say it like that, Harry; don't say it as if my mum was wrong to return to Denmark.'

He waves the comment about Sille away. 'Listen, if I don't work, I don't get paid. Ten months you were away. If it happened again – and don't forget the doctor said that there was a good chance it would – we'd lose this house for a start, and then what?'

'So, it's all about the money?'

'No, of course it's not all about the money, but we can't be stupid about this, Astrid, we really can't. It's you that wanted a mortgage in the first bloody place, not me, remember?'

'You have no right to stop me from having another baby. It's my body, it should be my decision.'

'I'm sorry,' he says, taking his jacket from the cloak cupboard. 'But, unlike you, I remember what happened last time. I really wish I could give you what you want...' He stops because he's picturing Astrid with electrodes on her head. He coughs away the image and then finishes his sentence, '...but I can't.'

'You could, you just don't want to.'

'That's not true.'

'Where are you going?'

'For a walk.'

'Slap bang in the middle of Chiswick High Road I hope.'

'Thanks for that, Astrid. Thanks for wishing me dead.'

She wants to tell him she didn't mean it but finds that she can't. Instead, she says, 'Well, if only I could go off when I felt like it.'

He leaves without saying another word and she shouts after him, 'And why don't you ever shut the cloak cupboard door after you?'

15: Resolution

Astrid feels she had no choice but to leave Harry for Keith. In the end, Keith said he would give her whatever she wanted if she divorced Harry and married him. She told him she wanted another baby. Back when they were courting, Keith always said he didn't want kids, but he thinks differently on the subject now. As a fireman in the London Fire Brigade, he works long and strange hours, but in return for his frequent absences he's promised to give her as many babies as she wants.

In the lounge of his two-up two-down terraced house, a house financed in part by his moonlighting job as a nightclub bouncer, they discuss their future baby.

'I really want to feed this baby, myself,' she says. 'I never got to do that for LJ. By the time I was well, he was ten months old and I had no milk. I missed out, Keith.'

She places her hands over her empty breasts. They ache as if they contain every drop of the milk that LJ should have guzzled in his first year, but didn't. She thinks of him as he is now, a seven-year-old boy with dark curly hair, big green eyes and long skinny legs. She glances at her watch and then pictures Harry helping him dress for school. He wears LJ's elasticated school tie like a headband and pretends to be a tennis player, and then a rock star, even though LJ is in danger of getting a red circle instead of the usual blue diagonal line in the school register. He makes LJ giggle, hiccup, gnash his pearly whites, and dribble down his chin. He manages to make a game of buttoning LJ's creased school shirt, but he can't make decent bunny ears with his shoe laces because they've been allowed to fray, and he can't find LJ's pom-pom hat, not because it's lost, but because he never looks for things properly. Picturing all this makes her chest feel pneumonic. She'd really like to go home to them but…

Keith takes her face in his hands and says, 'Of course you'll feed our baby, Astrid, I'll see to it.'

In his hands, her mouth shrinks and her head feels like a block of wood in a carpenter's vice. She reminds herself that she's doing all this for another baby, that she has no choice. 'I'd like two more children,' she says, struggling to move her distorted lips. She raises two fingers and repeats, 'Two,' because she and Harry never discussed numbers and her separation from him mustn't be for nothing. But, picturing him again makes her eyes water and a new pain in her stomach sallies forth. She can't stop dwelling on his gentle face. She already misses his laughter lines. And the fact that he'd stroke her cheeks rather than squash them is not lost on her.

'Yes,' says Keith, releasing her face. 'If that's what you want.'

'Things will be different this time,' she promises.

Keith nods.

'So two then?' she says, to make sure he knows.

'Yes,' he repeats. 'Yes, yes, two, but…'

'But what?' she cries.

'Hmm,' he says.

'Tell me.'

'I was just thinking about your bedroom.'

'My bedroom?'

'Yes.'

She thinks about her and Harry's bedroom, of the kaleidoscopic wallpaper; the angora blanket on their bed; the framed sketch of LJ in his nappy and wellies playing with his lorries in the sandpit that Harry built him; the collage of their black and white wedding photos on the wall; the vase of silk tulips on the window sill; the antique linen box at the end of the bed that doubles as the Christmas and birthday present hidey-hole; the mouldering wicker washing basket with a wire coat hanger and a copy of *Woman* stashed inside; the wardrobe with the whining doors that sound like tom cats scrapping every time it's opened or closed; the mahogany jewellery box with the silver 'A' on the lid that Harry made for her twenty-second birthday; the his 'n hers fluffy dressing gowns on the back of the pine door; the blood-red beads wrapped around the bed post; the impressions of their backsides in the mattress, and the pint glass of orange squash that Harry takes to bed with him and never brings down in the morning. The pain in her stomach gets worse.

'At your parent's house,' he says, as if he knows her mind has journeyed to the wrong bedroom.

'What about it?'

'It was a mess.'

'Was it?'

'Yes, it was. I pointed out the clothes on the floor and the buttery knife on the bed and the plate covered in toast crumbs and the half-drunk cup of Ovaltine. I told you it was disgusting. I said I couldn't, and wouldn't, live like that. I was so cross that I shouted at you. I vowed I wouldn't propose to you until you proved to me that you could pick up after yourself. I made you cry. I frightened you. I made you feel worthless. I insinuated that I was a thousand times better than you. Surely you must remember?'

'Hmm,' she says, mostly remembering that he kept a budgerigar in his bedroom, that it was often uncaged and that it crapped where it pleased.

'That's all you have to say, is it?' he snaps.

'I don't think I like the way you've decorated your lounge,' she says, vaguely. 'It's very, very plain and...'

'And what?

'I want to go home.'

'You are home.'

'This isn't my home.'

'It's the only home you've got now.'

She feels as if something has burst inside her; it's a fatal sort of pain. She bends over with her hands on her knees and tries to breathe.

'He won't want you back, you know. Not now. I wouldn't if I was him.'

She falls to her knees and thinks of Harry. He's shaving in the bathroom and re-enacting the advert that makes her laugh: pretending to be Tarzan, he says, *Golden Wonder Peanuts: Jungle Fresh*. He's very good at mimicking the actor, but this time it makes her weep.

'You seem to have forgotten that only I will give you what you want, Astrid.'

She thinks she might have a heart attack on Keith's swirly orange and brown carpet. She takes a deep breath and shouts, 'I don't care. I don't care about that anymore. I'm going home. I don't want to be with you, I want to be with Harry.' And she shouts this so loudly that she wakes herself up.

***

Astrid flips her pillow because life with Keith made her cry all over it. She reaches out for Harry, but he isn't there. She keeps her eyes closed and tries to come to terms with the events of her nightmare. She feels cross about the budgerigar: bird poo was a thousand times worse than a buttery knife. What an idiot Keith was. She wishes she'd told him that at Potomac Pond instead of all the other stuff. She opens her eyes. She wants Harry to come back to bed so that she can hug him tight, nuzzle his downy ear lobe with her nose, and say sorry with a kiss.

'Shall I wake Mummy up?' says LJ very loudly, from beyond the bedroom door.

'I'm awake,' says Astrid. The words are a comfort.

LJ bursts through the door wearing a balaclava and Harry follows behind slurping tea from her Portmeirion mug. 'Happy Mother's Day,' they chime.

'Goodness,' says Astrid. 'I forgot about that. Oh, God, did you post that card for Mor?' she gasps. 'And did you remember to send your mum one?'

'Yes,' says Harry. 'Calm yourself, it's all been taken care of.'

LJ gets under the covers and lies along the length of her body. He presses the soles of his icy feet against her calves and breathes Marmite on her face through the hole in the balaclava. 'I made you a Mother's Day card,' he chirrups, 'but I accidentally left it at school in my drawer... but I put a butterfly on it, and a daffodil, and I bought you some Milk Tray and I kept it a secret for... for... sixteen whole days.' He waggles his fingers in the air as if he has sixteen of them.

'More like three days, L, and you're not supposed to say what the present is, you're supposed to let Mummy find out for herself.'

'Oh, well,' he says, mimicking Astrid. 'These things happen.'

Harry laughs and Astrid tickles his armpits. 'Are you taking the mickey out of me?' she asks.

'No,' laughs LJ.

'Why are you wearing your balaclava indoors, darling?'

'I'm being someone.'

'Who?'

'Oh, Mummy, just a person you don't need to know about.'

'Oh, really?' she says with another tickle.

'We're going to try our best to make you breakfast in bed,' says Harry. 'Here's your tea,' he says setting down her mug.

She sits up and peers into the mug. 'Where's the rest of it?' she asks.

'I over-filled your mug, so then I had to drink a bit so I didn't spill it on the carpet.' He lifts her hand and kisses it. They both know he's talking nonsense.

'We've got all the stuff,' says LJ.

Astrid keeps hold of Harry's hand and says, 'I wondered why you asked me to buy bacon this week.'

'But, can you have scrambled eggs?' says LJ.

'I said LJ could crack the eggs if you wanted scrambled eggs,' explains Harry, sitting on the bed. 'But it's up to Mummy, L.'

'Do your impression, Harry,' says Astrid.

'Which one?'

'You know.'

'The Golden-Wonder-Peanuts-Jungle-Fresh one?'

'Yes,' laughs Astrid.

'No,' shouts LJ. 'Not again.'

'Yes,' shouts Astrid. 'Go on, Harry, do it.'

Harry takes off his pyjama top, stands on the bed, thumps his chest and cries, '*Golden Wonder Peanuts: Jungle Fresh.*'

Astrid giggles.

LJ pats her cheek and says, 'Scrambled eggs, Mummy? Please say yes.'

'L,' exclaims Harry, still in the jungle and still standing over Astrid.

'Yes,' she says. 'That's exactly what I want.' And it is.

1972

16: Odds and Sods

It's the day after Bloody Sunday. Bed-haired and sleepy, LJ wanders into the kitchen where Astrid is lobbing cubed braising steak and large discs of carrot at the slow cooker and says, 'I don't feel very well, Mum.'

She rinses her hands under the cold tap and rushes to his side. 'What's wrong?' she asks, automatically applying the back of her freezing hand to his forehead.

He steadies his dressing-gowned self against the kitchen side, buries his face in a tea-towel and says, 'My tummy really hurts.'

Astrid releases her clean tea-towel and immediately diagnoses a gangrenous appendix. In the *Ask Doctor* section in one of her magazines, a reader supposedly once asked the doctor about appendicitis. The doctor warned that the potentially fatal condition most commonly struck those aged between ten and twenty. At the time of that edition, LJ was nine. Consequently, Astrid took her pinking shears to the *Ask Doctor* section, cut out the signs and symptoms checklist, and preserved it in her odds and sods drawer. Five months before this moment, LJ turned ten; Astrid's been expecting his appendix to kick off ever since. She abandons his forehead and starts rifling through the odds and sods drawer for the saved appendicitis checklist. LJ lollops onto the kitchen side and groans with his head on his arms. Astrid rifles faster. The drawer is a who's who of objects that ought not to be there: spent batteries; half-cocked pens; a couple of tacks; a giant paperclip; a broken pair of aviator sunglasses; *An Owners Workshop Manual* for a Ford Cortina – a car they were going to buy but never did; a bottle of solidified calamine lotion with a rusty screw-cap; a tampon covered in battery acid; five pieces of macaroni; a six-inch screw with orange plasticine on the thread; one of LJ's playschool paintings depicting Sille on a Helter Skelter; a rabbit's foot still in the original packaging; an empty strip of aspirin; a tin of dried up boot polish; a feu orange car air freshener; assorted chipped marbles; a purple clip-on earring that resembles haemorrhoids; a palm leaf cross; several packets of spare buttons; Harry's bite guard; an edition of *The Watchtower* – Astrid didn't like to refuse the polite young American at the door; a sticky yellow fruit pastille; His and Hers Valentine's cards from 1961 – Astrid and Harry dig them out each year to acknowledge the sentiment but save on money; a plaque disclosing tablet attached to a pamphlet on tooth decay; an array of manufacturer's instructions for various appliances past and present; a crusty handkerchief; a plastic Airfix model of a World War II Commando with a bent Bren gun; and a pinking sheared *Ask Doctor* symptoms checklist for Rheumatic Fever.

Astrid has to accept that the drawer contains no nuggets about appendicitis, but it's hard. 'I could have sworn I put it in here,' she mutters under her breath. She wears a black pencil skirt, white long-sleeved shirt, black and tan wedges, flesh-coloured tights and rollers in her hair: she's supposed to be advising on the beauty counter at the department store in less than an hour. 'I expect your dad's moved it,' she says, as the roller in her fringe unravels and drops into the drawer. She slams the drawer shut, leaving the roller in situ. Then, she reopens the drawer and plucks out the Rheumatic Fever checklist because it's there and won't be ignored. She reads:

Sore Joints…

'Do your joints hurt?' she asks.

'What do you mean?' asks LJ.

'You know… your bones. These bits,' she says with a roll of the eyes and a pat of the elbows and knees. She looks as if she's demonstrating the actions for *Heads, Shoulders, Knees and Toes* to a playschool child.

'No,' says LJ grumpily.

Fever…

She considers this and then says, 'I don't think you've got a temperature.'

Skin Rash…

'What about a rash?'

'I don't know,' says LJ.

'Take your jimmy-jams off,' she orders.

'In the kitchen?'

'No one can see.'

'What about the postman?'

'He's already been. Anyway, what does he want to look at you for?'

'I haven't got a rash.'

'What a fusspot; just let me check your back.'

LJ tuts as she yanks the back of his dressing gown and pyjama top so she can peer down into the gloom. 'No,' she says, rubbing her cold hand along his spine.

'Told you,' says LJ shrugging her off.

Jerky Movements…

'Walk over there,' she commands, pointing at the Kenwood Chef.

'Why?'

'Because I said so, L, get a wriggle on,' she says, with an anguished glance at the kitchen clock.

LJ tuts but does as she asks; apart from looking as if he's about to turn a corner, she decides that his gait is normal.

Stomach Pain…

She abandons Rheumatic Fever and returns to appendicitis. 'Whereabouts does your tummy hurt?' She tries to remember whether the sharp pain of appendicitis is experienced in the right or left side of the sufferer's abdomen.

He faces her and, unhelpfully, rubs the entire width of his stomach, 'Everywhere,' he says.

She's not entirely sure, but she has a feeling that it's his right side that should hurt the most. 'So, not here?' she says, poking him.

'No, I don't think so.'

'Yes or no, L?'

'No.'

Just to be on the safe side, she prods his left side and says, 'Or here?'

'No,' says LJ. 'I told you, it hurts all over.'

'Do you feel sick?'

'No.'

'What about the trots?'

'Mum!'

'Oh, for goodness sake, L.'

He says, 'No, I haven't got that,' as if he's being falsely accused of a crime.

She goes back to feeling his forehead. Then she feels her own. The temperature of their foreheads feels much the same. 'What about a headache?'

He clutches his stomach. 'I didn't say my head hurt, did I?'

She realizes that she's the one with the headache and that LJ doesn't have appendicitis. Then she treats him to a stern expression because she doesn't like the tone of his rhetorical question. 'I'll give you some medicine,' she says.

'Can't I just go back to bed?' he asks meekly.

'No. You've obviously got a bit of a tummy bug and the medicine will help.'

He whines and imitates a cry.

'Yes,' she says. 'You're having some.'

'What medicine is it?'

'The usual?'

'What's the usual?'

'The one for upset stomachs.'

'Not that *Kaolin and Morphine*?'

She doesn't answer his question. Instead, she goes to the cupboard where she keeps the medicines. It's the cupboard that also houses her spice rack. She notices the jar of Asofoetida: it's the only jar in the rack that remains untouched. She removes the bottle of *Kaolin and Morphine* and the jar of Asafoetida from the cupboard.

'Mum…'

She reads the label on the spice jar as she retrieves a teaspoon from the draining board.

'It's not that disgusting runny chalk one, is it?'

The label recommends adding Asafoetida to meat stews.

He reads *Kaolin & Morphine*. His worst fears are confirmed. 'Oh, God, no,' he cries and then, with a shiver of revulsion, adds, 'That medicine will make me sick.'

She leaves the Asafoetida next to the slow cooker and says, 'That's not what it will do, L, and I really think you need it.'

He gags with enthusiasm.

'Are you going to be sick?'

He gags again. She grabs his wrist and rushes him over to the kitchen sink. 'Be sick in there,' she says, directing his head at the plug hole. He burps but isn't sick. 'Do you want to be sick?' she repeats.

'I don't want that medicine, Mum.' He resists her hand on the back of his head. He feels as if he's being made to confront what's been too big to pass through the plug-hole strainer: blackened sweetcorn, a slimy orange pip, a translucent piece of onion skin, a bloated strand of spaghetti, a grey blob of mince, and something that looks like hairy yoghurt. It's as if she's punishing him for saying unkind things about *Kaolin and Morphine* and the punishment is enough to make him sick for real. 'Please,' he says, as if he's begging for his life. 'Don't make me have it.'

'Alright, alright, what a fusspot,' she says, letting him stand.

He watches her return the *Kaolin and Morphine* to the cupboard and feels as if he's dodged an act of torture. She clears his fringe from his forehead and tucks his sideburns behind his ears. 'What am I going to do with you?' she asks, with one last touch of his forehead.

'I don't think I should go to school,' he says, glumly.

'No,' she agrees with a sigh.

'Can I go back to bed now?'

She shakes her head and another roller slips from her silky hair. She picks it up and shoves it in the odds and sods drawer. 'I've got to go to work today, L. I've got a new girl coming in for training.'

'What about me?'

'I'll have to sort something out.'

'Nobody else's mum works. Why can't you stay at home like them?'

'I only work part-time and it's not as if I leave you alone all day, every day.' She yanks the remaining rollers from her hair feeling guilty.

'Why can't I stay at home on my own? I can look after myself. I'm ten. All my friends are allowed to.'

She narrows her eyes and says, 'I thought you said their mums were at home?'

'I mean when they're not at home.'

She feels better about going out to work. 'Go and put something comfy on AND MAKE SURE ITS CLEAN... and brush your teeth while you're at it.'

Bent double like an osteoporotic pensioner and wondering if he'll be able to cadge some Lucozade from whoever's going to be looking after him, he slowly shuffles out of the kitchen while she tips a hefty dose of Asafoetida into the slow cooker and considers who to try first. Knowing that Maggie doesn't work regular hours, she hotfoots it to the phone, vaguely aware that the kitchen now smells of horse manure.

***

Maggie had put the phone down, scratched her mohair turban and mentally explored her home's storage spaces; each, she concluded, was already packed to the gunwales. Consequently, clearing a space for LJ on her settee hadn't been straight-forward because there was nowhere else for the hoard to go. And her assumption that he'd need to lay his poorly and long self across the whole length of the three-seater had also necessitated clearing off more junk than she'd have liked. In the end, and to a ditty of expletives, the settee junk had rained down on a small area in the corner of the room and the wastepaper basket, magazine rack, hoover, and small two-bar portable electric fire that was already there disappeared beneath it all.

Her bed clothes had been the cause of this haste. Even though it was a frosty January day and the air was heavy and still, and not so much as a dishcloth was ever going to dry on the washing line, Maggie wanted to strip her bed, get the bedclothes into her reconditioned twin tub and get them boiling before LJ's arrival. She should never have let Frankie back in to her bed again and she wanted every trace of her gone. She wished a regrettable act like that could be shaken from the brain and lost forever like a doodle on an Etch-a-Sketch. She was so cross with herself. If she hadn't gone to that pub, if she hadn't been drunk, if she hadn't felt lonely, if she hadn't fallen for Frankie's bullshit, and if she hadn't gone without for so long, it would never have happened. Why couldn't she have just told her to piss off the minute she felt her green-fingered hands on her hips? Later, when Frankie grasped her thighs, invaded her with her tongue and sucked at her as if she was siphoning fuel for her beloved petrol-engined mower,

Maggie knew she'd made a terrible mistake but it was too late: when she came, Frankie watched, just as she always had.

***

LJ spends the morning pretending that his auntie's settee is a sinking boat and her carpet a shark-infested sea. He tries to time his screams of 'Shark attack' and 'Man over board' and 'Ouch, he's got me leg' to when her washing machine is on a noisy spin. But on one occasion, he misjudges the spin cycle and hollers these things when there's no other noise to mask them. Afterwards, and just in case, he lies very still on the settee and pretends to doze until he hears the sound of his auntie going out into the garden with her washing. He hears the washing basket being kicked along the path as she goes from one end of the line to the other. *Tell me, who's this by my side?* she sings. *This girl with eyes like gems. And cool reactions to your lies. Lies. La la la la la la la lies.* He wishes adults wouldn't sing and congratulates himself for knowing what a group of sharks is called. Then he rolls off the settee while her back is turned, does back-stroke on her carpet and blindly shoots his speargun at the man-eating shiver.

Forgetting all about the two wooden washing pegs clipped to her turban, Maggie tiptoes to the patio door and watches LJ writhing across the floor of her sitting room with a length of bamboo cane. She thinks he must have found the cane under the settee. He makes a *shoom* sound and points the cane at her junk; she wonders what the junk's done to deserve being shot like that. Unlike Astrid, she knew he was pulling a fast one the minute she saw him hamming it up on her doorstep. She fancies an ice-cream sandwich. She wonders if she has any wafers in the cupboard. She knows she has a brand-new box of Neopolitan in the freezer. She steps inside the room and clears her throat. LJ freezes as if the tables have turned and the shiver's zapped him with a spear gun. 'Since you're only pretending to be ill, L,' she says, 'and there's nothing whatsoever wrong with your stomach, I wondered if you fancied an ice-cream?'

LJ thinks about clutching his tummy and emitting the groan of his life and then thinks again: when the game's up, it's up. 'But we never have ice-cream in winter, Auntie Maggie,' he says sweetly.

'Well I do,' says Maggie with a *so-there* nod.

'Are you going to tell mum?'

'What, that you've pulled a fast one?'

He shrugs. She shakes her head. He puts down his speargun because the shiver can wait, and very nicely he says, 'Please may I have some Lucozade instead, Auntie Maggie?'

1977

17: Christmas Crackers

It's a dismal Christmas day and fifteen-year-old LJ has just returned to the dining table having secretly downed another glass of his mum's Advocaat in the kitchen. The prawn cocktails are not long finished but the table already looks as if it's accommodated a five-day fiesta, and the holly leaves that Astrid had collected from the garden in the days before Christmas, and that she'd sprayed gold and silver on Christmas Eve, and that she'd artfully scattered amongst the condiments early that morning, have already drawn blood and been banished to the hostess trolley in the corner of the room.

The two younger Edwards women sit beside each other. Maggie wears a loose cashmere cowl neck jumper and Astrid, a beige challis blouse; silver combs keep her wavy hair in check and show off her angular cheekbones. LJ sits between his aunt and his Nan wearing his main present: an olive-green parka. He's hot but he doesn't care. His table present, the longed-for album, *In the City* by The Jam, is propped against the leg of his chair, but he still can't help but wish his parents had bought him the cherry red Vespa scooter he's been hinting about for the last few months. So what if he is still only fifteen, sixteen was next, and they had a garage for fuck's sake. Lil sits there suffering a hot flush and wishes people would stop buying her Lily of the Valley talcum powder and BHS petticoats and wonders how many more times she can disguise Alfie's mutterings with a cough, sigh or loud scrape of the plate. Alfie sits between his wife and his son with a serviette tucked in the collar of his shirt. The robin pictured on his festive bib looks as if a much larger bird has shit Marie Rose sauce over its plump red breast and the fence post upon which it perches. He can't place the fella sitting opposite. 'Bloody mirror,' he mutters in response to the stranger's hair: he thinks it must have been cut without one. He's glad the fella's got his coat on because it means he won't be stopping long. 'Sod off,' he mutters to his lap, before being troubled by his table present. Who the bloody hell is BRUT **33**? It rings a bell but trying to remember this brute sends him to places he doesn't want to go. His knees begin to bounce as he wipes his wet palms on the tablecloth. Periodically, Harry leans around the table, and thinking no one can see what he's up to, thrusts mistletoe at Astrid's thigh as if her coral painted lips have migrated south. She's given him a few coy kisses in response, but she's still trying to play down the knickers that were her table present from him: she doesn't want her nearest and dearest thinking she's some sort of nymphomaniac. Harry had intended for her to unwrap the emerald green satin and black lace knickers later, in the privacy of their bedroom. He'd been looking forward to feeling the silkiness of them against his mouth and tasting her through the holes in the lace. After the mix-up, which was due to Maggie 'finding' a present for everybody from under the tree without consulting the hosts, he thinks it probably won't happen because she'll be too worried about the overnight guests overhearing.

'In my day, we weren't allowed to leave the table to use the toilet,' says Lil. 'You had to wait, LJ.'

'Sorry, Nan, but I was busting,' he pleads.

'Hmm,' she says. 'We weren't allowed to talk either.'

Maggie rolls her eyes and LJ bursts out laughing. 'Good one, Nan,' he says.

Then Maggie announces her intention to wear nothing but purple when she gets old.

'Better start wearing purple, Aunt Maggie,' says LJ, briefly resting his drunken dark head on her shoulder.

'Don't you want your Christmas present?' she asks, with arched eyebrows.

'That sort of comment makes me doubt the existence of Father Christmas.'

'Sarky little sod,' she says. She wants to ruffle his hair but doesn't want to ruin his new hairdo, so strokes her own throat instead.

'Anyway, you've already given me my present,' he says, with a tincture of doubt.

'Have I?'

'Have you?' he mimics.

'How do you know there's not a little something else for Auntie's favourite boy?'

'Is there?' A cherry red Vespa scoots through his mind. Could she have forked out for it? He decides that it's the sort of thing a Godmother might do. Who else was she going to spend her money on? She could have hidden it in the garage last night.

'No,' she says with a zesty 'Hah!'

'Told you,' he says, trying to camouflage the fact that he feels a bit stupid and utterly tragic.

'Wearing purple?' interrupts Harry. 'How many have you had, Maggie?'

She turns to LJ's ear and whispers, 'Not as many as you, that's for sure.'

He tries to look as if he doesn't know what she's talking about and that makes her cackle. 'I read a poem about a woman who plans to behave badly when she gets old, Harry, and I thought to myself, what a good idea.'

'What's behaving badly got to do with wearing purple?' he replies, dunking a soggy Brussels sprout in a filmy lake of cranberry sauce. 'There's no law against wearing purple clothes, you can wear whatever you bloody well like.'

At this moment, LJ quite likes the idea of her looking absurd so he says, 'You could make it your New Year's resolution and start wearing purple next week.'

'What a great idea, L,' she says.

'I was joking,' he says, remembering that sometimes she gave him a lift home from school.

'I wasn't,' says Maggie with a wink.

'There were purple curtains in the bedroom of our first flat, do you remember, Harry?' says Astrid. 'Nothing to do with us, they were already there when we moved in, but they were such good quality. Shut out all the light. We were forever oversleeping, weren't we?'

Maggie puts Astrid's knickers on her head and says, 'You're blaming that on the curtains?'

LJ and Lil are assailed by an identical mental image that makes each of them frown and nearly resurrects LJ's undigested prawns. Maggie reaches for her Babycham and Brandy, and Astrid for her new knickers. Harry adjusts his paper hat and Alfie puts his head in his hands. 'One of the Goons had a fucking great purple birthmark on his cheek,' he shouts. 'He was a vicious bastard.'

Imagining his granddad's goon is, for LJ at least, better than imagining his parents shagging themselves senseless in the sixties, but, even though he'd like to know more about this goon, he knows to ask nothing.

'Don't upset yourself, Alfie,' says Lil desperately. 'Come on, have a pickled walnut, you haven't had any yet.' She marches out of the dining room and collects a jar from the kitchen side. When she returns, she fishes out a walnut with the cranberry sauce spoon and feeds it to Alfie as if it is medicine. Astrid retrieves her knickers and stuffs them in the pocket of her new dirndl skirt. As she does so, she catches sight of the size on the label and grimaces. She can't remember the last time she was that size.

Maggie clears her throat and says, 'So how long is this ceasefire supposed to last then?'

Astrid doesn't want to talk about the IRA on Christmas day but Harry finishes off an untucked pig-in-blanket with his fork and says, 'Five bloody minutes I expect but you can't really blame them: sure to be sure, Ireland belongs to the Irish.'

'Rubbish impression,' says LJ. 'Sure to be sure, Ireland belongs to the Irish.'

'Where did you say you were from?' responds Maggie with a raised eyebrow. 'India was it, L?'

'It was a better impression than Dad's,' insists LJ, waving his knife in the air.

With one eye on her father-in-law and the other on LJ's hyperactive knife, Astrid whispers, 'I've got a purple jumper you can have, Maggie.'

'Oh, no, Astrid, I wasn't hinting.'

'I know that, but it doesn't fit over my stomach anymore,' she replies, louder than she meant.

'What's wrong with your stomach?' says Harry, thinking there's absolutely nothing wrong with it.

'It's bigger than it used to be,' says Astrid, only just beginning to grasp the accuracy of this statement.

'Isn't everyone's?' he says, giving his a pat.

'No,' says Astrid, looking down at Maggie's, 'just mine.'

1978

18: The Alma Maters

LJ waits for the phone to be answered and when it is, says, 'Mum?'

'Oh, God, am I?' says Maggie. 'Not again, L, surely?'

She's at work. Her position at the women and children's refuge, and the refuge itself, are new, but the building that houses them is not. The council had thought to demolish the derelict and decaying Edwardian terrace but a successful campaign for a new women's refuge in Acton saved it from the wrecking ball. The council could have done better, but chose not to. In Harry's own time but with the help of some donated materials, and Dinky – a philanthropic homeless woman of undetermined age, who seemed to know an inordinate amount about architectural restoration and who, at Maggie's discretion, slept most nights in the refuge's vestibule – the place was freshened up and made habitable. Maggie's office was the last room in the house to be decorated. Harry and Dinky did as they were bid – in spite of Dinky's reservations about the shade – and painted it, not primrose yellow as Dinky would have liked, but sunflower yellow as Miss Howard liked.

Maggie wishes she hadn't given LJ her work number. She should have known he'd memorise and misuse it. She considers the grubby-faced toddler who dribbles on her plimsoll and his six-year-old sister who silently draws an octopus at her desk. She's supposed to be keeping an eye on them while their battered mother makes a complaint of marital rape to a deaf-eared detective in the common room next door. She's not supposed to be saving LJ's skin again.

LJ makes sure to keep the receiver pressed hard against his ear and confirms that he does require her to pretend to be his mum again.

'Seriously, L?' she asks, scratching her head with the end of a blunt pencil and making a mental note to get Tash – her deputy – to check every head in the refuge for lice.

LJ glances at his headmistress, Miss Allard, but she is busy repositioning a furry cactus in a macramé plant hanger. 'Yes,' he says crossly, and then, 'Yes, it's me, Mum… who else did you think it was?'

'Oh, I bloody well wonder,' says Maggie, 'one of my other phantom sons perhaps?'

LJ decides that the best response to this is silence.

'Well if I do decide to do this for you,' Maggie goes on, 'it's the last time, L, because if your mum and dad find out, I'll be for the high-jump.'

LJ wants to be facetious and say, *Oh, yeah, do you favour the scissors or the Fosbury?* but what he actually says is, 'Yeah, alright, Mum.'

Miss Allard turns and hisses, 'Ye*ssss*.' And then, making sure to roll every 'r', she adds, 'You're not an American, Master Edwards, so please refrain from saying 'yeah'.'

'Ye-Ha,' cries Maggie. 'Get off your horse and drink your milk, cowboy Edwards.'

The girl stops drawing and gives her a wary smile and the toddler shouts, 'Milk, peas, Mabbie.'

'In a minute my darling,' she replies, with a cursory glance at his wispy hair, 'when I've finished talking to this very naughty boy on the phone.'

Meanwhile, Miss Allard waits for LJ to correct his pronunciation. He glowers at the receiver as if expressions can travel down the telephone wire as well as words, and then says, 'Ye*ss*, Miss.'

Miss Allard suspects that somebody crept into her office when her back was turned and interfered with her macramé beads. She nods at LJ and then undertakes their repatriation.

'So then, *son*, what have you done this time?' asks Maggie.

'Erm…' says LJ.

Miss Allard spins on her heel, clears her throat, and once she's got his attention, shows him her watch and taps it for good measure. He notices that her watch stopped three hours and thirty-seven minutes before this frustrating phone call. 'I've been in a fight,' he says, sourly.

'Are you hurt?'

'No.'

'What about the other one?'

'Maybe.'

'What does that mean?'

'Can you come or not? Miss Allard needs to know.'

'Miss Allard's still there? I thought she was a temporary measure? Well, I can't say as I'm surprised, she's a bloody good teacher.'

LJ wishes Maggie would stop talking shit and get on with saving his arse.

'What if I can't come?' she asks, mischievously.

'I don't know.'

'You'll have to ring your dad, won't you?'

'Mmm.'

'Who's your favourite Auntie?'

'What?'

Miss Allard tuts and with a shake of the head says, 'We say, 'Pardon', Master Edwards, not 'What'. You're hardly an imbecile.'

'Pardon,' says LJ. He could kill Maggie.

'Humour me,' says Maggie.

'My options are rather limited, wouldn't you say?' says LJ.

Miss Allard raises her eyebrows. She presumes the punishment for fighting is being discussed. She knows the previous head favoured corporal punishment over and above anything else and slippering in particular. Many a so-called wrongdoer, LJ included, was whacked across the buttocks with a size twelve leather upper for the most piffling of misdemeanours. But, when this head was summarily dismissed, he forgot to take his slippers with him. The first thing she did when she was appointed his temporary replacement was to throw the revolting things in the bin.

'But even if you had plenty of aunts to choose from, we both know it'd be me,' laughs Maggie. 'What's the magic word?'

'Peas,' shouts the toddler, thinking 'Mabbie's' on about the milk again. He pulls himself up her leg and rubs his fluff covered cheek on her knee.

LJ rolls his eyes and mutters, 'Please.'

Maggie rubs the toddler's back and says, 'That's right, 'Please' *is* the magic word, isn't it?'

'So, I'll tell Miss Allard you're on your way then,' mumbles LJ.

'Hang on a minute, L.' She covers the phone with her hand and calls to a shadow passing her office door. It's a long skinny shadow with big hair and a baby on its hip. 'Deirdre, is that you?' she asks.

A teenager puts her multi-coloured frizz around the door. All Maggie can see of her baby is a dimpled and bare leg that looks as if it's growing out of the teenager's protruding hip bone.

'It is,' agrees Deirdre.

Maggie notices the fresh bandage on Deirdre's wrist and says, 'Will you watch these two? Mum's next door with a peeler...'

The girl looks up from her picture. She decides that she and her brother must be having chips for tea but what she doesn't understand is why she isn't allowed to be with her mum while she peels the potatoes. She's usually allowed to, in fact, most of the time she has to do the peeling.

'...though she shouldn't be much longer,' adds Maggie. 'I've just got to nip out. Family emergency. Tash is also on today.'

'Yeah,' says Deirdre. 'Sure thing.'

'I've promised this one some milk,' she adds, with a sideways nod at the toddler.

Deirdre sighs but says, 'Come on, kids, I'm sure we can do better than milk.'

Maggie frowns because as far as she's concerned milk and toddlers go together like cheese and pineapple on a cocktail stick, or sausage and tomato crisps in a liver sausage sandwich. She thinks of Deirdre in terms of Margaret-Thatcher-the-Milk-Snatcher but forces herself to say 'Thank you' anyway. The girl takes her brother by the hand and with a backwards glance and one more reassuring nod from the-lady-that-saved-her, grasps Deirdre's hand and allows herself and her brother to be led off to the lady's kitchen.

'L?'

'Yesss, Mum.'

'Tell Miss Allard, I'm on my way.'

She puts down the phone and lifts the child's picture from the desk. The octopus isn't an octopus at all; it's something else, something vile: it's the lump of meat that passes for the child's father and a representation of some of the things he's done to the people he's supposed to keep safe. She walks to her filing cabinet, locates a folder

157

that bears the child's surname, and slips the evidence inside. One day, that picture *will* be used against him. She'll make sure of it.

***

Maggie's blue Austin Princess swings into the grammar school gates. LJ and his best-friend, Ralph, sit outside Miss Allard's office and watch her progress through the gaps in the window blind.

'That's not your mum,' whispers Ralph.

'No shit,' whispers LJ.

'Who is it?'

'My aunt.'

Ralph sniggers. 'She looks rare.'

'She is rare.'

'What's with all the purple shit?'

'It's her thing.'

'Purple hair?'

'Yep.'

'Jesus, Edwards, that's hilarious.'

LJ thumps Ralph's thigh and Ralph sniggers again.

***

On the way to Miss Allard's office, Maggie spies an old upright piano in the corridor. It wears a sign. The sign says: FOR TUNING. DO NOT PLAY. Maggie walks past the piano and then stops. She thinks: *Go on.* And then: *Alright.* She checks she doesn't have an audience, tiptoes to the piano, lifts the lid, and plays a rising glissando. Then she closes the lid and does a lady-jog back down the corridor.

***

'Do come in, Mrs Edwards,' says Miss Allard gravely.

LJ and Ralph bow their heads: they wear contrition like a detachable hood. Maggie follows Miss Allard into her office and shuts the heavy oak door behind her. The two women take their seats and Miss Allard kicks things off by saying, 'Am I given to understand that the Virgin Mary stands before me once more?'

'I'm afraid so,' says Maggie. 'Though I can assure you, I won't appear in this guise again. I've made that very clear to LJ.'

'This is the last time *I'll* be wool-blinded by your nephew anyway; I'm leaving at the end of the month. The board has finally made a permanent appointment.'

'In that case, I'm glad I came,' says Maggie truthfully. Miriam could be a bit stuffy and talked like an eighteenth-century governess, but at university they'd seen eye-to-eye on almost every one of the issues they'd taken issue with, and Maggie had been pleased to have become reacquainted with her even if it was under false pretences.

'I'm quite concerned for LJ,' Miriam confesses.

Maggie sighs and removes her coat.

'He's been quite the buffoon of late.'

Maggie rolls her eyes but they don't do a full lap of her sockets.

'Par exemple...' says Miriam dramatically. 'Last week, he sheathed Discobolus.'

Maggie frowns. 'Discobulus?'

'His statue stands in our gymnasium.'

'Are you saying that LJ stuck a jonnie on the penis of a statue?'

'I am,' says Miriam, dismissing a smile. 'And there it remained for a number of days.'

Maggie's lips recede and her eyes sparkle as she imagines the slow descent of Discobulus' rubber on to the gymnasium's varnished floor. She makes a kite shape with her thumbs and index fingers, rests the leading tip on her philtrum and waits for Miriam to go on.

'But there have also been instances of rudeness, laziness and now, fighting.'

'He's taken up boxing.'

'Has he now?'

'I did tell his parents that I didn't think it was a good idea,' lies Maggie.

'Yes, well, I'm afraid a detention is inappropriate in the circumstances, hence I intend to suspend LJ for the remainder of the day.'

'Right,' says Maggie.

'And Ralph, of course.'

'What was the fight about?'

'Ralph and LJ took exception to another boy calling Ralph's mother a dyke.'

Maggie's expression mirrors Miriam's. She blurts out, 'Is she?' before she can remind herself that this isn't any of her business.

'If she's got any sense,' quips Miriam, straight-faced.

Maggie tries to laugh quietly but isn't very successful. Outside the office, Ralph looks at LJ and LJ shrugs: they both know that there is nothing worse than a parent brown-nosing a teacher.

'Whether she is or she isn't, I don't know,' says Miriam with a sideways peep at her macramé plant holder: the thing seems hell-bent on dressing to the left. 'What I do know is that the boy gave Ralph a kick on the shins and in return, LJ gave the boy a bloody nose.'

'The lesbian defenders,' jokes Maggie.

'Quite,' says Miriam, trying to put the cactus out of her mind. 'The thing is, Maggie, LJ has a sharp intellect. I'd go so far as to say that he's Oxbridge material.'

Maggie's mind journeys to Uxbridge before it arrives at Oxbridge but once there, her mouth says, 'Really?' and her mind goes from picturing LJ biffing homophobes – which was a good picture to start with – to him cycling down the streets of Oxford in academic dress, which is, quite frankly, the best picture to end with. LJ at Oxford is the stuff of her dreams: it's where Miss Howard and Miss Hughes studied.

'Yes,' continues Miriam, 'but only if he applies himself and does well in his A Levels. Obviously, I wanted to discuss his suspension with you, or rather his parents, but also his potential, and to make manifest that unless there's a significant change of attitude toward his studies, that potential will be dashed.' She sighs, stands, adjusts the macramé plant pot holder and says, 'What I'm trying to say, Maggie, is, sort your little sod out before it's too late.' Then she walks around to the door, opens it, and says, 'Master Edwards, your aunt will take you home now.'

As soon as LJ gets a chance, he looks at Maggie as if she's grassed him up. It doesn't go unnoticed. 'My father once gave me a puppy,' says Miss Allard. 'Naturally, it was very playful, but its favourite game was chase. I would chase the puppy around and around the garden and he would evade capture. However, when I grew tired of the game, I caught him.'

She waits for the fable to sink in but once it's clear it won't be sinking anywhere, she turns to Maggie and says, 'Ms. Edwards, would

160

you mind giving Master Murphy a lift home? His mother refuses to collect him and what with the current transport strike, I fear the walk home is a trifle too long for his newly lame leg.'

***

'She's gonna kill me,' says Ralph. He and LJ each lean an elbow on the backseat armrest while Maggie watches them in her rear-view mirror. 'I promised I wouldn't get in to any more fights.'

'It wasn't your fault,' says LJ, watching Maggie watching them.

'Doesn't matter,' says Ralph. 'She'll still kill me. I was on my last warning.'

'What's she gonna do?'

'Won't let me live with my dad, probably.'

'Nah.'

'Wanna bet?'

LJ sniffs and turns to the window.

'It's all her fault. Stupid dyke,' mutters Ralph.

***

Maggie isn't sure of the protocol in this situation. Should she accompany Ralph to the door and speak to his mum, or leave them both to it? She feels a sense of obligation: to speak up for Ralph and to play the incident down. After all, it was LJ who bloodied the boy's nose. Ralph was merely sticking up for his mum and got booted in the shins for his trouble.

She assaults the handbrake and asks, 'What's your mum's name, Ralph?'

'Sylvie,' he grunts.

'Sylvie. That's a nice name.'

'Is it?' says Ralph.

'Out we all get, then,' says Maggie, deciding not to labour the point.

'What, all of us?' says LJ.

'Yes,' says Maggie. She knows LJ likes to deconstruct things and she doesn't want him deconstructing any part of her treasured Princess.

'What are you going to say to my mum?' says Ralph, worried.

'I think I'll start with hello and see where that takes me,' says Maggie, amused.

Both boys slide off the armrest and roll out of the Princess like a couple of Weebles.

'Look lively,' says Maggie.

They don't. She takes the lead and heads for Ralph's front door but as she gets to the bell, Ralph barges her out of the way, produces a key, opens the door, and yells, 'Mum?'

Then he disappears inside with a nod to LJ to follow, and a woman appears full of cold and wearing a long nightie and a blanket. She looks like a Titanic survivor. She smiles tiredly, offers Maggie her hand and says, 'I'm Sylvie, Ralph's mother. Thank you for bringing the so-and-so home.'

Maggie's seen Sylvie some place before. She scratches her head and tries to place her. It's her hair that rings the biggest bell: it's long, thick and copper-coloured and she remembers watching her twist it around and around her middle finger before securing it on top of her head with a fountain pen. Afterwards, she looked like Virginia Woolf. Where was that?

'I'm Maggie,' she says, gently taking Sylvie's hand. 'I'm LJ's auntie. I think we've met before?'

The women keep hold of one another's hand and consider the likelihood of this. In the end Maggie says, 'This might sound like a funny question, but are you a social worker by any chance?'

Sylvie sneezes all over Maggie, apologises, coughs into her matted plaits and says, 'Yes, I am.'

'It was at the annual conference,' says Maggie, clicking her unemployed fingers. 'That's where I know you from.'

Nodding, Sylvie reaches forward and touches Maggie's hair. 'I take it you're a social worker too?' she asks.

Maggie's eyes attempt to follow the progress of Sylvie's hand but the rest of her body keeps very still. 'Yes,' she breathes, somewhat taken aback by the rush of feelings inside her.

'That explains it,' says Sylvie.

'Explains what?'

'Why you have head lice.'

Maggie's free hand jumps to her head and pats it as if it's alight. 'Damn it,' she says. 'Are you sure?'

'I just caught sight of the mother louse I'm afraid.'

'The mother louse... how do you know it was her?'

162

'We go back a long way,' says Sylvie resisting the impulse to scratch her own head. 'She's plump: you must taste good,' she adds suggestively.

Maggie stops playing Simple Simon and checks Sylvie's greeny-gold eyes for the meaning of her words.

'You'd better come in,' says Sylvie with a tug of Maggie's hand. 'I've a nit comb somewhere and I'm not afraid to use it.'

19: Fiddler's Green

Maggie and Sylvie's first date doesn't start well.

Maggie chose the venue: an Irish pub in Brentford, because Sylvie was Irish and the billing was Live Irish Folk Music. The plan was to arrive separately: Maggie by Princess, Sylvie by bus. It was Maggie's idea: she didn't want Ralph putting two and two together and telling LJ, although Sylvie wasn't told this. But the bus is late and Maggie is early. She tasks herself with getting in the drinks: two halves of Guinness. She's keen to get the butterflies in her stomach sozzled. She sips her Guinness and feels self-conscious. She doesn't know Sylvie's bus is running late. She wonders if she is being stood up. Every time she thinks of Sylvie, her heart goes on strike. A man in a patchwork waistcoat takes up the Bodhrán, and a woman with a gentle face and a habit on her head, the fiddle. The music isn't Maggie's cup of tea but she taps her hand on the table in time with the beat to suggest that it is. She wishes she'd asked for a shot of blackcurrant in her Guinness. Each sip makes her shudder. She imagines it tastes like water from a rusty bucket. She notices there are more men in the pub than women just as a bucket is shoved in her face by a man who looks like Burt Reynolds. 'Collection for the Rah,' he bellows. The bucket is the colour of irony: it is orange. Maggie says, 'Oh,' and dives into her handbag. The search for her purse is frantic. She throws in some change and hopes it's enough. There is folding money in the bucket. She imagines Burt blasting her kneecaps in an alleyway crowded with rubbish bins because she wasn't more generous to the cause. He seems to consider her contribution before moving on. She wishes she hadn't opted for the Irish theme. She wishes she'd suggested a bottle of wine at her usual haunt.

Sylvie blows in just as a Natterer's bat is spotted in the rafters by a barmaid with a Belfast accent. Maggie waves at Sylvie shyly and Sylvie mouths a 'sorry' as she squeezes past tables and chairs to reach her. When Sylvie arrives at Maggie's table, she bends down and kisses her on the cheek. The extent to which Maggie is taken aback by this kiss means that she has to tell herself off for being silly: women kiss each other in public. She and Astrid kiss all the time; nobody ever thinks they're at it, do they? Then the bat sets off on its first dive-bombing mission. Sylvie shrieks, throws herself on Maggie's lap and hides her face in Maggie's shoulder. This people do notice and Maggie worries. 'Do you have a bat phobia?' she asks, with her eyes on the nun who demonstrates that she can saw her fiddle strings without looking at them.

'Not really,' says Sylvie. 'But I do have hair a bat could get lost in and, if I'm honest, the only mammal I was hoping to go home with tonight is you.'

Maggie smiles and then returns to the nun: she is still watching. Sylvie considers the half-pint of Guinness. 'Is that for me?' she asks.

'Yes, is that alright?' replies Maggie.

Sylvie downs the Guinness and says, 'Maggie, I might be Irish but I don't like Guinness, I don't like this music and, if I'm honest, I don't like Ireland. Why do you think I live in England?'

'Collection for the Rah,' says Burt.

'Fuck off,' says Sylvie, and pushes the bucket out of her face.

'Shall we go?' says Maggie with all the gulp of a cartoon character.

'Aye, I would if I were yous,' spits the barmaid from behind the bar.

Sylvie ignores her and says to Maggie, 'But you haven't finished your drink?'

'It doesn't matter,' says Maggie.

Sylvie picks up Maggie's glass. 'Cheers,' she says to the barmaid.

'Fuck yous,' says the barmaid.

Sylvie finishes Maggie's drink and then says, 'No thanks, you're not my type,' before leading Maggie out of the pub at the speed of a funeral march.

***

Now, Maggie and Sylvie walk down the tree-lined avenue in Walpole Park in the dark. The night-time temperature means the place is deserted – save for nocturnal creatures – but neither Maggie nor Sylvie feel the cold. They hold hands and grip waists for the connection, not the warmth.

'In Dublin, where I'm from,' says Sylvie, 'homosexuality doesn't exist: certainly not as unconscious choice, anyway. My family, apart from thinking I'm disgusting and destined for hell, actually believe I woke up one day and decided to be a lesbian.'

'My family don't know about me,' says Maggie.

'But you've always been single?'

'As far as they're concerned, yes.'

'They must wonder why you haven't married, surely?'

Maggie shrugs, 'Possibly, but they've never said anything. I think they're a bit like Dublin, although, when we lived in Waldeck Road, a lesbian couple lived in the maisonette below us and Mum made it clear that I wasn't to go near them. Looking back on it, perhaps she did know what they were. Perhaps she thought their sexuality was contagious or something. She didn't like them, I know that, and yet, they were lovely. I used to visit them when Mum was at work. I read their books. When I was growing up, the only time I didn't feel strange was when I was with them.'

'What happened to them?'

'When I was about fourteen they emigrated to Canada, and that was that.'

Sylvie sighs.

'I wanted to go with them.'

Sylvie squeezes Maggie's waist and says, 'I only realized I had feelings for women once I was married, but by then I'd had Erin and Ralph was on the way. I couldn't leave the children.'

'I would have liked children,' says Maggie.

'I've lost mine,' says Sylvie. 'Erin lives in Dublin with my mother and since the incident at school, Ralph's gone to live with his father in Ruislip. Des thinks fighting is fine. It's what boys are supposed to do, apparently. You know he's actually worried that I'll turn Ralph into a quote-unquote 'nancy-boy' if he continues to live with me.'

'The kids will come round,' says Maggie, but she knows this is fluff.

'Not if Des has anything to do with it. Poor bastard did his best to fuck it out of me but failed. He hates that and he hates me *for* that. The thing is, whatever Ralph thinks of me, he still needs his mother.'

Maggie says, 'hmm' but thinks of her own mother and how she would rather have gone without her.

***

They arrive at the bandstand in silence and abandon the sides of each other for the fronts. Sylvie is an inch taller than Maggie but most of this is hair. She buttons Maggie's coat and rearranges her scarf. Then she talks about cheesecake. 'We could go back to mine for a slice.'

'I don't like cheesecake,' laughs Maggie.

'Do you want some anyway?' says Sylvie.

Maggie nods and says, 'Sure to be sure,' and Sylvie smacks Maggie's bottom and says, 'Very cheeky.'

1980

20: Stay That Way

The curtains are drawn in Lil's bedroom but the light is such that Maggie can read. She sits in an armchair chair close to the bed and watches her yellowing mum drift in and out of sleep. Outside the door stands Alfie. When Lil is quiet, Maggie can hear his disciplined breathing: in through the nose and out through the mouth. It's worse than a ticking clock, but she's grown tired of inviting him in to the bedroom or telling him to go downstairs and sit with Harry.

For Alfie, some areas of the house are out of bounds and the boundary lines are clear, particularly when the carpet on the landing disappears and the papered walls turn into concrete. He's used to standing in a pillbox and guarding an airfield and he's had the training on German spies, saboteurs and honey traps; he knows his duty and he won't be distracted. Downstairs, Harry stirs a saucepan of tomato soup that nobody upstairs wants to eat, while Astrid worries about them all from the perfumed confines of her beauty counter, and LJ determines *the exact value of the area of the region bounded by a curve* in his maths A Level exam.

Lil's bedroom is austere like a nun's cell and the olive-green bedspread is proof that she didn't pooh-pooh the British Ministry of Information's 'Make Do and Mend' pamphlet back in 1943: it could almost be framed and called a sampler. There are no knick-knacks, mementos, pictures, or accoutrements in her room and the mirror is both tiny and cracked. Each of her things has its place and each of those places is out of plain sight, except for the one lace doily on the glass-topped dresser. Maggie has no idea where it came from – Lil doesn't knit or crochet – but the stocking filled with pudding rice that sits at its centre is there because Maggie didn't know where else to put it.

Lil had repurposed the pudding rice following the total mastectomy of her left breast. After the surgery, she'd felt lopsided. Also, it had seemed that people talked to her absent breast instead of her face. She'd never felt normal but she'd always tried to look it, so she'd decided to stuff the left side of her brassiere with a handful of pudding rice. Just as she'd suspected, beneath her clothes, the rice had looked and moved like the saggy breast next to it. But the improvised prosthetic had had a down side: she couldn't bring herself to make rice pudding anymore, and it had always been a favourite of Alfie's.

When Lil's condition had deteriorated, Alfie had forced himself to lift her from the sofa in the sitting room and carry her up the stairs to her bedroom. His eyes had never strayed from looking straight ahead and he'd muttered all the way, 'Just to the bed, just to the bed…' Afterwards, Maggie had undressed her and made her comfortable and Alfie had lain flat out on the landing with his face turned to the cold skirting board trying his very best not to re-visit Dresden.

Now, Lil wakes and says, 'Margaret,' when, thinks Maggie, she means to say 'Maggie.'

Maggie frowns, closes her book and tucks it down the side of the chair. 'I'm here, Mum,' she says. 'Can I get you anything?'

'I'm missing The Sullivans.'

'Don't worry,' says Maggie, surprised to hear she watches the soap, surprised to hear anybody does. 'Try to go back to sleep.'

'I'm sorry I made you look after LJ,' Lil says, suddenly.

Maggie is taken aback: her mum has never apologised for anything before and Maggie doesn't understand why she's apologising for this. It was such a long time ago and there was nobody else to do it, was there?

With the palm of her hand, Lil lightly sweeps the vacant space on the bed beside her dead legs and adds, 'It was cruel, I think.'

Maggie does as she is bid and sits beside Lil but it feels strange.

'It's a horrible word, isn't it?' says Lil.

Maggie frowns.

'Why do they have to call it that?' asks Lil.

'What else should they call it?' says Maggie, hoping this might prompt her mum to reveal the word that's troubling her.

Crossly, Lil says, 'Perhaps they shouldn't call it anything,' and grimaces with pain.

Maggie wishes her mum was in hospital. She thinks of nurses, strict visiting hours and a morphine pump. Lil wonders why her legs had to go numb instead of the parts of her body affected by the cancer. She wishes her body could have got one thing right, given her some relief, before it gave up completely. 'I didn't want you to be one of those… women,' she says. 'Sille and Bill wanted LJ, but I put my foot down. I wanted you to want children. I thought wanting children would make you want to marry.' She grabs Maggie's hand.

Being touched by her mum is as alien to Maggie as being touched by her dad. Once her dad came home from Germany and it was made clear that he was never to be touched, all touching between everybody else in the family seemed to stop too. They'd never been the most demonstrative of families but it was as if they all contracted her dad's phobia the minute he returned home. She thinks about the word on her mum's mind. She thinks about it until she's not sure it's a word at all.

'But you fell in love with LJ, didn't you?' says Lil. 'And then you had to give him back.'

Maggie stares at her mum's swollen ring finger and wonders where her wedding ring has gone, if it is lost and whether it matters.

Lil allows one small tear to slip over the ledge of her lower eyelid and says, 'I should have known better.'

Maggie tucks her mum's cold hand under the bedspread, wipes away the tear with her thumb and nods. She has a lump in her throat too big to be swallowed: it feels like a tumour, like something requiring surgical removal. The words her mum has spoken are unhelpful: it has to be the morphine talking. She pets her mum's thigh as she might a dog's head and returns to her chair determined that her blurred vision won't get in the way of her finishing her book.

Lil closes her eyes and permits her mind to wander to the final time she saw Margaret. It was a warm September afternoon in 1977. Up until then, September had been her favourite month of the year: not hot, not cold and the trees full of her favourite colours. It was the month where happiness seemed less preposterous. It was the month where she'd sit in the park with her face raised to the sun, her fingers anchored in the grass, her stockinged feet free of shoes and she'd think about leaving. She'd leave Alfie a note, or not leave Alfie a note. Either way, she wouldn't leave a forwarding address. She'd pack a small suitcase, empty the bank account by half – it was as much her money as it was his – and she'd leave. For as long as September lasted, leaving seemed plausible. Until the meeting with Margaret.

It transpired that Margaret had spotted Lil at the pictures a few months before and had followed her home. That was how she'd known where to send the invitation asking Lil to afternoon tea. Lil hadn't liked the fact that Margaret had followed her home. What if Margaret had seen her in her cleaning clothes? What if she'd seen Alfie being strange? *I didn't approach you at the pictures, Lil, because I didn't like to put you on the spot.* Lil thought that that was exactly what Margaret should have done; that way she could have put an end to Margaret's thoughts of afternoon tea right then and there.

Margaret's front garden was heaving with roses grown fat on apple-sized lumps of moist horse manure. The voluptuousness of each bloom was obscene: the stem of each buckled under the weight. Pink, apricot and cream-coloured petals perfumed an evaporating puddle on the harlequin tiled path. Lil remembered adding rose petals to jam jars of water to make perfume for her mother when she was a little girl but she didn't dwell on the memory because Margaret opened the door before Lil had a chance to ring the bell. Margaret said hello and then chattered on about the housekeeper. The housekeeper had made cucumber fingers and fruit scones fresh that morning but had been given the afternoon off so that she and Lil could have the entire place to themselves. Margaret's Georgian terrace smelt not only of baking but also those awful French cigarettes combined with something else… damp, perhaps? Lil glared at the delicate white fingers on the gold plate and the fruit scones with their shiny tops, and the butter curls and strawberry jam in their silver dishes and decided not to eat any of it. And she knew that Margaret wouldn't either because her frail frame suggested that she survived on nothing but thin air and those awful… Gauloise. What a horrible word that was… Gauloise. It sounded like a disease of the throat. And that cigarette holder was ridiculous and the colour of Margaret's hair completely wrong: it was always auburn, never black. The only thing Alfie and Margaret had in common. Now, she looked like a medieval man in a skullcap or even worse, that awful Wallis Simpson woman. Surely silver hair was preferable to that? Lil half-expected a gaggle of overweight pugs to come trundling into the room. Simpson always seemed to have one sniffing around her. She thought of the late Duke of Windsor and then, of course, his equivalent, Geoffrey. Margaret dropped a slice of lemon into a pink teacup with an unnecessary flourish. The joints of her heavily ringed fingers were bulbous and the black tailored suit she wore funereal. She deplored the brewing of English Breakfast Tea in the afternoon. Lil thought about the PG Tips in the Tupperware box on the kitchen side at home. She didn't know what sort of tea was used in PG Tips. With a pair of ornate silver tongs, Margaret selected a sugar cube that had lost the points from its corners and sharp edges from its sides. Lil had no time for sugar tongs. What was wrong with a spoon? Margaret stopped to scratch her throat. She scratched it as if she had fleas. Her throat reminded Lil of the silver sinew she removed from a leg of lamb before putting it in the oven to roast. She wondered if Margaret was as thin back then when they were... friends. She felt plump in comparison. She hid her stomach with her hands and wished she hadn't worn tights. They were Astrid's fault. Astrid insisted that tights were better than stockings but the shade was wrong: her legs looked like two hot dogs and the nylon suffocated a place she didn't like to provoke.

'What a stroke of luck seeing you at the pictures that day,' said Margaret. 'Of course, I recognized you as soon as I saw you. You haven't changed a bit, Lil.'

What Lil didn't know was that Margaret had wanted to find Lil for months and had been on the verge of hiring a private investigator to do it for her. But then *Airport '77*, a film in which Olivia De Havilland had a starring role, went on general release. Margaret's hunch that De Havilland's role would prompt Lil to go and see the film proved correct, although she had to endure *Airport '77* a total of nine times before the hunch paid off.

'Won't you sit, Lil?' said Margaret, when Lil didn't respond to her compliment. 'Please.'

Lil took the nearest chair.

Margaret smiled. 'Shall I make a plate for you?'

'No… thank you,' said Lil, and after a pause added, 'I'm not hungry.'

Margaret insisted. 'Do have something.' She put two cucumber fingers on a plate. Then she collected a painted table from a nest of four and placed it beside Lil. The table was the smallest of the four. Lil fixed her eyes on its painted top. A man was playing the flute to a woman who clearly had nothing better to do with her time than listen to him. She couldn't discern the artist's signature. Margaret handed Lil the plate and set the pink teacup directly on top of the musician's head. Lil stiffened at Margaret's indifference to the lacquered table top and also her proximity. She forced herself to nibble the corner of one of the cucumber fingers to divert her mind. Margaret lit another Gauloise and perched on the arm of a nearby chair.

'I'm so happy you came,' said Margaret. 'I wasn't sure you would.' She blew a long column of smoke at the pale yellow ceiling. Lil abandoned the cucumber finger and balanced the plate on the arm of her chair. 'I can't stay long,' she said.

Margaret looked crestfallen but soon rallied. 'In that case,' she said, jumping up from her chair, 'let's skip tea and have a proper drink.'

Lil watched her stride over to the drinks cabinet and said firmly, 'No, I won't, thank you, Margaret.'

'Oh, come on, Lil, one won't hurt,' said Margaret. She poured two large glasses of brandy and told a lie, 'I never drink alone.' She chinked their glasses and said, 'Chin-chin.' Then she swallowed a large mouthful of the autumnal liquid.

Lil took a small sip; it made her shudder. She wanted to go home. 'I should be going,' she announced.

'But you just arrived,' said Margaret.

'Nevertheless…'

Margaret finished her brandy and cried, 'Will you come to Venice with me, Lil? Please say you will.'

'Venice?'

'Have you ever been on an aeroplane before?'

Lil shook her head.

'Oh, they're such fun… if you don't mind heights. Off we'll fly to Venice and have a tremendous time.'

Lil's cheeks burned. 'But why would you want me to come to Venice with you? We don't know each other anymore.'

'We simply lost touch, Lil. It was the war. We'll soon be back to the way we were.'

'I can't go to Venice with you, Margaret.'

'Or somewhere else,' said Margaret. 'Wherever you like… I don't mind.' She didn't mean to but she looked Lil up and down. 'I'll cover all our expenses naturally… you mustn't worry about that.'

Lil rose to her feet and stood her glass of brandy on the flute-player's legs. Margaret dashed over to the drink's cabinet and poured herself another drink. 'Let's discuss it, Lil,' she said, standing in the doorway.

'Perhaps we should discuss Geoffrey,' said Lil.

'Geoffrey?'

'Yes, Geoffrey… your husband.'

'Geoffrey was my fiancé, Lil.'

'Yes, I know that…'

'He was never my husband.'

'What do you mean?'

'He was killed… not long after our engagement and then Tom, less than two weeks later.'

Lil returned to her chair.

'You didn't know?'

Lil shook her head and rubbed her teeth against the knuckles of her right fist.

Quickly, Margaret said, 'Did you know about Tom?'

Lil didn't care about Tom; Margaret was never going to marry her brother. Margaret advanced on the occasional table, picked up Lil's glass of brandy and shoved it in her free hand. 'Drink,' she ordered.

Lil did as she was bid and downed the liquid. She glanced round the room looking for photographic evidence that Margaret went on to marry a different man. 'But you did marry?' she said.

Margaret sucked her cigarette holder. 'Actually, Lil, I didn't,' she admitted. 'Once Geoffrey died, I was off the hook so to speak. Mother believed that I was too grief-stricken to consider marrying anyone else.'

'I have to go home,' repeated Lil.

'No you don't.'

'Yes… yes… I do. I have to go home… immediately.'

'To Alfie?' sneered Margaret.

Lil frowned and then considered Alfie. He was probably on guard duty. He generally went on guard duty when she went out. He had to protect their house from the Nazis of Chiswick. He had to sit on the stairs with his gun pointed at the front door. 'To my husband,' she spat.

Margaret changed tack. 'But you don't have to. You could live with me…'

Lil frowned.

'…as my companion, Lil. You need never see that man again.'

Wordlessly, Lil got up and thrust her empty glass at Margaret's bony chest.

Margaret looked from the glass to Lil and said, 'Are you seriously suggesting that you'd rather live with him than with me?'

Lil sniffed. 'Yes,' she said.

'Why?'

'You should know the answer to that.'

Margaret's lips twisted into a cruel smile. 'Because you love him?' she laughed.

'Don't be ridiculous.'

'I can think of no other reason.'

Lil said nothing.

'For goodness' sake,' shrieked Margaret. 'Whyever not?'

'Because,' shouted Lil, 'don't you remember? It was you that said it. There is no other way!' And it was shouted with such conviction that it made her smile.

21: The Professional Mourner

Of all the mourners at Lil's funeral, it is Sille who puts on the greatest display in the crematorium chapel. She holds Maggie as if to prevent her from being swept out to sea. She whispers 'Poor darling' at Maggie's Vivienne Westwood inspired hair-do as if she is nine and orphaned and the next stop for her is the workhouse, a meagre serving of gruel and a spot of oakum picking. Dry-eyed and silent, Maggie counts the chapel's arches, lets herself be hugged and wishes the vicar hadn't said 'Gillian' instead of 'Lillian' even if it he did just say it the once. Beside Sille stands LJ. The shirt he's been forced to wear is new and the collar stiff: his neck glows like a hob ring and stings like a scratch from his mum's new cat. This is his first funeral and he finds himself completely underwhelmed by the lack of pomp, ceremony and people: Jesus, didn't his Nan have any friends? To his left sits Astrid still thinking that the piano tie LJ wears is inappropriate for the occasion and that Maggie was wrong to intercede and say that the tie was fine because it was as much black as it was white. Like a real piano, it was definitely more white than black and it was bought for his school leavers disco, not his Nan's funeral. Harry sits at the end of the pew, next to Maggie, in the black velvet pinstripe suit of his wedding day and bites his nails. (If Astrid could get at him, she'd gently lever his fist away from his mouth, but she's at one end of the pew and he's at the other. If he's not careful, she'll paint them with that nail biting solution again. Mark her words.) He fidgets in his seat but is the last to stand when it's time to sing and is late with every 'Amen'. His belated 'So Be Its' make the chapel sound like a well but it isn't really his fault. It's the fault of the woman in the gallery above. For the life of him, he can't place her. He wonders if she's a left over from the funeral before or an early arrival for the funeral to follow. Perhaps she was one of those professional mourner types? He saw a documentary on them once. They were the in-thing in Victorian times and in Egypt if memory serves... Well, whoever she was, she was certainly doing her bit for the occasion: he's never seen so many crocodile tears. He resists the urge to look at her again, or at his dad, or at his mum, or rather her coffin. Best stare at the ceiling, the cream-painted ceiling: Christ Almighty, it could do with a touch-up.

Alfie sits alone in the front pew on the other side of the chapel. He grips his kneecaps and bites the inside of his cheek with his dentures. He stares at Lil's coffin as if it's about to hatch. He doesn't hear a word of what the vicar says. He just worries about Lil being trapped in that shitting wooden box and being burnt. Trapped and burnt. He fumbles for the button in his pocket. Why did she want to be burned? *How much ash does a burnt body make? A cupful? A bucketful?* He wipes his clammy face on the sleeve of his jacket and licks his dry lips. He hates those bloody curtains. When they move again... He rises to his feet, enters the aisle and hurries towards her coffin, his arms outstretched like, LJ thinks, the Scooby Doo ghost-of-the-week.

'Oh, Christ, here we go,' mutters Harry.

'Oh, no,' whispers Astrid.

'Shall I go to him, darling?' whispers Sille to the back of Astrid's head.

'Yes, Mormor,' whispers LJ. 'Go and get him.'

Maggie pictures her dad on the receiving end of a Sille manhandle and all but shouts, 'No, Sille, leave him.' Then after a pause she adds, 'Please.'

'Are you sure, darling?'

Maggie nods sharply and Sille tightens her grip, kisses the top of her head and murmurs, 'You know best, darling.' Harry returns to staring at the ceiling and sets about estimating the height of the scaffold tower that would be needed to reach it, while Astrid, unable to catch Harry's calculating eye, blinks back a tear and begins to rub LJ's back. LJ, experiencing the onset of a runny nose, begins to wonder if he's allergic to Mormor's Chinchilla waistcoat. He turns away from the rodents and buries his face in his mum's neck just in case. When Alfie reaches Lil, he rests his bitten cheek on her brass coffin plate, upsetting the floral tributes in the process, and closes his eyes. The vicar continues reporting Lil's life to those who actually knew her, but reads the script faster than before, hoping to goodness that that coffin lid is well screwed down. Meanwhile, the professional mourner watches Alfie's performance with the greatest of contempt: thanks to him, her wreath of orange roses sets off down the steps of the marble platform like a trundling hoop and disappears from view. Nobody else seems to notice though.

***

Once it had been arranged that Astrid and Harry would host Lil's wake, Sille had said, 'Leave the buffet to me, darling. How many do you expect?'

Astrid got out her fingers. When she reached the thumb of her left hand she said, 'Six.'

'Six?'

Astrid nodded, 'If Dad comes.'

'What do you mean, if? Surely Alfie will come to his own wife's wake?'

Astrid shrugged. 'There's no surely about it, Mor. He doesn't do well in a crowd. You know that.'

'Six is hardly a crowd, darling.'

'I was just going to do a few sandwiches.'

'Ach,' Sille said. 'If it's only going to be six, we could have *frikadeller med stuvet hvidkål eller flæskesteg med rødkål og kartoffelsalat og æblekag* for dessert.'

'*Rødkål*,' Astrid repeated. Then, with a shake of her head said, 'My mind's gone blank.'

Sille frowned: she should have insisted that Astrid learn Danish. When Astrid was just a few days old, she'd said to Bill, 'I want Astrid to speak Danish. I want her to be bilingual.'

'Good idea, love,' Bill had said.

'But you'll need to learn it too, Bill,' Sille had warned.

'What? Why's that, love?'

'We'll need to speak Danish at home, Bill, otherwise all she'll ever hear is English. If all she ever hears is English, that's all she'll ever speak.'

'Well perhaps we shouldn't bother, love. I mean, what good will knowing Danish do her, eh? It's not as if anybody else speaks it round here, is it? Anyway, everybody speaks English nowadays, don't they? It doesn't matter where you go in the world; you're proof of that, love. Praps she's better off sticking to English. Save a lot of confusion in the long run, won't it? Nobody would know what she was on about. They'd think she was talking double Dutch or something. The other kids would make fun of her. You can't do that to her, love, you really can't. Just think of the upset.'

So, in the end, save for the odd word that Sille had stood firm on such as *Mor* for Mum and *Far* for Dad, or the names of a few Danish dishes that had, over time crept into the Gordon vernacular, it never actually happened. Still, it was ridiculous that Astrid had forgotten what *rødkål* was: it was a Christmas tradition for *Guds skyld*. 'I'll roast some pig, knock up a potato salad and bake an apple cake,' she said sourly. '*Min guldklump* loves my crackling,' she added, brightening at the memory of LJ crunching cracklings past.

'Dad doesn't eat pig,' Astrid said, supressing a smile. 'And by the way, Mor, LJ doesn't like being called a gold nugget anymore.'

Sille threw up her arms in defeat. 'Sandwiches it is then.'

Now, outside the crematorium in the courtyard of remembrance, Sille, Astrid, LJ and Harry huddle, like black sheep in a pen, in the small paved square where Lil's floral tributes lay. They stare down at the 'MUM' tribute from Harry, Astrid and Maggie; the 'NAN' tribute from LJ; the heart tribute from Alfie; the small spray of white lilies from Sille, and the anonymous wreath of large-headed roses from God knows who. Sille bends down to the latter looking for a card. She picks through the expensive foliage like a forensic officer.

'If you're looking for a card, Mor, there isn't one,' says Astrid. 'I've already checked… but there is a card holder so there must have been one at some stage.'

'Must have fallen off,' says Harry.

'Hmm,' says Astrid.

'Oh, what a shame,' says Sille. 'Somebody, somewhere, is missing their flowers. These roses are gorgeous; such a warm shade of orange, aren't they? I always think it's a bit of a waste sending flowers for a cremation. At least with a burial they can sit on the grave and be appreciated.'

'Can they?' says Harry.

Astrid grips his hand.

'You have to send flowers, Mor. It's still a funeral whether it's a cremation or a burial. You can't have a funeral without flowers. It would look like nobody cared.'

'That's right,' says Harry.

'It would be cheaper,' says Sille.

They all agree about that.

'I think this wreath must belong to the person next door,' says Astrid, discreetly gesturing to the paved square beside Lil's.

LJ reverses three paces and reads the relevant placard. 'June Elizabeth Valent,' he says too loudly. Astrid puts a finger on her lips. 'Not so loud, L,' she says.

LJ looks about him. 'What?' he protests. 'There's only us here and it's not as if June's going to give a…'

Astrid narrows her eyes.

'…going to mind,' he finishes.

'Oh, yes,' says Sille, 'I think you're right, darling. All June's flowers are bright. Isn't that a lovely touch?'

'I don't spose it matters where the flowers go,' croaks Harry. 'Spect they bin em the minute we leave.'

LJ looks worried. 'Are you crying, Dad?' he asks, hoping that he isn't.

To LJ, Astrid says sharply, 'No, he's not, L.' To Harry, she gently says, 'I'm sure they don't, love,' and wraps her arms around him.

Meanwhile, Sille maneuvers the wreath of orange roses into June's square with the outside of her shoe and says, 'There you go, June; sorry for the mix-up, darling.'

***

Alfie hadn't wanted to view Lil's flowers. What he'd wanted was five minutes to himself. Once he'd been shielded from the vicar's outstretched hand by Maggie and her poncho, he'd trundled across the crematorium's grounds and plonked himself down on the nearest memorial bench. Now, listening to the sway of bough and the tee-tur-tee-tur call of a lone blue tit, Maggie watches him from the trunk of a Douglas fir. Until, that is, someone clears their throat from somewhere behind her. Whisking round, she finds a well-dressed woman with a

180

tear-stained face. A handkerchief, heavily stained with make-up, pokes out the top of the woman's black patent handbag in testimony of her grief.

'Sorry to impose,' the woman says, extending her left hand. 'I just wanted to offer my condolences on the loss of your dear mother.'

Maggie steps forward and takes the proffered hand but thinks this woman must have confused her with somebody else. 'Thank you,' she says, too drained to put her straight, too dazed to reflect on the intimate manner of their hand-holding.

'Lil and I were friends many years ago,' she explains.

'You were a friend of Mums?' says Maggie.

'Yes,' says the woman. 'We were the best of friends once.'

Maggie blinks in surprise.

'Before she was married.'

Maggie can't act today. She can't pretend that her mum used to talk about a best friend from the old days. She can't pretend that this woman meant anything to her mum. She can't stop herself from saying, 'Oh,' and giving all of what she's too tired to pretend, away.

'You're like her,' says the woman, but it's clear from Maggie's face that this isn't good news. 'I shouldn't keep you,' she adds, glancing at Alfie's back.

Maggie squeezes the woman's hand to herald the end of the shake and wonders if she ought to invite her back to Harry's house for a sandwich and a cup of tea. She searches for the woman's name thinking that it must have been given but no name comes to mind. In the end she feels obliged to say, 'I'm so sorry, I didn't catch your name.'

'It's the same as yours,' says Margaret, wincing at the sight of the smoking chimney.

1983

22: Thin Red Line

Astrid is in the conservatory doing *The Sunday Times* crossword with Percy, her rag doll cat, warming her corduroy lap. Winter seems to have come early this year. She sits with a black and gold snood around her long neck thinking she should have waited till the following spring to have her long hair cut short and worrying about LJ.

The previous winter, when LJ was in the second year of his history and politics degree, Astrid and Harry had visited his university digs to take him out to lunch. As they'd stood waiting for him in the lounge, Astrid watched her own breath and surveyed the mushrooms growing on the ceiling with mounting hostility. Over lunch, she learned that he was going to bed in his coat, hat and gloves. (He didn't mention the women.) Astrid expected better from the city of Oxford. She wished he'd chosen a university closer to home so that a damp and dingy dig wouldn't have been necessary at all. She decided that all she could do was equip him with a mountain of thermal underwear and instruct Harry to throw some more money his way because his grant obviously wasn't covering all his expenses. Now, she hopes LJ's done what she asked and put some of that extra money aside for heating because she's heard it's going to be a very cold winter this year. Harry suggests they break their October rule and put the fire on; as far as he's concerned, if she needs to wear a scarf indoors, its cold enough. But she won't have it. 'I only notice the draught because I have a long neck,' she says.

'You're a gi-raft,' he puns.

She rolls her eyes. 'You inherited your parents' sense of humour.'

'You can't inherit something that isn't there,' he says truthfully.

'Exactly,' she says, solving *'Thin Red Line (7)'*.

'Nothing made them laugh.'

'I know, darling, I was only joking.'

'Not even when they were young, or we were young, and we hadn't got tired of trying. Once, Mum trimmed the ends of her hair and tossed them in the garden...' he starts to laugh. 'Then in comes Maggie...' He can't stop laughing.

'Oh here we go. Will I hear the end of this one? In comes Maggie...' says Astrid writing *Equator*.

'And...'

'And...' says Astrid chewing her pen and doing a royal wave.

'In comes Maggie from the garden and she's cupping the bits of Mum's hair in her hands and she says to Mum...'

'Yes...'

'She says...'

'I don't know why you start these stories, Harry.'

'She says, "Look, Mum, I found a moustache in the garden".'

Astrid forgets that Percy is on her lap and catches him as she slaps her thigh; he bolts into the garden ignoring her cries of *sorry* and *come back*.

'I found a moustache! What a daft bugger she was... is.'

'How old was she?'

'Oh, I don't know. Seven? Eight? Something like that.'

'Poor Maggie.'

Harry stops laughing and says, 'And Mum just told her off for bringing the hair back into the house. How could she not find that funny?'

'Oh, poor Maggie.'

'I'm not like them.'

'No, my darling,' she says, throwing down the crossword onto the rattan sofa. 'You're not, and neither is Maggie.'

'Maggie thinks she was swapped at birth but I'm almost certain the old girl had us at home.'

Astrid yawns and says, 'She told me about two sisters that used to live in the maisonette below yours.'

'That must have been at Waldeck Road.'

'I don't remember where it was, she just said that you had the top part of the house and they had the bottom.'

'In that case, it was Waldeck Road. I didn't like that place. It was poky and dark.'

'She said she wanted them to adopt her.'

'Back then, I'd have been all for it - she could be a right pain in the arse; used to agitate the old man no end.'

'I would have liked a sister.'

'You and Maggie are as good as...'

'I mean growing up.'

'I bet you got more roast potatoes on a Sunday than I did.'

She thinks about saying nothing but finds that she can't. 'I didn't like being an only child,' she says, 'extra roast potato or not.' She sounds like a greeting card when she adds, 'An only child is a lonely child, Harry.'

'What do you want for Christmas?' he says, thinking she isn't a giraffe, but a bloody elephant.

She returns to her crossword and says, 'Oh, I don't know. I'll have a think.'

'You have to tell me now; Maggie's picking up a few bits for me in town tomorrow.'

'A scarf then.'

'Another bloody scarf?'

'Yes, you can never have too many.'

'Oh.'

'That will be nice, Harry.'

'It's not much of a present.'

'Why isn't it? I don't need anything. When I need something, I go and get it.'

'If you say so.'

'Tell Maggie not a purple one though.'

'I better write that down.'

'Put it in capital letters and underline it.'

'I will.'

'Cup of tea would be lovely, thanks,' she says, having a stretch and another yawn.

'What was that you said: "When I need something, I go and get it"?'

'Off you go, Harry, there's the best husband in the world.'

'Do you mean that?'

'Yes, Harry,' she says, 'you know I do.'

1983

23: The Social Workers

When Stewart first joined PizzaExpress, the branch manager, an American named Todd (real name Colin), suggested that Stewart might want his name badge to read 'Stu' because 'Stu' sounded more 'hip and cool' than 'Stuart'. Stewart – who had never allowed his name to be shortened to Stew because 'stew' was the 'unhip' and 'uncool' dish of left-over roast meat and gritty root vegetables favoured by the sweaty school-cooks of his childhood and, to this day, his mum every Monday tea-time – reiterated that his name badge should read 'Stewart' and 'Stewart' with a 'w' because *och aye the noo*, he was actually a fraction (improper) Scottish. The branch manager duly wrote on the name badge requisition form: "Stuart with a 'w'". Five days later, a name badge for 'Stuwart' arrived by internal post. Two hours later, a Japanese tourist read Stewart's name badge as 'Stu-wart' with emphasis on the second syllable. Because the restaurant was quiet that day, a teenage girl seated two tables away from the Japanese tourist, accoutred in an impressive arrangement of orthodontic headgear, overheard the emphasized syllable and sniggered, loudly. In Stewart's opinion, a Metal Mickey had no right to laugh at anyone, let alone him. He flushed the name badge down the customer toilet before adding his very own personal touch to Metal Mickey's Coppa Gelato. Two months later, the following edict arrived from Head Office: ALL STAFF <u>MUST</u> WEAR NAME BADGES AT ALL TIMES. Other than changing BADGES to read BADGERS, Stewart took no notice of the memo.

***

Maggie had met Sorrel, and Sorrel's partner of several years, Chrissie, when the three of them worked together on a protracted child protection case, the offences of which spanned one decade and five London boroughs. The case necessitated many lunch-time meetings, though never in public places owing to the horrific details of the offences committed by the first-aid volunteers of the charity concerned. Once the case had gone to court and the ring of offenders to Wormwood Scrubs, Maggie, Sorrel and Chrissie decided that the lunch-time meetings should continue indefinitely with the addition of Sylvie and in venues licensed to sell alcohol. The next meeting was to take place at the Chiswick branch of PizzaExpress. Maggie and Sylvie arranged it to coincide with a mutual day of annual leave and to fuel a planned day of Christmas shopping.

***

The day Maggie and Sylvie were due to meet Sorrel and Chrissie for lunch also happened to be the same day that the Chiswick branch of PizzaExpress were due to receive a visit from the company's managing director. 'He's coming all the way from Uxbridge,' Todd declared with something of the Oh Me Oh Mys. 'Badges,' he clucked, 'badges-ON, people.' Luckily for Stewart, a full-time waitress called 'Jules' ('hip and cool' for Julie) had phoned in sick. Stewart found her name badge buried in a milk and creamer basket and hastily pinned it to his shirt.

***

Seated at the table and with drinks already ordered, Sorrel reads the menu and says, 'Chicken Caesar Salad, for me please, Jules.'

Stewart winces while Chrissie treats Sorrel to a raised eyebrow.

'My bum cheek wobbled when I cleaned my teeth this morning,' Sorrel explains. 'That's a sign that is, that it's getting too big and that I should go on a diet.'

Stewart's not sure how to respond to this analysis. Clearly, he's waiting on a bunch of lezzies ergo, whatever he says or does, or whatever face he pulls, it will be wrong because he's a man and they hate men. In fact, the bum comment's probably a set-up so they can get all huffy and demand to be waited on by Jo-Jo, the drop-dead gorgeous Spanish waitress covering Jules' shift. Just because Jo-Jo's got short hair, they think she's one of them. But does Jo-Jo wear two or more studs in the queer ear? And another thing: why is this lezzie worrying about the size of her arse when her hair is blue? He assumes it must be some sort of lesbian code, to dye your hair a primary colour.

'But salad dressing is hugely calorific,' points out Chrissie.

'Oh, great,' says Sorrel.

'Well, it's oil, isn't it?' says Chrissie.

'No salad dressing, please, Jules,' says Sorrel.

Stewart winces for a second time and then does a squiggle on his dog-eared note pad.

'What about the parmesan cheese?' says Maggie. 'And the fried croutons?'

Chrissie laughs.

'Leave her alone, you two,' smiles Sylvie. 'Your bum cheek wobbling is only a sign that you're going at your teeth too hard.'

'Why don't you just have a pizza, doll?' says Chrissie kissing Sorrel's ear. 'Your bum's a peach.'

Sorrel feels conflicted: pizza in place of salad induces relief, but her lack of will-power induces dismay. Why did her bum cheek have to wobble on a day they were going out to eat? She reminds herself that they haven't seen Maggie and Sylvie in ages and, as such, she should just pig out and have a laugh. She thinks: *Why do today what you can put off till tomorrow.* She reconsiders the menu and then orders a Sloppy Giuseppe pizza with a side-order of garlic bread.

Stewart runs through the order and then slinks off in a fashion that he imagines must look 'hip and cool'.

'I know we shouldn't talk about work...' says Chrissie.

'No, we shouldn't,' says Sorrel firmly. 'We're having a day off.'

'But...' continues Chrissie.

Maggie smiles. 'I got the file, Chrissie,' she says, 'but I haven't had chance to look at it yet.'

'There's no rush, there's no rush,' says Chrissie waving a hand. 'I just wanted to check you'd got it alright.'

'I'll read it first thing on Monday morning,' says Maggie slapping a decisive hand on the table, 'and give you a bell.'

Chrissie nods gratefully, forgetting that she's off on Monday; Sorrel says, 'Okay, gals, no more boring job talk,' and Todd starts hip and cooling it all over the joint because he's spied the managing director outside the restaurant. 'Badges,' he yells in a hushed whisper, 'the MD is here.'

Frowning at a pink milkshake stain on the restaurant window, the managing director gives it a scrape with his key before shaking his head long enough for all inside to see.

***

'I shave all the relevant regions, except the nethers,' declares Maggie in response to Sorrel's declaration that women should embrace their body hair and stop shaving themselves. She is on her third bottle of Peroni and speaking louder than usual. 'I haven't got anything against personal deforestation. And, I don't think that's because I'm a subjugated woman, either. I shave because I like smooth skin and don't like hairy pythons, I mean nylons.'

Sylvie laughs and Sorrel sprays a mouthful of Rosé over the table cloth.

'When Des was being an arse, which was always,' slurs Sylvie, 'I'd use his razor on my nethers. It was great. He'd get flolli...flolli...'

'Folliculitis, my love?' says Maggie laughing.

'Folliculitis,' confirms Sylvie, 'and I wouldn't have to kiss him.'

Maggie rests her head on Sylvie's shoulder.

'Mink trim knickers,' says Chrissie, raising her glass as if to toast them.

'We're all for them in our house,' adds Sorrel gravely.

'Speaking of *your* house,' says Sylvie. 'We got you a little housewarming present, didn't we, Maggie?'

'We did, Sylvie.'

'We should say, "Oh, you shouldn't have", but we love presents, don't we, doll?' says Chrissie excitedly.

'You do,' says Sorrel finishing her second glass of wine. 'When are we going to be able to buy you two a housewarming present?'

'When we live in the same house,' says Sylvie, reaching under the table.

'When will that be?' asks Chrissie.

'Ask Maggie,' says Sylvie from underneath the table.

Maggie swigs her Peroni and then says, 'Eventually.'

Sylvie grapples with one shopping bag and then frees another from a chair leg. 'Maggie's stuck in the closet,' she grunts. 'Well and truly stuck.'

Maggie looks about the restaurant and says, 'Not anymore.'

'Good,' shouts Sylvie.

Maggie feels the need to expand. 'It's only my family that don't know. Dad's very…' She wants to say 'strange' but doesn't. 'Old-fashioned,' she finishes.

'What about your brother and sister-in-law?' says Sylvie. 'Are they old-fashioned, too?'

'It's not that long ago that I told my family,' admits Sorrel.

'Should I close my eyes for this pressie, Sylvie?' asks Chrissie.

Sylvie says, 'No,' from between her knees.

'For much the same reason as you, Maggie,' continues Sorrel. 'But they were fine with it. I don't think it was much of a surprise to be honest. You might find the same.'

'I sincerely doubt it. Anyway, we'll get a house together when the time's right and whether my family know about us or not,' she says, rubbing Sylvie's back in a placatory manner.

Sylvie finds the framed Patrick Nagel print she's been looking for, wrapped in the sky-blue cashmere scarf that Maggie's bought for Harry to give to Astrid on Christmas day. She unravels Astrid's scarf, places the print in Chrissie's waiting hands, carefully refolds Astrid's scarf and replaces it in the carrier bag.

'Please stop moving house,' says Maggie. 'You're bankrupting us.'

'We won't be moving again,' says Sorrel as Chrissie begins to pull the print free of its tissue-paper wrapping.

Stewart arrives at their table to check if they want more food or drinks because he wants a decent tip but nobody is listening to him. Sorrel and Chrissie gasp with delight at Nagel's image of two women embracing. 'Look, Sozzles, it's us,' exclaims Chrissie. 'Albeit slightly chiselled, but it's definitely us!'

Stewart gawps at the painting and thinks: *these lezzies are obsessed.*

'What do you think, Jules?' Sylvie asks.

Stewart asks if they'd like to order anymore food or drinks.

'We thought you could hang it in your new bedroom,' says Sylvie ignoring him. 'I've bought myself the same one,' she adds turning to Maggie, 'and I'm going to put it in *my* bedroom above *my* bed.'

1988

24: The Beginning of the End

Astrid's oncologist has eczema on his forearms; Maggie thinks they look like a couple of Rainbow trout. The meaty scab on his wrist also makes her think of Bisto. Her stomach rumbles even as the combination of Rainbow trout with gravy makes her blanch. She wishes he'd worn a long sleeve shirt because the state of his arms makes her secretly doubt his ability to keep Astrid alive: how can he successfully treat ovarian cancer, if he can't sort out his own bloody eczema? While Astrid agrees to a hysterectomy and a course of chemotherapy, Harry stands by the door, one palm on the handle, and stares at the doctor wondering how they got from irritable bowel syndrome to this. The oncologist insists that the surgery must take place immediately.

'But I'll need to go home first, to get some things,' says Astrid.

The consultant glances at Maggie.

'I can get them for you,' she says, 'don't worry about that.'

He arranges her admission to the hospital before discussing cancer staging and life-expectancy. Maggie misses some of what he says. She tells herself that he said it will take Astrid, on average, five years to beat the disease rather than five years, on average, for the disease to beat her. Then he asks Astrid some more questions. 'We're trying to establish correlations,' he explains. Astrid answers that she has never taken the contraceptive pill and that she has only been pregnant and given birth once. She wants to know why this is relevant.

Warily, he says, 'We think the risk of developing ovarian cancer decreases with each pregnancy and the taking of the pill.'

Before she even asks the next question, Harry hangs his head in shame.

Astrid ignores him because she's getting to the crux of the matter. 'So, what you're saying, doctor, is that if I'd had more than one child, I might not have got this ovarian cancer?'

'We can't say for certain that you developed ovarian cancer because you only had one child, Mrs Edwards, but our current research into the disease suggests that it could be a factor.'

She says, 'Oh,' and then stares at the top of Harry's head wondering why she's only just noticing that he's thinning on top.

***

Maggie's nose bleeds. She tastes it in her mouth. She takes a damp tissue from her sleeve, twists it into lengths and shoves one up each nostril. She does this without using the sunshield mirror so she doesn't know that both her mascara and foundation wandered off her face during the quick cry she had in the hospital when nobody was looking. Her displaced maquillage, abject misery and nose plugs give her the appearance of the last sabre-toothed tiger to walk this earth. If the circumstances were different, Harry would have noticed and made a joke of it, but he's forgotten she's there. She decides to compile a mental list of all the things Astrid might need and want during her stay in hospital, while he thinks about driving into a tree. He wonders which species of tree is more likely to cause instantaneous death in a head-on collision. He suggests oak to himself until he remembers that Mark Bolan died after the Mini he was travelling in crashed into a sycamore tree. He has a vague idea that it's the sycamore tree that produces those helicopter seeds that LJ used to love throwing into the air. It makes him remember LJ as a little boy: it reminds him that he was a lovely little thing, so bright and funny. Now, twenty-five years on from the birth of his son, and thirty minutes on from getting the worst news of his life, he finds it easy to despise himself for not letting Astrid have more children, more LJs. He finds himself thinking about those morons who assumed it was LJ's fault they'd only had one. It wasn't LJ that had put him off having any more but the fear of having to live with Lady Astrid again; of putting her back in that awful place;

of letting them do all that terrible stuff to her head; of having to move back in with his parents; of watching what he said and what he did; of not knowing when Astrid would come back and life would begin again. But, as Astrid always said, things might have been different the second time round. He wishes he hadn't been such a coward. He wishes he'd bitten the bloody bullet and let her have another. Lady Astrid was nothing to this. A tear rolls down his cheek and he is back to thinking about trees. Even if it wasn't rush-hour and he could get his Bedford Rascal out of second gear, where was the tree that would take him out? He leans over the steering wheel and squints at the horizon. A skinny silver birch is ahead but it's on the opposite side of the road; he'd collide with the oncoming, also stationary, traffic before he got anywhere near it and sustain whiplash at the most. He wonders what has happened to all the tree-lined roads of his childhood – to the whopping fat trees with the black railings around their trunks. A second tear spills down his cheek as he considers the destructive potential of a pillar box on an uncongested road.

This tear, Maggie notices. 'I haven't had any children,' she says, her upper lip dislodging one of her tusks, 'but I haven't got ovarian cancer. Astrid might have had ten children and still developed the disease. I know you think it's your fault, Harry, but it isn't.' A blood clot slithers out of her nose and plops onto her lap looking like a spoonful of strawberry jam. It makes her think of Sylvie's home-made stuff and it makes her feel sadder than ever.

Maggie's voice, appearance and the realisation that he was a pillar box away from killing her, startles him. And she's wrong: it is his fault. Ahead, a small flock of rose-ringed parakeets noisily abandon the heavy grey sky for the skinny silver birch. He doesn't know how he's going to do it, but he knows he'll have to watch his wife die just at the point in their lives when they should be learning a new skill, or joining the National Trust, or hiking in the sticks with a rucksack full of goodies to eat at lunch-time. He wipes his cheek on his sleeve and stalls the Bedford Rascal just as the traffic lights turn green.

1990

25: Inheritance

Maggie is with Astrid in the conservatory. They sit with their arms linked like primary school children and laugh as if someone's just invited them to play kiss-chase until Astrid says, 'I don't think I've ever been less than average at anything but it turns out I'm less than average when it comes to cancer.'

'What do you mean?' says Maggie gently.

'The consultant said that, on average, I could expect to live for five years following my diagnosis but here I am about to die and it's been less than three years since he said that.'

Maggie bites her lip and inhales sharply.

'Harry thinks Mor's death's to blame,' coughs Astrid. 'The shock of it all.'

Sille's death had been unexpected. One minute she was on the phone sounding bunged up and assuring Astrid that what ailed her was, 'Just a silly cold, darling,' and the next, she was on her kitchen floor curled up in the foetal position beneath the kitchen table, dead. There was talk of suspicious circumstances until it was determined that she'd died of hypothermia and had, in her confused hypothermic state, regarded the table as something that might cover her up and make her warm. Back then, Maggie had thought it was the shock of learning that her *darling Astrid* had been diagnosed with terminal cancer that had killed Sille. Now, she doesn't like the idea that a mother and daughter who loved one another are in any way to blame for the death of one another. She prefers to blame the scabby oncologist for Astrid's impending premature death along with her dinosaur GP for failing to look beyond IBS. As for Sille, it later transpired that her heating had packed up during the coldest month of the year.

'Since I'm half-Viking, I'd like a Viking funeral,' Astrid says. 'On the day I die...'

'Oh, don't,' says Maggie.

'It's alright,' she says. It isn't really, but somebody has to allow her to start a sentence with these words. She finishes a coughing fit and then says, 'On the day I die, I'd like to be sent out on the water in a burning boat with someone blowing a horn.'

Maggie thinks of her sailing down the dirty Thames on a barge with tyre fenders, the shouted commands of a weedy coxswain raining down on her sunken face from the wide end of a megaphone. 'What boat should we use?' she reluctantly asks. 'I'm afraid my gondola's currently out of action.'

Astrid smiles. 'Don't you think it's better than being pumped full of chemicals, stuffed in a fridge and then weeks later, you know when there's a free slot, being burnt behind a pair of cheap polyester curtains?'

'Possibly,' says Maggie, but she doesn't like the idea of seeing Astrid's face on fire.

'I don't want to wind up a wonky cross on a paving slab. Just take me home and scatter me on the roses, will you? It's where the cats are.'

Maggie rests her head on Astrid's shoulder.

'And don't let the undertakers put blue eye shadow on me. The last thing I need is St Peter mistaking me for Agnetha when I get to the pearly gates.'

Maggie wants to say, *I don't much like Abba, but I quite like Frida,* but what she actually says is, 'I don't much like Abba, but what's wrong with Agnetha?'

But Astrid is on a roll. 'And that's another thing, I don't want *Abide With Me*; I want something more cheerful like...'

Maggie claps and sings, '*Oh, oh, the hokey, cokey.*' She sounds like a tone-deaf Pearly Queen.

Astrid laughs and then sucks air through her teeth because it hurts to laugh.

'Sorry,' says Maggie, 'I shouldn't make you laugh. What hymns were you thinking?'

'What about *Morning Has Broken*?'

'Right,' says Maggie. She thinks that's just as depressing.

'Harry's got it on a Cat Stevens' album somewhere if they don't have an organ.'

She lifts her head and thinks of Sylvie. Sylvie likes Cat Stevens too but he makes her cry. Maggie refuses to listen to music that can do that.

'Harry will know where it is,' says Astrid. 'It's either in the loft or in the garage.'

'I don't mind the one about his dog.'

'His dog?'

'You know: *I Love My Dog*. Can we have that instead?'

'Oh, that one,' she smiles. 'If it was, *I Love My Cat* I'd say yes; I'm going to miss Percy. I hope there's a cat heaven. Wouldn't it be great if I could catch up with all the cats I've ever owned?'

'I suppose they have mad cat ladies in heaven,' says Maggie with a shrug.

Astrid doesn't like the thought of being mad again. 'Maybe I'll leave the cats where they are,' she says, 'and find somewhere else to wait for you lot.'

Maggie shakes her head. 'You've never been without a cat.' Then she sings, '*I love my cat much more than I love you… sod you all, my cat will always come through.*'

'You could sing that at my funeral if you like. I'd rather people laughed than bawled.'

Maggie pictures herself at Astrid's funeral; she can't even say a few words let alone sing. She re-rests her head on Astrid's shoulder. 'Come on, you,' says Astrid, 'what else could I have?' but she's had enough of this subject too.

***

Eleven years before this moment, Harry's new and expensive Sony TV failed to live up to his expectations. Following a disappointing response from Vincent, the then-head of Sony's customer complaints department, he commissioned a sweatshirt emblazoned with the white-felted words: My Sony TV Is Junk. Later that week, Vincent

197

received a recorded delivery. Inside the PLEASE DO NOT BEND envelope was a three by five-inch photograph of Harry, sweatshirt clad, funereal-faced, and pointing at the Cooper Black font with a frown that vowed to express the complaint every day and everywhere for the rest of the sweatshirt's life.

Now, he stands in the hallway at the foot of the stairs wearing a faded blue sweatshirt that reads: **My Son V s unk**. He rifles through a cardboard box of Alfie's belongings because, owing to a move from sheltered accommodation to a local care home that specializes in dementia, he no longer needs the contents of his house. Brandishing Alfie's gun he asks LJ, 'What the bloody hell am I supposed to do with this?'

LJ shrugs.

'What shall I do with the old man's gun, Maggie?' he shouts. 'Do you want it?'

'Sure, Harry,' she replies. 'I'll take it to Barclays: I could do with some free cash.'

Maggie and Astrid titter.

'It was a simple bloody question,' grumbles Harry. He sets the gun down on the stairs.

'It's good to hear Mum laugh,' says LJ.

'Yes, Maggie's always been able to make your mum laugh.'

LJ picks up Alfie's gun.

'Christ Almighty, son, you'd better check that thing's not loaded. It would be just like the old man to have left it in a dangerous bloody condition.'

As if his granddad is already dead, LJ says, 'He wasn't really one for rules, was he?'

Out of habit, Harry mutters something about the war. LJ checks the top of the gun and sees that his granddad left the safety on. He presses his thumb against the top lever, pushes it to the right, breaks open the gun and exposes the back end of the barrels. Neither barrel contains a cartridge. 'It's safe, Dad,' he says, closing the gun.

'There's a leather trunk case for it somewhere,' says Harry, searching the cardboard boxes. When he finds it, which he does after ten minutes of concentrated effort, he asks LJ to disassemble the gun and put it away. LJ grips the fore-end and inserts his index finger in the notch between the barrels.

'I remember when he bought that gun,' says Harry, 'must have cost him a small fortune.'

LJ attempts to pull the fore-end away from the barrels but finds that it is stuck.

'About seventy bob, or thereabouts,' Harry adds. 'That was a lot of money back then.'

He repeats the action. The fore-end comes away but not without jarring his shoulder first. 'Fuck,' he mutters.

'I don't think my old mum was in favour of it, but she would never have said anything.'

He clasps the fore-end between his knees, grips the barrel with one hand, the stock with the other and depresses the top lever.

'He never went shooting, I know that.'

He separates the barrels from the stock and disassembles the gun.

'You were only a baby when he bought it.'

He places the fore-end, barrels and stock on the floor, kneels beside the trunk case and opens it.

'You weren't even walking.'

He reads the label inside the case: *Fabrira de Esropetas. Aguirre & Aranzabal. Eibar Espana.* Next to the gun maker's label is a label that bears his granddad's name.

Alfie was fond of making labels with his Rotex machine. He made one for LJ's school dinner money tin but he printed LJ's name in full irritating Astrid and confusing the teacher.

'Do you remember any of this?' Harry asks.

'I remember the gun,' says LJ, placing the stock, barrels and fore-end in the case. 'He showed it to me when I was a kid.'

'He thought it was smashing the first time you took his gun apart and put it back together again without him giving instructions.'

LJ remembers that this is true. 'My prize was a toffee,' he says. 'I had to catch it.'

'Hmm.'

'He liked the way I smacked my lips when I ate it.'

'That's because he always smacked his.'

'I remember.'

'You could take up shooting,' suggests Harry.

'So could you.'

'I can't leave your mum alone all day, and shooting things has never appealed to me.'

'Yes, Harry,' shouts Astrid. 'You can leave me alone all day.'

Harry mutters something about there not being anything wrong with her hearing and then delves into another box as Astrid, wrapped in a blanket and wearing a headscarf, shuffles into the hall.

'Do you need something?' says Harry, standing up.

'I'm okay,' says Astrid.

Harry returns to the box and, shortly after, resurfaces with a tattered lamp in his hand. 'I bet this wouldn't look out of place in Maggie's house,' he says.

'We don't want that old thing,' says Astrid, wearily. 'It's already like Blackpool illuminations in there.'

'In where?' says Harry.

'In the sitting room, Harry, where do you think? Have you seen Dad's new reading lamp, L?'

LJ shakes his head and tries not to think about how many weeks she has left.

'I call it his interrogation lamp.' She winks at LJ and then falls against the wall. He hurdles over the boxes and throws his arm around her waist to stop her from sliding all the way to the floor. Harry drops the lamp and swears. Astrid rests her head on LJ's arm but gently loosens his grip on her waist. 'I'm a bit sore there, darling,' she whispers. LJ kisses her headscarf because he wants to hide his face from his dad.

Harry loses his rag. 'What are you doing out of your chair? Go and sit down,' he says.

'I need the toilet, Harry,' she says, tersely. 'Is that all right with you or would you like to start piddling for me as well?'

'What's going on out here?' says Maggie, joining the fray.

'Oh, nothing, Maggie,' lies Astrid. 'We were just talking about Harry's new lamp.'

'Hah,' says Maggie. 'You need a specialist subject or else be in possession of a bloody state secret if you want to sit beneath that thing.'

LJ smiles at Maggie because he knows she's trying to lighten the mood but it takes a lot of effort. Harry retrieves the lamp from the box and says, 'Do you want this, Maggie?'

'You think my place is a dumping ground for any old piece of tat, don't you?' she accuses.

'I don't know anything about your place, it's been so long since I was in it.'

'Mum needs to sit down.'

'I'm okay, L,' says Astrid.

'Astrid needs the toilet, Maggie,' snaps Harry. 'She can't go on her own, she just went arse over tit a minute ago.'

'Astrid did not go arse over tit a minute ago,' says Astrid, 'bit of an exaggeration, Harry.'

Harry returns the lamp to the box and sighs deeply.

'And thank you for the public announcement about my bodily functions,' she adds wearily.

'Come on, dear,' says Maggie, 'I'll help you with your drawers and then I'll make you a nice cup of tea. You'd like that, wouldn't you? A nice cup of tea.'

'Don't make me laugh,' says Astrid.

'No chance of that,' says Harry, bleakly.

Maggie pulls a face at Harry's bent back and then takes Astrid from LJ.

'Stick the gun in the loft, grumpy,' says Astrid as she passes him. 'We'll decide what to do with it another day.'

'There's no room in the loft, Astrid.'

'Stick it in there anyway,' she says, holding Maggie's hand to make the slow and painful progress up the stairs.

Harry reflects on Astrid's chest infection. She's had it for weeks. No amount of antibiotics seems to have helped. Sometimes, it sounds as if she's suffocating. Every morning now, as soon as he wakes, the first thing he does is check for the rise and fall of her chest. The thought of waking up to her dead body terrifies him. That she won't hear of having a stair-lift installed makes him cross: he doesn't care what it costs, or how much use it will get. He wishes she would use the commode during the day; that way, she'd only have to climb the stairs once a day. He wishes she would do more to help herself, to make things more bearable.

Once they are out of sight, LJ says, 'You can come out of the box now, Dad.'

'Jesus wept,' he says shaking his head. 'When will it end?'

They ignore the answer.

'You can't keep Granddad's gun in the loft. You'll have to pay a gunsmith to store it for you while you decide what to do with it.'

'Look what I found amongst the old man's things,' says Harry. He hands LJ a crumpled and dusty letter. LJ reads: *Louis' Illustrated Guide To Sexual Positions For Virgins.* 'I found it tucked away in one of his drawers. I don't suppose your Nan ever saw it.'

LJ smiles at Louis' cartoons.

Harry remembers his uncle Louis and says, 'Poor sod.'

LJ nods, smiles at the <u>THE WHEEL BARROW POSITION,</u> and then hands the letter back.

Harry takes a look at the <u>THE DOUBLE-DECKER POSITION</u> before dropping the letter into a box labelled 'Miscellaneous.' He can't remember the last time he and Astrid made love. It occurs to him then that they'll never make love again. His life seems to be full of 'lasts' now: *the last holiday abroad; the last meal out; the last visit with such and such; the last Christmas; the last birthday; the last spring; the last trip to the cinema; the last walk round Kew.* And last minute wishes: *a day-trip on the Orient Express; Swan Lake at the Royal Opera House; Afternoon Tea at the Ritz; Fossil hunting at Lyme Regis.* Things she never mentioned wanting to do before the diagnosis. And very soon, she will be taken to the hospice and that will be the day she leaves their house, the house they now own in full, for the very last time. And it will be the hardest last of all.

LJ returns to the gun. 'Dad, you can't keep a gun in the loft.'

'Yes, son, I heard you the first time, but it won't hurt to keep it there a few days.'

1990

26: Cobblers

Astrid hadn't wanted this sort of carry on and Maggie doesn't think Harry should need reminding of this. 'She gave me clear instructions and I've delayed for long enough.'

'I'm not ready, sis.'

'I've brought bin liners with me.'

'That's not what I meant.'

'I know what you meant.'

'What difference does it make if her stuff stays? What difference does it make if I never get rid of it?'

'It makes a mausoleum of your house, Harry, that's what.'

'That's a posh word.'

'It's an accurate word.'

'So what if the house becomes a posh word?' He can't bring himself to say 'my' house.

'It's not good for you.'

'Who says?'

'Astrid did.'

'Did she now?'

'Yes, she did.'

'Well it doesn't have to be done today, does it?'

'What else have you got on today? Going back to work, are you?'

'What's it to you?'

'You should get back to it.'

'I'll get back to it when I'm good and ready.'

'You'll lose the business if you wait too long.'

'*The* business is *my* business, Maggie, not yours.'

'What do you want with a wardrobe full of women's clothes, anyway?'

'Not today,' he said, thinking how easy Maggie's life was; how selfish she could be.

'When?'

'When I'm ready,' he repeated slowly.

'Astrid wanted the women in the shelter to have her clothes,' she said, as if talking to a difficult child.

'Grave robber,' he said, turning his back on her.

Maggie wanted to smack him in the chops. She hadn't wanted to do this job either but she'd made a promise, and she wanted it over and done with. It had been a job she'd been dreading, too. How much longer was she supposed to let it hang over her? 'I'm carrying out her wishes,' she said.

'Wishes?'

'Yes, Harry, it was her wish. You know it was.'

'Wishes are cobblers,' he said, yanking open the cloak cupboard door.

Maggie said nothing.

'Well, aren't they?' he shouted, emptying the cupboard of Astrid's things.

'Not hers,' she said, as she watched coats, shoes, a brolly, handbags, hats, scarves, gloves and a wicker shopping basket scud past her.

'What about mine?'

'What was your wish, Harry?' she said, as if she didn't know.

'Forget it,' he said, closing the cloak cupboard door. 'What does it matter now?'

***

Standing in his and Astrid's bedroom, leaning against the window sill, Harry looks pregnant. The scarf he hides beneath his SONY jumper puts him somewhere in the second trimester. It's the scarf Astrid wore the day she entered the hospice. The one she then had to remove because the Macmillan nurse said that wearing a scarf in bed was dangerous.

'She's worried... I... might die... in.... here,' she'd wheezed from behind an oxygen mask.

Harry had frowned and she'd tutted. 'Lighten...up,' she'd managed.

'How can I?' he'd asked.

'It was... a... Harry... joke.'

'Your timing was off,' he'd said, with a lump in this throat.

She'd tried to laugh but had gasped instead. 'Just rest, love,' he'd pleaded, taking her hand in his.

Now, he cradles his bump like an expectant mother.

Maggie should notice Harry's distended stomach but she doesn't because she's come across Astrid's brogue-patterned platform boots. Maggie was with her the day she bought them. She was the one who convinced her to buy them. Thereafter, the bottle green boots were worn with everything, even with outfits that didn't call for them. They were known by the cobbler before they became a relic in the wardrobe. Maggie wants to hug them to her chest and weep into the tops of them but Harry is watching her. She'd like to step inside the wardrobe, close the shuttered door, and stand amongst Astrid's clothes in the dark. She'd like to find a chiffon blouse and breathe her in.

27: Raclette

The staff at the care home police Alfie's television viewing. Every week, they go through his *TV Times* with a red biro and circle the programmes he's allowed to watch. Cookery programmes have never been a problem before, provided the chef isn't called Louis or Joe. And Delia never causes him any trouble because he thinks Delia is Lil. That was why he was plonked in front of the television that morning: Lil was supposed to be making Toad-in-the-Hole from her bespoke cottage kitchen in the Suffolk countryside. But, without warning, a French chef supplanted Lil to demonstrate the versatility of Raclette. With mounting despair, Alfie watched as the chef scraped off one oozing layer of molten cheese after another from a block of the stuff that was the colour of human fat and was roasting on a spit. The dolloping of melted cheese on a pile of cold meat prompted him to remember that people can melt as easily as Raclette. Then, when the chef cheerfully declared, 'Sacre bleu, melting is magic,' Alfie lost it because it was clear to him that Maggie, somewhere along the way, had melted to the size of a button and it wasn't down to a shitting magician, it was down to the RAF. The channel was swiftly changed. But not even Judy Finnegan chortling over a novelty suspender belt or Richard Madeley thigh-slapping at the prospect of her wearing it, could divert Alfie from his conviction. So, the staff convened and decided that Maggie should be phoned.

***

At this moment, Maggie sits in her bed, a cup of coffee on her lap with *The Guardian* covering it like canvas. Everything feels wonderful: the sheets are fresh – the room still smells of fabric conditioner; the sun streams through a chink in the curtains; the night wasn't spent dreaming that Astrid was lost and lonely in the after-life, Margaret Thatcher has been ousted from politics, and Sylvie sits beside her sipping syrupy coffee and reading *Trumpet*. She pushes Harry from her mind and then kisses Sylvie's shoulder. Sylvie finishes her page and then returns the kiss.

While Maggie considers *The Guardian's* analysis of Margaret Thatcher's final address to the press, Sylvie puts down her novel and thinks about one of her cases: two-week old Josh. On the home visit the day before, she found him asleep in a cot beneath a soiled double duvet. When she mentioned suffocation and cot death, his mother played dumb: 'One of the other children must have dumped it on him; it wasn't me.' Then she picked him up and shifted him from one bony arm to the other. Sylvie thought he should have objected to all the toing and froing; it wasn't normal that he didn't. About the mother she wrote: *Evidence of continued abuse of amphetamines* in her report. She asked to see the kitchen cupboards. Each one was empty.

'What are you feeding him?' Sylvie asked.

'Milk.'

'I gathered that. What sort?'

'That Smar stuff.'

'Smar?'

'Yeah.'

'Oh, do you mean S… M… A?'

'Yeah, well, whatever you stuck-up bitches call it.'

Sylvie thought Smar sounded more stuck up than S.M.A. 'Where's the Smar then?' she asked.

The baby's mother stabbed a finger at the eldest girl and shouted, 'I told you to go to the shops and buy some milk for Josh, didn't I? You're in big trouble now, you lazy bitch.'

Sylvie could tell from the girl's face that her mother's claim was fabricated; she was a rubbish actress. She wrote: *Josh is failing to thrive* and then took the girl to the chemist. She paid for a tin of S.M.A for the baby and a pack of sanitary towels for the girl. Her report recommended that all four children be taken into care

IMMEDIATELY. Now, as always, she wishes that *IMMEDIATELY* meant that day, or the next at the very latest.

Maggie can tell that Sylvie is thinking about work when she doesn't want her to. 'Isn't this great?' she says. 'I can't remember the last time we stayed in bed all day.'

'Hmm,' says Sylvie.

'We should do it more often.'

'We could if we lived together.'

'Hmm,' says Maggie and thinks of Frankie.

'Hmm,' echoes Sylvie.

'I've got some face packs,' says Maggie. 'We could do them now, if you like?'

Sylvie puts down her book. 'Are they those ones you peel off?'

'No, I know you don't like them. I got mud masks this time. It's supposed to be very special mud. It's blue anyway.'

'Alright then,' says Sylvie, brightening, 'let's give them a whirl.'

***

Maggie and Sylvie are discussing French and Saunders' take on *The Exorcist*. Sylvie laughs at Maggie's impression.

'I'm cracking up,' says Sylvie touching her cheeks. 'I'm eroding.'

'You're Barton-on-Sea,' says Maggie, referring to the location of a recent romantic weekend away.

'I'm worse.'

Maggie checks her watch. 'It's been twenty minutes. We can wash them off now.'

'I wish I didn't have to; I look so much younger with a face pack.'

The phone rings as Maggie wishes that Sylvie wasn't so hung up on age.

'Do you have to get that?' says Sylvie. She watches dried flakes of turquoise-coloured mud flutter to the duvet. It reminds her of standing around in crematoriums, trying to ignore the big chimneys and the falling ash. It's the one thing Catholics are right about: burials are better than burnings.

'It might be Harry,' says Maggie. 'I'll only spend all day worrying if I don't answer it.'

Sylvie licks her mud-caked lips while Maggie belts down the stairs looking like a wild apparition to get to the phone. Sylvie goes to the bathroom and looks at her face in the mirror: no wrinkles, age spots or sun damage. The face pack makes her eyes stand out. With her mouth shut to hide her tea-stained teeth, she thinks she looks a good ten years younger. That would make her almost the same age as Maggie; she wishes she was. She sighs and fills the sink with lukewarm water; didn't she read somewhere that hot water aged the skin, or was it just the breasts? She splashes water on her skin and thinks about Harry and Alfie. She wonders if Maggie will ever introduce her to them. She tries not to get cross about it but it's the nineties, not the fifties; surely, they must have an idea that she's a dyke for God's sake? Jesus, Mary and Joseph, wasn't the writing on the fecking wall? LJ must know. And if Ralph could swallow it... She pats her face with a towel, drains the sink of the chalky blue water and wonders why, at sixty-two, she allows herself to remain Maggie's dirty little secret.

***

'I'm alright, Dad. I promise you,' says Maggie, excavating her chalky face with her nails. Why is it always her that melts? Why can't it be Harry for once? 'I'm as big and solid as ever,' she adds, crumbling flakes of mud between her fingers and staring at her thighs. She must start doing some exercise.

'You've melted,' Alfie insists.

'I haven't.'

'I saw you do it. You melted all over my hands.'

'I didn't, Dad, I promise. I'm okay. Harry's coming to see you tomorrow.'

'Who?'

'Harry.'

'Not him again; I don't want my hair cutting.'

'Not the barber, Dad, Harry... your son.'

'I've run out of smokes.'

'What?'

'He'll only cut my hair if I give him twenty smokes, Lil.'

'Listen to me, Dad, just listen to what I'm saying: Harry isn't the barber, he's your son and anyway, you don't smoke anymore.'

'HE IS NOT,' he shouts. 'HE'S THE SHITTING BARBER.'

'Don't swear, Dad, you'll get into trouble.'

He starts to cry and says, 'Sorry, Lil, I didn't mean to swear.'

'It's okay, Dad, don't cry… Is Pearl there?'

He continues to cry down the phone.

'Is Pearl there, Dad?'

'Don't be cross with me, Lil.'

'I'm not cross with you, Dad, it's alright, don't cry. Ask Pearl if you can watch *This Morning*.'

He turns to Pearl but asks the phone, 'Can I watch *This Morning*? Lil wants to know.'

Maggie rolls her eyes. 'You have to ask Pearl, Dad, not me.'

'I did.'

'No, you asked me. Where is Pearl?'

'I don't know.'

'Ask someone.'

'WHERE IS PEARL?' he shouts at the phone.

Maggie shakes her head.

Pearl says faintly, 'I'm here, lovey, what's up?'

'I have to ask you something.'

There are footsteps and Pearl's voice gets louder. 'What do you want to ask me?'

'I don't know.'

'*This Morning*, Dad,' shouts Maggie, losing her patience. 'Ask if you can watch it.'

'*This Morning*,' he repeats.

'You want to watch *This Morning*, lovey?'

'Hmm.'

'Go and sit yourself down, and I'll sort that out for you.'

'I have to tell Lil.'

'Alright, lovey.'

'I'm going to watch *This Morning*, Lil.'

Maggie leans her head against the wall and says, 'Great.'

'Will you watch it with me?'

She sees Sylvie standing at the top of the stairs. Her face looks shiny like a glazed bun. 'Sure, why not?'

'Alright, Lil,' he says and breathes down the phone.

She sighs, 'You have to give the phone back to Pearl now.'

He doesn't.

'Give the phone back to Pearl, Dad.'

Without saying another word, he hangs up, forgetting about Pearl.

Maggie tuts and looks up at Sylvie. 'I have to go and see Dad.'

'I could come with you?' she says, hopefully.

'No, no,' says Maggie. 'There's no point ruining your day off as well. You stay here and finish your book.'

28: Secret Smoking

Maggie leans out of Harry's bathroom window and blows smoke rings at the sky. It's mid-morning on her least favourite day of the year: Boxing Day. Outside, the day already looks over and done with. On the lawn below lies Percy's latest victim, disembowelled and mostly pink in colour. She thinks about the deceptiveness of appearance, of the well-dressed man with the bruised knuckles who stormed into the shelter and threatened to kill her if she didn't send his wife and children home for a Christmas punch-up. She taps the ash from her cigarette and sighs with a well-versed weariness: Percy's a fluffy haired, blue-eyed pussy until he finds something smaller to pounce on. He mews at her from the conservatory roof. She steps away from the window to let him in. He pauses on the window sill expecting a stroke. 'Sorry, puss,' she says, 'but you literally make me sick.' She unlocks the bathroom door and waits for him to take the hint. He dusts Harry's collection of ageing aftershaves with his seal-grey tail before leaving. She shuts the door on him and Harry's ludicrous snoring before returning to the window to finish her cigarette.

She can't remember the last time she smoked in the loo. Yes, she can. Of course she can. It was in her final year at school with Connie. The cubicles were tiny. They had to stand close together to fit inside. Connie stole the gasper from her dad and hid it in her bra. It was warm between her lips and she delighted in its recent proximity to Connie's tits. They puffed in turn and tried to choke quietly but it was nigh on impossible. Their bodies touched as their lungs expanded. They stayed pressed together long after Connie had flushed away the filter. They ignored the bell for lessons and blew on each other's face to check for fag breath. Then, when it was Maggie's turn to blow, Connie closed her eyes and opened her mouth. The stuff they did afterwards prompted Connie to demand that they each go out and get a boyfriend to prove that they weren't really one of those *lesbo* types. Maggie settled for Alistair, and Connie went for Jonathan. Alistair made up for his big nose and shocking acne by being very funny, but his monstrous hands made her tits seem like a couple of coconut macaroons which was a crying shame because personally, she liked them big and presumed everybody else did too. When she dragged him into the school loo to try the Connie stuff on him, he made a mess of *his* trousers and *her* jumper but predictably no impression on her nether regions. That evening, she told her mum that she'd slopped custard down her front at lunch-time because everyone knew that ice-cream was never on the menu at school. Then her dad lost the plot because custard was yellow. Then Harry sent her to Coventry because she'd set Old Looney Tunes off. Then her mum brought laundry day forward to appease her dad, and made her do the whole bloody lot on her tod as punishment for her slapdash eating style and for upsetting everybody. As she set to work on Alistair's mess with a bar of sunlight soap, she began to think that her dad would have preferred the truth to custard. She'd told herself that in truth, she didn't like custard either and dumped Alistair the following morning. Silly old Connie, however, went the whole hog and married Jonathan in St Nicholas Church at the age of sixteen. Maggie followed her down the aisle as chief frilly in long white gloves, an ice-blue damask dress and with the expression of the lobotomized.

Now, Maggie doesn't understand Harry's penchant for the smoke alarm. He doesn't smoke but he has five in the house? Christ, it must have been nearly twenty years ago that he accidentally extinguished his Chesterfield on Astrid's chin at a New Year Tarts and Vicars fancy dress party. Thank goodness the bathroom escaped the unnecessary installation: chilly tits at the bathroom window were preferable to frost-bitten ones on the garden patio. Of course, if she were taller, she'd have removed the batteries from the alarm on the landing and smoked her first cigarette of the day where she did at home, in bed.

And that's where she should have stayed: at home. It was silly to attempt Christmas with Harry this year. Trying to be happy was worse than being sad. She lights another cigarette and sits on the edge of the peach-coloured bath. She stares at a textured bathroom tile and perceives a woman's face; she is reminded of Sylvie but doesn't want to think about her now. The row they had about spending Christmas apart was fierce and regrettable. Maggie had to agree to give serious consideration to Sylvie's request that they buy a place together to stop Sylvie from dumping her. She lies down in the empty bath tub, with her legs outstretched, and wonders what Astrid would have made of macaroni cheese for Christmas Day lunch. This makes her think about Percy's reaction to the bauble-free Christmas tree and her reaction to the news that LJ would be out of the country, not just for Christmas, but for months. When the smoke alarm finally does wake up to the fact that she's chain-smoking in a bathroom that has a big gap under the door, she finds that it's a bloody relief.

1991

29: The Good Old Days

At this moment, Harry wishes the hour was ten minutes longer so he could have woken at eleven and at least contemplated a shave. He tries to calculate ten minutes multiplied by twenty-four hours but can't hold on to the numbers. He leans against the van in a car-park close to Gunnersbury station and then checks that he didn't just think about winding the windows down. He considers air fresheners for vehicles. The choice available at Halfords implies that the colourful bits of perfumed cardboard are mandatory, but they seem like a waste of money to him, a gimmick that dangles from the rear-view mirror, distracts, and like furniture polish, induces headaches. LJ's only going to be in the van a few minutes; he can stick his head out the window if he's that bothered.

He tries to remember if he met LJ's train last time, but this sort of information eludes him these days. He just remembers being desperate for a drink in the kitchen and LJ putting the kettle on. He'd wanted to slip a shot of vodka in his mug without LJ seeing but his slight frame had made an inadequate screen. He'd pulled at the sides of his SONY sweatshirt to make it bigger but he may as well have been pulling at knicker elastic. It was only when LJ had decided to go for a catnap later that day, that he'd been able to quench his thirst.

Now, he watches a man wearing a tweed flat cap, turquoise shell-suit, and scuffed grey slip-on office shoes scan the ground for some dropped change by the car park's ticket machine. He notices a yellow granular stain on the tracksuit top and guesses chicken korma: he decides that the tracksuit bottoms have recently doubled up as a lav. He turns away in case he's asked to help with the hands-and-knees search for coins and wonders if the silly sod is really up to driving a car. With a shake of the head, he takes a box of peppermint Tic Tacs from the pocket of his ratty dressing gown, throws a handful in his mouth and waits for LJ's train: the bloody thing's already ten minutes late.

***

Reading between the lines of the weekly bulletins that Maggie has left on his answerphone, the man LJ expects to find waiting for him at the station is now utterly fucked. He wishes she'd believed him when he'd said that he was going abroad for work and wouldn't be home for months. She was an A1 tout, but what she reported was old and unwelcome news. Now, looking out the window at the fleeting snapshots of graffitied walls, terraced houses, shops, parks, railway signs, and station platforms, he thinks about the last time he visited his dad. It had been five weeks after his mum had died.

LJ had spent the previous eight days at his desk in Thames House responding to the IRA bombing of the London Stock Exchange and was knackered; within an hour of arriving at his childhood home, he announced he was going to bed.

'Your bed's not made,' said Harry. 'But you know where your mum keeps the stuff.'

Crossly, LJ wondered where dead people kept stuff. On the stairs, he heard the twist of a bottle top and a long drink being poured. He threw his bag into the bedroom that had once been his, and went to the airing cupboard. He passed his dad's bedroom *en route*. The door was shut and he was glad. The airing cupboard looked as if it had been burgled: he half expected to uncover a turd amongst the crumpled bed linen and not just Percy. He found the multi-coloured brick-patterned sheet and duvet-cover that his mum had bought him when he was a teenager and then turfed Percy out. He spread the sheet over the mattress of his old single bed and stepped out of his jeans. He wrapped the duvet cover around his body and fell onto the bed like a carpet-roll. Harry sang, 'Don't Bring Me Down' loudly and tunelessly, replacing forgotten lyrics with lyrics of his own that didn't rhyme and projecting them thoughtlessly up the stairs. Bastardizing tunes was a habit his parents had shared. LJ turned onto his front and covered the back of his head with a pillow. Later, he found his dad passed out on the settee, slacked mouthed and snoring like a brachycephalic dog. There was less than a finger of vodka in the bottle beside him. He frowned at Harry's muddy shoes and then booted them. His dad went from collapsed to standing with the rapidity of a wooden push puppet. Then, after LJ lied and said he was hungry, off he bounced down the walls of the hallway like a cold squash ball, to zap two frozen kebabs in the microwave. It was at that moment that LJ decided he wouldn't make a habit of coming home.

Now, on his way home to attend a tea party for his dad's fiftieth birthday, he calculates how many months have passed since that last visit and finds that it is six. It doesn't feel long enough.

***

'Maggie and her parties,' exclaims Harry. 'Your granddad has no idea who I am let alone that I'm about to turn fifty, the poor sod. I've tried telling your aunt that I don't want a party but she won't have it, son. I think it'll make him worse. She's worried about him missing out. He wouldn't bloody well know if he was. It's my bloody birthday and I get absolutely no say in the matter. She says it will just be cake: "We'll have a piece of cake with him and then go". If only it were that simple. On average, it's not really the way I'd like to spend the day.'

LJ opens the back door of the van and swings his bag from his shoulder. 'How would you like to spend it, Dad, in your dressing gown?'

Harry ignores the question and says, 'Stick that in the front, son, the back's a mess.'

LJ eyes the shit hole that is the back of his dad's van but says nothing because he thinks that what he keeps in the glove-box is worse: Mum's reading glasses, a lipstick and one of her scarfs. He gets into the passenger side, winds up the window, searches his jacket pocket for some chewing gum and wonders when his dad's going to get his arse in gear and return to work.

Harry climbs awkwardly into the drivers' side and says, 'I'm getting old.'

'Cod liver oil.'

'Do you take it, son?'

'No, I eat fish.'

'When I was a kid, a spoonful of cod liver oil was a treat.'

'The good old days.'

'Yep,' says his dad sighing. 'The good old days.'

LJ offers him a stick of gum even though he knows he won't take it. He just wants to derail his train of thought. He doesn't want him to visit the good old days. As far as he's concerned, he fucked up the second he mentioned them. It works: 'Keep your chewing gum and I'll keep my crowns,' he responds.

He returns the gum to his pocket and turns his attention to the carrier bag he finds at his feet.

'I picked up tea. A meal-for-two,' says Harry, demonstrating poor clutch control as he pulls out of the car park.

'And a bottle of vodka,' says LJ, sharply tugging his seat belt to release the lock.

'Buying a meal-for-two makes a change. There's more choice when it comes to buying a meal-for-two. Why do you think that is?'

'Because pleasing one miserable bastard is easier than pleasing two.'

'Funnily enough, I never looked at it like that, L.'

'Why don't you learn to cook, Dad?'

'Who's going to teach me? The only person I see these days is your aunt.'

'Ask *her* then.'

'Maggie? Maggie teach me how to cook? Christ Almighty, son, that's a very bad idea.'

LJ closes the bag, stares out the window and wishes he was already on his way back to central London. Harry farts and LJ winds down the window. 'God almighty,' he complains, 'even your arse has got an accent.' He does an impression of Donald Duck saying, '*What's the big idea?*'

'I can't help it,' laughs Harry. 'It's those bloody meals; God knows what they put in them.'

'Stop eating them then.'

'You know I must have eaten every meal-for-one at least a hundred times.'

'Like I said...'

'Alright, alright, I get the message.'

'You used to cook.'

'Did I?'

'On Wednesdays.'

'Christ, you've got a good memory, son. I forgot about that.'

'I wish I could.'

'It wasn't that bad, was it?'

LJ remembers the greasy beef burgers, the half-baked potatoes, and the cold baked beans that were always on the table by the time his mum walked through the door reeking of lotions and complaining about some fussy bitch or other. 'You were shit at cooking but great at timing,' he says, and then considers whether he can be arsed to have a deep and meaningful with him about the severity of his DTs.

'Let's have some music,' says Harry, switching on the car's cassette player.

He watches the progress of his dad's trembling hand and says, 'What about Shakin' Stevens?'

'Shakin' Stevens? You don't like him, do you, son?'

He grabs his hand and says, 'No, Dad, I fucking hate him, but you could give him a run for his money. Look at the state of this.'

They both look at his hand before LJ returns it to the steering wheel. Harry trains his eyes on the road and says, 'Have a look on your side, son, and see what tapes I've got knocking around in there.'

30: A Knee's Up

'Why do these places always smell like beef casserole?' asks Maggie. She's talking about Alfie's care home.

'Is that what it is,' says Harry, sniffing the air.

'I'm not saying it is beef casserole, I'm just saying that it doesn't matter what day I come, it always smells like beef casserole.' She wrinkles her nose and adds, 'I go home reeking of it.'

'Who's there to notice?' says Harry.

'Me, Harry, I notice,' she snaps.

LJ has no thoughts on the matter. He elected to carry his dad's birthday cake and he'd rather concentrate on getting it from the boot of his aunt's car to the care home's day lounge without dropping it. Maggie ordered the biggest sponge the bakery did. The wording: 'Happy 50th Birthday, Harry'; the colour of the icing: Blue; and the decoration: Plain, was almost an afterthought. 'As long as there's a slice for every one of the poor old sods,' she'd said, 'that's the main thing.' She'd collected it that morning, *en route* to Harry's house after she'd dropped Sylvie home. To keep it fresh, the baker had sealed the edges of the large yellow and white striped cake box with a myriad of blank bakery price stickers. 'Let's see it then,' Harry had said when she'd arrived at his house.

'No,' she'd said. 'It's a surprise and I've left it in the car.'

'It's not a surprise; I know you've got me a cake.'

'You don't know what's on it,' she'd said, frowning at the strong smell of alcohol on his breath.

'Let me guess: Happy Birthday, Harry.'

'If you say so, Harry. Where's LJ?'

'No, wait, it says: Happy *Fiftieth* Birthday, Harry.'

'Shut-up, Harry,' she'd said. 'LJ?' she'd called. 'Where are you? We'd better sing Happy Birthday to old beaky here.'

Now, standing in the reception area of the care home, a space dominated by spider plants, Thank-You cards, and a mobile commode, Pearl comes bustling up to the three of them looking sweaty and flustered. 'Hello, hello,' she tweets. 'We had a little emergency this morning so we're running a bit behind. Lovely to see you again, LJ. We're just finishing lunch. Shouldn't be much longer. Alfie's had a spruce; we sprayed him with some cologne. Just to warn you, he wasn't very happy about it but he's alright now. If he tells you we sprayed him with toilet freshener, I can assure you that we did not. Anyway, we're all very excited about the party. Oh, sorry, Harry, many happy returns by the way.'

'Thank you,' says Harry, worrying that Pearl might have party games planned in his honour.

'What was the emergency?' asks Maggie, because emergencies in the refuge always necessitate the calling of the police.

LJ imagines the emergency had something to do with bowels. He thinks about the nameless emergency in conjunction with the beef casserole and decides that, if he is to avoid adding to the stains already on the reception's carpet, he should swiftly direct his thoughts to his dad's birthday cake. He thinks about jam and buttercream. He hopes the jam isn't apricot. Apricot jam is just pointless.

Harry glances at his watch. Lunch should have been over and done with ages ago. Now, he'll have to spend even longer in this place and on his birthday as well.

'Oh, it was something and nothing really. I won't bore you with the details but Alfie wasn't involved so nothing for you to worry about. LJ, you know where the kitchen is, don't you?'

'Yes, Pearl,' he says, charming her as always with a smile.

'Would you mind popping the cake on one of the counters? I'll get one of the girls to bring it through to the day lounge when everybody's ready.'

He nods and heads off in the direction of the kitchen.

'Wait, L!' says Maggie reaching into her handbag. 'I've got some candles. Close your eyes, Harry.'

'Hells bells, sis, I know what candles look like,' he protests.

'Just do as you're told,' she says.

'Fifty blue candles,' he mutters, with one hand covering his eyes.

She places five packets of ten blue candles on top of the cake box and says, 'Smart arse.' Then she indicates to LJ that she could quite happily strangle her brother.

As LJ disappears through the double doors, Maggie hears a parrot squawk.

'Go on through to the day-lounge,' says Pearl cheerfully.

The parrot squawks again. Maggie didn't realise pets were allowed in the home but she's heard of pet therapy, and she knows that stroking dogs is good for the heart. She supposes a parrot is just the thing. 'When did the parrot arrive?' she asks.

'What parrot?' says Pearl.

The parrot obliges Maggie with another squawk. 'That one,' she says and points at the ceiling as if it's flying overhead.

Harry perches on the commode and closes his eyes.

'Oh,' says Pearl with a pained expression, 'that's not a parrot, that's one of my gents. He makes that sound when he's agitated.'

Maggie claps her hand over her mouth to hide a smile wide enough to crack concrete, and says, 'Oh, sorry.'

Harry's eyes flicker open and then shut again.

'Me and my big mouth,' says Maggie.

Harry nods in agreement and then takes a packet of Polos from his jacket.

***

A blue-glazed plate spattered with egg yolk and pocked with broad beans sits on a glass-topped coffee table in the day lounge – an oversight from the previous day. And from somewhere distant, an old man shouts 'SEX'. Maggie is enthralled. 'It's unusual for someone of their generation to say "sex" don't you think?' she whispers loudly. 'Surely, it's 'making love' for the older generation.'

Harry huddles by the radiator and stares at the brise bise nets at the window and wishes he was outside, and LJ looks daggers at the blue-glazed plate and wishes it wasn't there.

'It's your generation that says 'sex', LJ, even when they claim to be in love,' she adds.

LJ is reminded of the time he was sixteen and his Nan blamed him for all the McDonald's packaging littering London. He could tell his aunt that he doesn't say 'making love' or 'sex', but he doesn't think this is the time or place for a discussion on fucking.

'His generation say "bonk",' says Harry, with his hands tucked under his armpits.

LJ doesn't want to think of old people having sex, making love, fucking or bonking; it's as horrific as putting fried eggs with broad beans. He diverts his thoughts back to the blue glazed plate on which egg yolk and broad bean inappropriately mingle.

The plate reminds him of the week he spent at Pontins in Weymouth when he was nine because the plates they used at the holiday camp were the same. Maggie organised the break and dragged the rest of the family along. Only his granddad was excused although his Nan left after two days because she had a problem with men showing up to the bar in their speedos. Most days, his dad went AWOL, while his mum spent the majority of the week lying on a sun lounger by the pool with a book covering her face. She entered him into the fancy dress competition along with the daughter of a fat woman she met at the pool. On the morning of the competition, the two women made 'Jack and Jill' costumes out of crepe paper in the empty bar while he slid from one corner of the parquet dance floor to the other, and 'Jill' picked a scab on her knee and blew bubbles in a glass of lemonade with a curly straw. During the fancy-dress parade, which started on the dance floor and finished on the stage, he held 'Jill's' hand and it felt wet and he imagined that the wet was wee. Then a Bluecoat dared 'Jill' to kiss him and to his horror, she did. Before he started crying, he noticed that her breath smelt of dry roasted peanuts. They came second and each received a jumbo sugar dummy as their prize. It was a prize he could wear around his neck and suck at will but it was a dummy and dummies were for babies. He would have preferred one of those giant red lollipops with the writing on one side that turned your tongue white when you licked the letters. He saved the dummy as a present for his granddad because his granddad loved sweets and he didn't think the dummy shape would bother him, and he got rid of 'Jill' by telling her that before the competition, he'd puked green, might die and she might too if she didn't buzz off. Helpfully, his aunt nodded when 'Jill' asked her if he was telling the truth and then she took him down to Weymouth beach and paid for him to have a go on the sunken trampolines. It was at Pontins that a bearded lifeguard called Brian taught him how to swim. He was practising the doggy-paddle, trying to remember all that Brian had told him, when his dad got bundled by a gang of other dads, stripped down to his Y-fronts, and thrown into the pool for a joke; it made him so angry he had to wee in the pool. At Pontins, he ate fish for breakfast and the waiters put candles on the table at tea-time. His aunt's hair caught fire as she leaned over her blue-glazed plate to whisper something to him, and his mum put out the flames with her hands and then passed out and bumped her head. The next day, his aunt joined the queue for breakfast with a boys' haircut and was very happy about it. The worst thing about Pontins was the nightly cabaret because it was loud and the closing song had a miserable tune.

Now, it's easy to imagine Pearl making his granddad and all the other old duffers sing *Good night, Campers, see you in the morning*, but with a caveat: *if I don't it croak it before then*. He turns away from the plate knowing he'll eat fried eggs again, but never broad beans.

***

Slowly, and in batches, the frail and the infirm are shepherded into the day-lounge by Pearl and her staff. Every few seconds the promise of a piece of Harry's birthday cake is repeated. LJ pictures donkeys snaffling carrots. Maggie quickly ascertains that Alfie is not among the aged throng. Her face asks Pearl for his whereabouts.

'Don's just taken Alfie to the loo,' says Pearl.

Maggie nods and then feels guilty because a delay to dealing with her dad, no matter how short the duration, is a bit of a relief. She turns her attention to the old girls. The white, lemon and pink coloured clothes they wear makes her think of sherbet pips; her mouth waters until she spies an old boy with orange lipstick on his cheek. His cheek looks like orange peel gone white with mould. It makes her think of the tangerines, conference pears and black grapes in the fruit bowl at home. She'd bought the fruit for Sylvie because she likes to eat fruit with every meal. Picturing the fruit bowl still full of fruit reminds her that Sylvie's visits have been sporadic of late.

'Es-SEX,' shouts an old boy in the manner of a darts caller as he motors past Maggie on a Zimmer frame. 'THAT'S WHERE I'M FROM.'

'That's right, Ernie,' says Pearl with a sigh. 'But not so loud, lovey.' Ernie ignores her. 'Es-SEX,' he shouts.

Maggie glances at Harry: he wipes his clammy forehead with his sleeve and plans his visit to the jewellers; he's going to buy a hip flask that he can keep in his trouser pocket for emergencies such as these.

As the day lounge fills up, Harry and LJ vacate their seats and with unnecessary solemnity, stand either side of a plastic yucca plant in the corner of the room; Maggie thinks they look as if they're guarding the horrible thing. She tells them to smile with an exaggerated smile of her own. LJ ignores her command but Harry gives it a go; the result, she decides, is quite maniacal. He resembles Jack Torrance from *The Shining*. She shakes her head and leaves him to it.

While Alfie's pants and trousers are being swapped for dry ones and special care is taken to ensure that his skin isn't touched, or that the little button he likes to keep in his trouser pocket isn't lost during the change of clothes, Cherry, Pearl's newest and youngest member of staff, bursts in to the day-lounge firing sing-song apologies above the heads of Pearl's charges and reeking of a Fisherman's Friend. She wears a batik dyed scarf round her head, a ruby stud in her nose that looks more blind boil than gemstone, and a large black hole in her tights. Maggie stares at the hole and wonders if those legs have ever seen a razor: somebody ought to tell the girl that it's 1991, not 1971. Cherry talks to Pearl as if there's nobody else in the room. Making sure to sing from her diaphragm she trills, 'Sorry, sorry, sorry, sorry, bus was late.' Maggie thinks she sounds a bit like the lead singer in that band Sylvie likes: all squeals and grunts and nodules on the vocal chords, although there's a touch of the German Shepherds about Cherry's voice too. Oh, what is that singer's name? Or the name of the group? Sylvie has the album. It's no good: she thinks of Björn Borg and sugar lumps even though she knows she's barking up the wrong tree.

Pearl heaves dead weights into chairs and elevates elephantine ankles onto leatherette pouffes. The trapped gas she liberates as she lifts and lowers limbs makes a bassoonist of her. 'Not again, Cherry?' she says, trying to stay upwind of a woman called Muriel who is quite obviously rotting on the inside. 'This is getting to be a bit of a habit with you.'

Cherry makes a moue: Pearl might be on to her and her singing lessons. 'Sorry,' she sings again, but she isn't really because she wants to be a famous vocal artist, not a poorly paid care assistant, and her singing teacher is right: a serious vocal artist does not watch the clock. Worried she might be for the dole queue before her demo tape is finished, a record deal is secured, and next month's rent is paid, she decides Pearl must be reminded of what a blessing she is when it comes to the afternoon sing-alongs. She glances at the entertainment notice board but worryingly it reads, 'Birthday Party' in place of 'Sing-along'.

'Never mind for now,' says Pearl. 'There's a birthday cake in a box on the kitchen counter. Put the candles on the cake, light them, and bring the cake through.'

'I could do that if you like?' says Maggie, trying to be helpful.

'Oh, no,' says Pearl. 'Best stay put for Alfie's sake. He'll worry if he thinks you're not here. Go on, Cherry, off you go.'

Cherry nods at Pearl and then flashes Maggie her best filthy look because nobody must get in the way of her bringing in the cake and belting out *Happy Birthday*.

***

Alfie trudges to the day-lounge with Don. 'How old am I today?' he asks.

For the fifth time in a matter of minutes, Don reminds him that it's Harry's birthday, not his.

'It's my birthday,' says Alfie.

'It's your son's birthday.'

'How old am I?'

'You've just turned seventy-one.'

'I'm twenty-one.'

'You remember Harry, don't you?'

'The barber?'

'Your son.'

'He's the wotsit,' shouts Alfie.

Don hands go up in surrender. 'Alright, Alfie, take it easy,' he says gently.

'The shitting barber... I know what's what.'

'I think I can hear the party,' says Don.

'Well, you're not deaf, are you?' shouts Alfie.

'Maggie, Harry and LJ have come to see you today. That's your...'

'Where's Lil?'

Don gives up trying to jog Alfie's memory and pushes open the double doors with a jovial, 'Here we are.'

Upon seeing Alfie, Maggie gets out of her seat, Harry takes an unsteady step away from the wall and LJ raises a hand in greeting. Smiling broadly, Alfie says to Maggie, 'Lil, it's my birthday, excuse the shit-fresh I'm wearing, they put it on me,' and then shouts across the room to LJ and Harry, 'Louis, Joe, you couple of ...' He stops and wracks his brain and then has a Eureka moment, 'cunts,' he finishes.

LJ grins as if he's been correctly identified while Harry gets reacquainted with the wall. Maggie stares at the Mary Whitehouse who's raised her spinster-claws in distress and tries her best to wonder why she wears a cameo brooch on her bed jacket.

'Es-SEX, THAT'S WHERE I'M FROM,' shouts Ernie.

'I don't think that was the word you were looking for, Alfie,' states Don.

'No,' says Pearl sternly and keen to move the day-lounge on from talk of vaginas and the county of Essex, she pumps her arms like a pair of bellows, and with wild nods of the head to anyone who will look at her, shout-sings, '*Happy Birthday to you...*'

In general, the rest of the room take the hint and sing the next line, '*Happy Birthday to you...*' (Though, some of the residents sing it to Alfie instead of Harry.)

Then Cherry struggles though the door with the whopping great birthday cake and, with two rifts mid-chorus and a run after the final note, belts out: *Happy Birthday, dear Pa-a-a-nsy, Happy Birthday-ay-ay-ay to you, mm-mm-mm-mm-mm-mm-mm-mm.*

Maggie glares at a pink birthday cake covered in purple sugared pansies and reads:

Happy 95th Birthday, Pansy

From All Your Friends At Church

***

And back at Maggie's house, Sylvie seals an envelope and tapes it to the mirror by the front door. She avoids her reflection before resting Maggie's spare door key on the newel post of the staircase. Then she steps outside and leaves Maggie to get on with the rest of her life in the closet.

1991

31: Adapting

It is the day of woe and Harry's decided not to bother with the rest of the week. He thinks Bob Geldof had a problem with the wrong day. Tunelessly he starts to sing, *Tell Me Why I Don't Like Wednesdays* and surveys the washing-up: it spills out of the enamelled sink and onto the grey kitchen counters. The bin needs emptying, it smells worse than the toilet and there's a housefly trapped inside growing fat on liquidized remnants of a ready-meal lasagne. The sun beats down on the kitchen window sill where fragments of egg shells and spent tea-bags bake companionably in a cracked blue ice-cream container. Next to the provisional composter sits a potted Aloe Vera plant, the leaves of which have withered like the chin of an old-aged pensioner. Damp laundry lurks in the washing machine and a pair of his dirty underpants lay beside the machine on the tiled kitchen floor. He snatches up his pants, holds his breath, opens the bin and throws them in, smothering the housefly with navy-blue Marks and Spencer cotton that's done a straight shift of ninety-six hours. He crosses the kitchen and lunges at the cupboard under the sink. He extracts a black bin liner and into it deposits the contents of the washing-up basin and the mess from the counters. He remembers leaving an empty vodka bottle behind the roll of patterned kitchen paper and mopping his curried chin on a tea towel. He seizes the bottle and searches for the tea towel. He finds it in the fridge. He thinks he must have mistaken the fridge for the washing machine during one of his 'moments'. He tosses the bottle and the tea towel into the bin liner. He unlocks the back door and dumps the bin-liner outside ignoring the sound of breaking glass and china, and the certainty that the snowdrops won't flourish beneath it all. He returns to the kitchen bin, picks the entire thing up, takes it outside, and drops it into the mouth of its much larger relation. Before liberating the last of the Battenberg cake from its plastic film and slinging it into the cat's food bowl, he removes his left slipper and wedges it in the back door. Then, half-shod and armed with a litre of Smirnoff, he leaves the kitchen and shuts the door behind him.

***

The dining room, directly across the hall from the kitchen, is as Astrid left it: clean, tidy, and fit for purpose. He squeezes past the table and chairs and goes to the sideboard. He opens one of three drawers and fishes out one of her 'everyday' table cloths. He covers the dining table with it because he wants to avoid scratching the veneer: she was always very precious about the furniture. The table cloth is white and yellow check, crisscrossed with sharp lines that form ridges and dips according to the fold of the cloth. He thinks about her and pictures her needle bruised hands folding and smoothing and ironing the spot that he touches. He lifts the cloth to his face and inhales sharply, craving the smell of her. He tries to remember the scent of her moisturizer or perfume. He remembers her dabbing pink lotion on her skin and the way her fingertips moved in tiny circles on her cheeks and in long upward strokes on her neck until the lotion had disappeared.

When the morphine drip had gone up and she'd lost consciousness, his painter and decorator fingers – newly red from cleaning another batch of brushes in turps – had assumed the role of moisturizing her skin. He'd worried aloud about doing it right. 'You can't go wrong,' a nurse had said, as she cleaned Astrid's mouth with a mouth swab that was pink and had made him think of lollipops. But Astrid had attended training courses on these things. Even he'd known it wasn't simply a case of slapping the stuff on. 'You can go wrong,' he'd replied.

Now, he is disappointed because he smells nothing but washing powder and spray starch on her table cloth. He carefully refolds it and returns it to the drawer. A hacksaw lies on the room's crimson coloured carpet and his father's shotgun rests against a silvery wall. He collects Alfie's shotgun, picks up the hacksaw and lays it on the dining chair next to the one he then sits on, to save the table. He grips the stock of the shotgun between his thighs and rests the barrel on his left shoulder. He takes a stick of white chalk from the breast pocket of his creased blue shirt and holds it in his right hand. He rests his chin on his chest and with the chalk, marks an inch beneath this point on the barrel of the shotgun. He picks up the hacksaw and begins to shorten the barrel. He thinks about leaving a note but he doesn't know what to write except for:

I've had every meal-for-one.

Or:

I don't like Wednesdays.

Or:

I've had every meal-for-one and I don't like Wednesdays.

He thinks LJ would see the funny side, but not Maggie. He decides to keep the note in his head and leave nothing for whoever finds him but Maggie's home address and telephone number. Then he collects a tumbler from the sideboard and the cordless phone from the hallway. He fills the tumbler with vodka and takes a swig. He picks up the cordless phone, presses the nine button three times, and waits.

32: Answering the Call

'You're through to the police,' says the dispatcher, while trying to rescue a lapsed bra strap from her perma-tanned arm. 'What's your emergency?'

'I'd like to report a suicide,' says Harry.

'Can I take your name and address, please?'

'Sure,' he says, and gives his details as casually as if he were booking a ticket to watch Brentford play next month.

The dispatcher inputs Harry's details on the computer in the box entitled: INFORMANT, and then does a thumbs up to a colleague that's just mouthed 'Coffee?' at her. 'Do you know the person who's committed suicide?' she says, preparing to dispatch an ambulance and a panda to the victim's address.

'Yes, it's me,' says Harry.

'It's you?' she asks, and stops typing.

'Yes, me.'

'What's your date of birth?' she asks, with the belligerence of a doctor's receptionist.

He tells her and glugs down the tumbler of vodka.

She shakes her head and starts typing: 'Timewaster', in the box entitled: INCIDENT. 'Sorry, Mr Edwards,' she snaps. 'You've lost me, and I have calls waiting on the other line. This number is for emergency calls only...' She does a PNC check on Harry's details to see if he is known to the system.

'Yes, I'm sorry,' says Harry sighing. 'I didn't mean to confuse you and I don't mean to tie up the line but I didn't know who else to phone. It *is* me I'm talking about.'

She frowns at the result of the PNC check: No warning markers; nothing to suggest the informant has a history of threatening suicide or is known to suffer from a psychiatric condition, or is suspected of possessing a firearm or any other weapon with which he might do himself harm. In the PNC box she types: *No Trace*. 'But I'm talking to you, Mr Edwards. You can't be dead if I'm talking to you?'

'I'm going to do it after we've finished talking,' he says, overfilling his glass so that it spills onto the table. He wipes the Russian puddle with his sleeve.

'Is this a joke?'

'No, I have my dad's old gun.' It stares up at his chin like a faithful springer spaniel.

'You have a firearm in your possession?'

'That's correct… I have a firearm in my possession.'

'Is it loaded?'

'I don't think the thing works unless it is.'

'Look, Mr Edwards…'

'Yes, it's loaded,' says Harry. 'It's loaded, I'm sorry.'

'And you're telling me that you're going to commit suicide with this firearm?'

'Yes, that's exactly what I'm telling you.'

'And you're at home, are you?'

'Yes, I'm in the dining room.'

She deletes the word 'Timewaster' and then wastes no time in dispatching an ambulance and several firearm units to Harry's address.

'Okay… now… listen… Mr Edwards,' she says, half-rising from her swivel chair and waving her arms at the Control Room Supervisor as if he's a Sea King helicopter and she's drowning in the North Sea. 'Whatever's happened…'

'When the police arrive, they'll find the back door open and me in the dining room. I don't want my family to find me.'

'Mr Edwards… I want you to…'

'We've got a cat. His name's Percy. We'd like him to go to a good home. Please tell his new owner that he likes tuna but not salmon, well, he likes salmon, but it gives him the squits. Also, chicken, on average, is fine, but that cat milk stuff's a no, no.'

He wishes Maggie wasn't allergic to Percy, or that LJ wasn't always off gallivanting: Astrid would prefer Percy to live with a familiar lap. Then he wonders if the Battenberg cake's a hit.

The Control Room Supervisor – a police inspector and enthusiastic born-again Christian who believes that no resident of Greater London has God's authority to murder themselves – hoofs it over to the dispatcher and speed reads her screen. He grabs a piece of paper, scribbles, 'KEEP HIM TALKING' and momentarily covers her screen with this instruction. Then he turns to the centre of the control room and starts clicking his fingers at the ceiling as if he's a John Travolta tribute act doing *Saturday Night Fever* at the local workingman's club.

The dispatcher vaguely considers whether she'll get a commendation for her role in this incident but then cautions herself that it's only likely if she actually manages to talk the *chicken oriental* out of topping himself. 'You said, "We've got a cat." Is somebody else with you, Mr Edwards?' she asks, glancing at the Control Room Supervisor. He places his right index finger on his temple and nods at her while finger-touching his crucifix tie pin with his left index finger.

'I was referring to my wife. Percy's Astrid's cat really.'

'Can I speak to your wife?'

'No, I'm afraid Astrid's already gone.'

'Gone where?'

'Where I'm going, I hope.'

'Mr Edwards, is Astrid hurt?'

'She's dead.'

'Right...'

'And it *was* my fault.'

'Have you shot your wife, Mr Edwards?' squeaks the dispatcher.

The Control Room Supervisor throws his hands over his face and shakes his head as if the second coming has decided against coming.

'God Almighty, no, you've got the wrong end of the stick there,' Harry laughs, mirthlessly.

'Okay... okay... I got it wrong... I'm sorry, Mr Edwards... Listen, why don't you tell me where Astrid is?'

The Control Room Supervisor nods, clutches his tie-pin and puffs Mellow Birds in to the dispatcher's personal space while Harry quaffs another glass of shop-bought anaesthetic.

'Astrid died... months ago... well, eight months ago to be precise... of cancer which... well... I won't go into details... but it *was* my fault.'

'Mr Edwards... I'm sure that's not...'

'I'm going to go now.'

'... true... No don't go... Wait... Stop... Tell me about Percy...'

But Harry has waited for eight months and he thinks that that's long enough; he hangs up.

'He's gone, sir,' she says, just as the first firearm unit screams silently onto the scene.

'I'm sure you did your best,' says the Control Room Supervisor.

'Yes, sir,' she says, wondering what that means. Then she presses a button on her switchboard and thinks: *Bang goes my commendation.*

33: The Death Message

A policeman comes to Maggie's house to tell her that Harry has killed himself. He stands on her doorstep looking for signs of life. His stomach growls and he thinks about the bacon sandwich he's missed out on back at the nick. He feels the sharp February air attack the bare skin above the collar of his coat and wishes he'd remembered to wear his black scarf. He hears the sound of an aerosol, the scrape of plastic on frosty glass and a car engine idling, further up the street. The house produces no sounds. He thinks that the next of kin must have left for work or is still tucked up in bed. He looks for a bell but finds none. He finds no knocker either. He takes off his calloused leather glove and assaults the weary front door with his knuckles. He lifts the red flaking varnish from the tiled door step with the toe of his polished Magnum boot and waits.

Meanwhile, Maggie is upstairs in the back bedroom purging her antique pine wardrobe of old clothes with the detachment of a stranger. She thinks this job can't wait any longer even though it only occurred to her that it needed doing just a few days before. She shakes open a black bin liner as if she's reprimanding it and throws in brightly coloured jumpers, blouses and trousers. She is careful not to rid the wardrobe of anything belonging to Sylvie. She thinks of the women in the refuge where she works, of Shelagh, Janice, Lesley and Carla and wonders what they'll make of her cast-offs. She thinks it unlikely that Shelagh's breasts will fit inside any of her jumpers. She was the only one she knew with tits like Norfolk.

When she hears the knock at the door, she considers ignoring it but then glances at her watch. The time of day concerns her; the postman's already been and it's too early for visitors, but then she thinks of Sylvie. It might be her; she might have changed her mind. She drags the bulging bin liner to the landing and descends the stairs feeling nervous.

The policeman tots up the number of death messages he's given during his fifteen years of service. He hears the turn of a key in the lock just as he is reflecting on the fact that he's never had to give a death message involving suicide before. He's still deciding on what face to wear when the next of kin appears in front of him. He takes in her age, her athletic frame and short greying hair, her ruddy skin and bright red spectacles and her pale blue pinstripe pyjamas, and decides that she's someone who copes. He throws on a frown and asks her if he can come inside and speak with her.

Maggie wants to tell the policeman to go away but finds herself saying in a voice that sounds like somebody else's, 'Has there been another burglary?'

She doesn't feel strong enough to deal with bad news today. Fear covers her like Clingfilm does a bowl of leftovers. She thinks of Sylvie and Harry and of LJ and her dad. She wonders which one she can bear to lose for good. She finds herself thinking of her dad the most.

'No,' he says. 'Could I come in and speak to you, please?'

'It can't be bad news: you haven't got a WPC with you', she says.

She is irritated with herself for saying that. She wishes she could just tell the policeman to go away. He wishes that she would just let him in to the house so that he can say his piece. He thinks about stepping into the hallway uninvited.

'I'm afraid I have got some bad news for you,' he says, 'but I would rather tell you inside, Mrs...'

'Maggie,' she says, dully. She puts away her thoughts and fixes her eyes on the blue and white 'Police' badge on his coat. She traces each letter, P through to E and when she finishes doing E, she starts again with P.

'Maggie,' he says, apologetically. 'It's about your brother, Harry.'

She drifts away from the door and he enters her house. The chilly morning falls from his uniform and grasps the thin material of her pyjama bottoms. She wishes she'd bothered to dress or hadn't answered the door. She notices that he holds his right hand in the palm of his left as he tells her that her brother has shot himself. Then she feels the blood inside her head rushing away to somewhere else and her legs collapse beneath her. She feels his hand on her arm before everything turns black.

***

Maggie sits on her sofa with a cup of tea in her hand watching the policeman search for a place to set his own cup down. Finding a clear surface in her house is no easy task. She doesn't think that she hoards things, just that she forgets to throw things away. 'I won't pretend that my house is usually much tidier than this,' she says.

He puffs out some air and raises the palm of his hand as if he is stopping slow-approaching traffic in her sitting room. He smiles and asks her if it is okay to rest his mug on a pile of stacked books. She nods even though she never permits herself to do the same.

'*Dessert of the Heart*,' he says, reading the title of the book that tops the stack. 'Never heard of it.'

She thinks about laughing, but finds that she can't. Instead, she imagines Sylvie laughing and this drags the corners of her own mouth down even more so that it feels as if her lips are going to slide off her face.

'I see you smoke,' he adds, nodding at a pack of cigarettes she's left on the floor. 'Do you mind?' he asks, removing a pack of Hamlets from his breast pocket.

Happiness is a cigar called Hamlet, she remembers.

'No,' she says.

'Do you want one?'

She shakes her head because she's recently given up smoking. But then she thinks how silly it is to deny her body nicotine when she's just discovered that Harry has denied himself the rest of his life. She stops shaking her head and nods furiously. She thinks she has nothing to gain from giving up cigarettes now. The policeman bends down to the floor and grabs the packet.

'Thank God we smoke,' he says, handing her the box.

She imagines God handing out nicotine habits to those He knows will have to deal with suicides. She holds her cup of tea in her left hand so that her right hand is free to hold a cigarette. A combination of adrenalin and a weak wrist from a childhood fall down the stairs means that her left hand shakes more than her right. She lets her tea swell over the rim of her cup in waves and watches impassively as it slops onto the carpet. She could steady her hand or balance her mug on her knee, but she doesn't feel like it. She doesn't care that the spilled tea stains the light beige carpet.

She lights a cigarette and inhales deeply. She closes her eyes and inhales again. She sips the remaining tea in silence and wonders why it has to be so sweet and milky. She thinks about the cup of tea she made for Carla when Carla ran into the refuge with her baby and a broken nose two days before. She thinks that she'll ask the women who come into the refuge if they want sugar next time.

She can't remember the policeman's name. Has he introduced himself? The only name that comes to her is 'Harry'. She feels sure that if the policeman shares the same name as her brother, he wouldn't have told her his name. She remembers that Sylvie never forgets a name.

They use her plate from breakfast as an ashtray passing it between them with slight nods of the head and twitches of the lips. She jumps when his radio begins speaking, '*Alpha-lima-zero-seven-for-an-update.*'

'That's me,' he says. 'Excuse me one moment.'

He clamps his Hamlet between his lips and fumbles with the brooch mike that is clipped to his jumper. She notices his wedding ring. It is one of those Irish rings with two hands holding a heart. She didn't detect an Irish accent, but then, she reflects, Sylvie didn't have one either, not really, not unless you listened very hard.

The length of ash looms over his woollen jumper. She lifts the makeshift ashtray from her lap and offers it to him. He nods and grabs the plate. He sets down his cigar and then transmits, 'Alpha-lima-zero-seven-all-in-order.' He taps the ash onto the plate. Then they listen to the ensuing radio silence until she says, 'I fainted.' She feels that it's necessary to check this with him.

'More of a half-faint,' he replies, drawing heavily on the tobacco.

'Who will clear up the mess?' she asks.

He looks around her sitting room, baffled.

'Who will clear up after my brother,' she says, taking the plate from his hand and stubbing out her cigarette.

'Not you,' he says frowning. 'That's not something you need to worry about.'

34: Purple

LJ is on the phone to Maggie. She wants to keep talking. 'The police couldn't get hold of you,' she says, 'so a policeman came to my house and told me first.'

He thinks of her house as a bigger version of the back of his dad's van. She tells him that his dad's body must be officially identified by a relative. She finds she can't say the word gun, much less contemplate viewing the damage one has done to her brother, so she says, 'Will you do it, L? I just don't think I can.'

'Yes,' he says, because he has no choice. 'I'll do it.'

She weeps with relief. 'The policeman gave me a telephone number for you to ring. If you let them know the time you expect to get to the hospital, they said they'll meet you there, to save you hanging around.'

He imagines his dad swinging from a rope, his eyes on stalks and his tongue poking out the side of his mouth, swollen and blue.

'Shall I meet you at the hospital?' she asks.

'Yes,' he says, because he isn't thinking straight.

***

Maggie can't tell if her hearing has deserted her or the people in the hospital foyer have stopped talking. Her head sails like a freed helium balloon. She hears the rush of the sliding doors behind her and feels a cold blast of air on her neck. She decides to wait for LJ outside. She turns on her heel and leaves the foyer with the intention of smoking her thirty-fourth cigarette of the day just as LJ gets out of a cab. He hands over a note and nods. She thinks he looks like one of those moody fashion models. But he also reminds her of her mum. She finishes her cigarette and lights another as he hastens up the steps towards her. He has to bend down a long way to kiss her cheek. She blows smoke across the top of his ear and wonders what to say to him. He takes a step back and sets off the automatic doors. He sees a policewoman spying on them from the confectionary kiosk and ignores her.

'I gave these up,' says Maggie, addressing her cigarette. 'I said to your dad, "I'll give up the smokes if you give up the booze." We lasted a week, just one lousy week, but that's his fault not mine.' Her words catch in her throat. She drops the cigarette to the ground and crushes it beneath her purple Doc Marten.

He glances at the policewoman. He knows she's after a sign from him that he and Maggie are the people she's waiting for. He gives her a nod. She smiles ruefully and stands up.

'Come on,' he says. 'Let's get this over with.'

35: Formal Identification

The policewoman likes dealing with the dead. They make for a quick job compared with the other shit she has to deal with: one short statement of identification and one form to record the circumstances and that's it. Provided they haven't been murdered, she considers a dead person to be the least bureaucratic job of them all. And suicides are much more interesting than old people who die of natural causes. And she's not squeamish; top spot in her list of favourite films goes to, not only *Bill and Ted's Excellent Adventure*, but also, *The Texas Chainsaw Massacre*. She holds her clipboard to her chest and stands up; the relatives have given her the nod. The son's a bit of alright. She tries to look sad even though the afternoon is shaping up well; if she times it right, this job will take her to the end of her shift and she'll be able to make it to Legs, Bums and Tums tonight at the leisure centre. She wishes there was no need to sort out her arse. She wishes Cheese and Wine from traffic hadn't said it was big, or that she hadn't overheard them, or that she didn't care what they thought. She hates LBT: she can't walk properly after it and she can't use her thighs for forty-eight hours either. It makes hovering over the toilet for a widge a nightmare. She re-visits Cheese and Wine. Then she pictures her thighs straining against a toning band and tells herself that this time next year, from the arse down at least, she'll look like Winona Ryder. Then she thinks about the job at hand and Rodney, the mortician. Rodney is the only down-side to dealing with the dead. She half-suspects him of being a necrophiliac. She wonders if she could put it in writing that, should she die on duty, her body is to be taken to a different hospital mortuary. The thought of Rodney washing her bits and pieces makes her shudder with revulsion. She updates control that the relatives of the suicide have arrived to identify his body, and heads to the automatic doors wondering if the suicide's son is married.

***

LJ wonders why they have to walk so fast to get to a dead body. It's not as if his dad's going anywhere. Maggie is unfit and the pace adopted by the policewoman to get them down to the Chapel of Rest means that she fills the narrow corridors with her fag breath. LJ doesn't like smells. Just this once, he wishes he was like one of those tossers at Thames House who keep a handkerchief in their breast pocket. He would have no compunction in smothering his nose with it. He decides to take his mind off the smell by counting the orange hexagons on the hospital's brown modular carpet. By the time they reach the room containing his dad's body, he's counted one hundred and seventy-six. Maggie leans against the wall and tries to regulate her breathing. LJ wishes there was something on the walls to look at; an advertisement for an undertaker would be better than nothing. The policewoman stands in front of the door as if she's guarding a crime scene and says, 'Before we go in…'

'I'm not going in,' gasps Maggie.

'That's fine, I know you don't want to, I meant LJ.'

'Sorry, sorry, of course you did.'

'Before I take you in, LJ, I have to ask: do you know where your father's wound is?'

Maggie jumps in with the answer as if it might earn her a prize. 'Chest,' she says, with a conviction that irritates him.

The policewoman frowns and takes a step towards her. 'I'm sorry; I was hoping they would have told you. They should have told you,' she says, trying to conceal her irritation that the copper who delivered the death message failed to deliver the entire message. She feels as if he's dropped her in it. She decides she'll have a moan to him about it tomorrow.

It takes a while for the penny to drop but when it does, Maggie says, 'Oh Christ.'

The policewoman throws down her clipboard and marches off back down the corridor. She picks up a blue plastic chair, brings it back down the corridor and gently forces Maggie onto it. 'I'm very sorry,' she says turning to LJ, 'but he put the gun in his mouth and pulled the trigger.'

This is not news to LJ. Maggie holds on to her neck while her throat makes some uncharacteristic sounds. The policewoman fears her face isn't acting sad enough so she makes it sadder by making her bottom lip disappear. Then, retrieving her clipboard from the floor, she adds, 'I'm sorry but Mr Edwards adapted the shotgun.'

'Adapted? But Harry was never interested in guns,' croaks Maggie.

'Dad must have shortened the barrels, Maggie, to be able to fire the fucking thing in his mouth,' says LJ impatiently.

The policewoman ignores LJ even though she generally goes for the mean and moody type, and, crouching down by Maggie's chair, begins to rub her arm. Maggie's face reddens. 'I see,' she says. 'I didn't mean to be obtuse, LJ. I'm not really helping, am I?'

'Perhaps we should go in,' says the policewoman, glancing at LJ. 'If you're ready?'

LJ thinks he'd need to be seriously fucked up if he was ever going to be ready to see what she wants to show him. Then he nods because it occurs to him that, at that moment, he probably is.

***

The policewoman opens the door into a room that is windowless, white and dimly lit. A small table stands against one wall displaying a basket of dusty yellow plastic primroses that LJ wishes weren't there. He ignores the large table in the middle of the room on which his dad lies, and eyes the mortician who is standing in the corner, twitching like a stoat.

Rodney takes the eye-contact with LJ as his cue to approach him. He takes a step forward as LJ takes a step back. Rodney hovers on his tiptoes and says, 'I'm sorry for your loss.'

LJ nods and puts his hands in his pockets.

'I've done the best I can for your father,' he adds, wanting more than a nod, 'but his head's a bit blown up, so it's not been easy to make him look normal.'

The policewoman glares at him. Her face screams: FOR THE LOVE OF GOD, RODNEY, YOU SAID "BLOWN UP". THE DUDE SHOT HIMSELF IN THE HEAD. SHUT THE FUCK UP,

YOU BLOODY NECROPHILIAC. He fingers his greasy comb-over and slopes back to the corner of the room.

LJ tells himself that he can't leave the circus until he's checked out the big top. He turns to the large table and sees a white sheet. He's aware of something dark at the top of it but focuses on the bare arm lying outside of it and the hand resting on top of it. From a distance, he studies the hand. He stares at the mole beneath the knuckle of the middle finger and remembers that when he was small, he used to put his finger over that mole because he didn't like the look of it. He recognises the wedding ring: a gold band so thick that he once compared it to the ring fittings plumbers use. Even though he hasn't looked much beyond his dad's left hand he says, 'This is my dad,' because he doesn't want to look at his dad's new face and then say, *This is my dad.*

'Okay,' she says. 'What would you like to do now?'

Rodney fidgets in the corner. He holds a small pot. LJ doesn't know what it contains but he knows it has something to do with his dad. 'I'd like to stay for a bit,' he says.

'Of course,' she says. 'I'll wait with your aunt. Stay as long as you want.'

As far as LJ is concerned, the mortician's twitching is getting out of hand; it looks as if he's touching a live wire. He wishes the little twat was. The policewoman knows that Rodney wants to get his hands on the suicide. 'I'll let you know when we've finished here,' she says. He bolts out of the corner, pockets the jar, flashes LJ a pitying look and scurries from the room.

***

LJ thinks his dad smells like a chemistry lab and his face looks like stretched pizza dough. One of his eyes is where it should be, but the other looks as if it slid down his cheek but ran out of steam at his chin. His mouth and the top of his head are sewn shut. The stitches are crude and do not match the colour of his flesh. Grey, white, pink, and red coloured particles nestle amongst the strands of his greying hair. His nostrils and ears are plugged with wax but blood oozes out of his right ear and runs down his neck like cold black treacle. His hair is wrong; he has the same parting as the mortician. LJ rectifies this, not caring that his dad's brain matter sticks to his fingers. He wipes the treacle with the sleeve of his white shirt. His eyes wander to the plastic primroses and back again. He doesn't know where to plant a final kiss.

***

Harry's suicide makes the fifth page of *The Times*. This is because he reported his own suicide to the police before he killed himself. It's this detail that makes his death nationally newsworthy. LJ notes the cheery tone of the article just as his pager bleeps from the lid of the bread bin. He finishes the article and checks the message: *PIRA have launched three mortars at 10 Downing Street. All leave cancelled.* He folds the newspaper in half, takes a lighter from the drawer, and burns the article in the sink. Then he heads to the bathroom for a shave and wonders if he needs to iron a shirt just as Maggie picks up the phone beside her bed and dials Sylvie's number.

The End

Thank you to...

My beautiful and fiercely intelligent late mum, for answering questions such as: What did people call vaginas in the 40s? without query or judgement; my hero and beloved late dad for wearing the sweatshirt that read My Sony T.V is Junk during my formative years – I couldn't have made that up; my wonderful children, Hugo and Matilda, for excusing me from many a family game so that I could write my book; my late pugs, Pablo and Juno, for keeping my lap warm as I typed and drying my tears with their fur on difficult days; my aunt, Diane Wilkins, for so generously gifting me her late father's war memoir; my late great-uncle Ron Stone, for his service and his testimony; my doctoral supervisors, Rebecca Smith and Professor Will May – aka my dream team – for everything, but in particular for their friendship and continued belief in my writing; my sensitivity readers, Karen Ellis and Kate Shaw, for their warmth, generosity and validation; Dr Ros Ambler-Alderman, my very precious and ingenious friend, for kindly reading drafts and offering unending support; my audacious reviewers: Nemone Lethbridge, Kate Pullinger, Paul Reid, Rose Ruane, and Rebecca Smith – that each of you brilliant people have read my work and garnished it with munificent words sticks me nicely in the territory of Dream Central; my publisher Stairwell Books, aka Rose Drew and Alan Gillott, for picking up The Other Way and not running The Other Way... (see what I did there?), but seriously, thank you for all the big-ups along The Way; and lastly my husband, Ig Dawson, for always holding my hand, making things better, and for being my one true love.

Other novels, novellas and short story collections available from Stairwell Books

For further information please contact rose@stairwellbooks.com

www.stairwellbooks.co.uk
@stairwellbooks